METAPHOR FOR MURDER

MYSTERY WRITER'S MYSTERY #3

BECKY CLARK

Any references to historical events, real people, products, or places are used fictitiously. Names, characters, and places are products of the author's imagination.

Cover design by Steven Novak

ISBN: 978-1-7346893-7-2 (paperback)
ISBN: 978-1-7346893-8-9 (ebook)

www.BeckyClarkBooks.com

For everyone who got mad at me when they saw themselves in my previous books. Brace yourselves.

ONE

I jumped when he licked my calf. Behind me I heard the wheezing and huffing that signified the unmistakable arrival of Peter O'Drool.

"Hey, Pete," Ozzi said. "You trying to steal my girl?" He bent to pet the rambunctious pug who lived upstairs with Don and Barb Singer.

"Oh, honey," I said to Ozzi, squatting down to rub Peter's face. "That ship sailed. I fell in love with Pete long before I met you." Peter rubbed his face on my leg before bouncing back toward Ozzi. I locked the front door of my apartment.

Peter dashed away then came right back, impossibly but valiantly chasing his minuscule tail that curved up toward his back, and finally, as his big flourish, got down in the play position, butt in the air, front legs on the ground. Well, that was the play position for normal sized dogs. Pete had so little clearance he was already mostly on the ground. But I knew what he meant.

"I wish I could, Pete, but I'll be dead if I screw this up. I promise I'll see you later and we'll have a romp." I gave him a chuff under his nutmeg-colored chin.

"Big day, eh?" My eighty-something neighbor Don Singer descended the outside stairs and met us at the bottom.

"Today is Charlee's big workshop and book signing with Rodolfo Lapaglia." Ozzi held out a book he was hoping to get autographed. "He's coming into town just for this. We're on our way to meet his train at Union Station." Ozzi could hardly contain his excitement, eyes bright, butt wiggling. He looked remarkably similar to Peter. Not nearly as much drool, though.

"That's a good boyfriend, going with her." Don nodded approvingly at Ozzi. "Baby Boomers get a bad rap, but you're all right."

"Geez, Don, how old do you think I am? My parents are Boomers!" Ozzi said with a chuckle.

Don shrugged. "We're the Greatest Generation. That's where I quit paying attention."

I barked out a too-loud laugh. "You ARE the greatest. And while Ozzi is a good boyfriend, he's not going to this event for me. He's got an enormous man-crush on Rodolfo Lapaglia and can't wait to meet him." I tugged at Ozzi's sleeve but he gave me a reassuring pat on the arm, as if that would banish the butterflies in my stomach. The only thing I had control over today was not being late to the train station, and that ticked away the longer we stayed here chatting with Don.

This entire event today was the brain child of Stephanie Szabo, my new editor at Penn & Powell. She was also Lapaglia's editor. After all the turmoil from the murder of my agent and the withdrawal of my manuscript "Mercury Rising," she thought it would boost buzz for me, maybe sell some of my back titles. And I had to agree, since my agent had been completely ineffective in selling any of my new book proposals. Henry had learned nothing from his wife before he cavalierly assumed control of her literary agency after her murder. Melinda was tough and unlikeable, but fully professional and astute in the realm of book publishing.

Henry, on the other hand, made completely unreasonable demands and editors—even Stephanie who had worked with me before—wouldn't agree to take on any of my new work. She told me in no uncertain terms that as long as Henry Walter was my agent, I'd never sell another manuscript. I was keeping my fingers crossed I could just run out the clock on my contract with him.

But then a bona fide miracle happened. Not one the Pope would bless, but still. Henry Walter closed up shop and sent letters to all of Melinda's clients that he was going back to his tech business and releasing us from our contracts. Apparently my editor wasn't the only one he'd antagonized.

Then the next thing I knew, my friend Viv Lundquist had signed with a new agent and convinced her to sign me as well. As relieved as I was, though, you can be sure I scrutinized every word of that contract.

But when both my new agent and editor thought this event would be a boost for my career, I believed them. Plus, I wanted them to know I was a team player and not some literary diva.

Stephanie confided that she was keeping her fingers crossed for a miracle that our event today would not only raise my profile, but also humanize the reclusive Lapaglia a bit, make him less of a jerk.

Seemed like a lot of pressure for a one-day workshop for writers. I didn't have the heart to tell her I'd already been the recent recipient of a miracle.

"Who is this Lapaglia?" Don asked. He pronounced it "La-page-lie-ya."

"Lapaglia. Just the best thriller writer who ever put pen to paper, that's who," Ozzi said, puffing out his chest.

"Told you. Man-crush."

Don raised his eyebrows.

"Seriously? You've never heard of him?" Ozzi asked.

Don screwed up his face in an exaggerated manner to

mimic extra-hard concentration. I hid my grin by bending down to rub Peter's belly.

"You're killing me, Don! Rodolfo Lapaglia ... has thirteen books in his Mob Busters series? Won the most Dark Dagger Awards ever? Bestsellers in like, every country you've ever heard of and some you haven't?"

After each fact, Don looked even more quizzical. I was afraid Ozzi might hyperventilate. And then we'd *really* be late.

I knew Don was pulling Ozzi's leg because I'd seen Lapaglia's books on his shelves. I hung around Don and Barb more than Ozzi did, so I was a bit more immune to Don's pranks. Not that he didn't fool me on occasion. The most recent time was when he had me convinced that a house being built near us had actually been blown down in a recent windstorm. I believed it longer than I cared to admit.

Don slapped his thigh and guffawed. "Of course I know Lapaglia's work. I own most of his books. Been reading them since you were still in knee-britches."

"Pretty sure I've never worn knee-britches," Ozzi said.

"I bet you'd rock them. I'd kinda like to see you try." I waggled my eyebrows and gave him a lascivious leer.

Ozzi shot me a pin-up girl pose, complete with pout and finger in dimple.

"On second thought, no time. We should go." I held out my hand to him.

Ozzi scritched Peter O'Drool once more then took my hand.

I let him lead me across the sidewalk toward the apartment complex parking lot, calling over my shoulder, "See you, Don. Stay out of trouble, Pete."

"Can I ride in your new car?" Ozzie headed toward my covered parking spot.

I rolled my eyes. My long-paid-off Kia had gone to the big scrap heap in the sky so I bought a used Chevy Sonic that, while cheap, still didn't feel affordable. I stared at its backend. "It looks like they lopped off the rear to save money. Or maybe the previous owner got rear-ended and they just left it smushed in like that."

"If that's true, they buffed out the accordion folds nicely." He studied it for a minute. "What do they call that color?"

"I don't know. But I call it *olive red*."

When Ozzi and I got to Union Station in downtown Denver, I was frantic we had missed Lapaglia as it had taken us forever to find parking. I checked with the Amtrak employee in the booth who assured me the train had not come in yet, despite it being almost twenty minutes past its arrival time. I collapsed on one of the benches in the main hall to collect myself.

The last thing I needed was to have to wrangle a furious Lapaglia all day.

Ozzi sat down next to me on the wooden bench and immediately stood. "That is the most uncomfortable seat ever made." He pulled me up. "Let's sit on the comfy-looking chairs instead."

"I think these are the original benches. You know, from history."

"Doesn't make them comfy."

"No, but I can see the door from here. I don't want to miss him."

Ozzi gave me a kiss and a neck rub. "You can watch the door from here. Or we can go outside and wait." He looked over my head and through the window to the tracks outside under the canopy.

I nodded and followed him out the door. The huge canopy covered much of the plaza, casting it in a muted glow, like looking at the world through a gauzy soft focus.

We wandered near track four where the train was to come in. At least two hundred people were queued up in a serpentine line, some with luggage, some without, waiting for the train to arrive to deliver them to points west. Several people wandered like we did, perhaps waiting for their own passenger to arrive.

Even though the sun hadn't been up long, it was hot and uncomfortable outside under the canopy. The planters overflowing with multi-hued petunias brightened the bland civic space, but the cloying sweetness of broiled petunias made me feel like I was drowning in saccharine. I liked that the train wouldn't arrive in some dark underground tunnel, but didn't like that it wasn't even eight in the morning and already seemed to be ninety degrees.

"Let's go back in," I said. Sweating through my sundress before the day even began seemed ill-advised. "You still want to go hiking tomorrow? I think it's going to be hot."

"I guess the better question is, will you? We'll have to get up early to beat the heat, but after today I bet you'll want to sleep until noon." He kissed her. "Maybe brunch at the Brown Palace instead?"

"You're the best boyfriend in the world." I'd been dying to go to the ritziest brunch in Colorado at the historic Brown Palace Hotel. "Are you sure your project team won't call you to bail them out of an emergency the minute we sit down?"

"No." Ozzi frowned. "Maybe a rain check for a better weekend. The project is hitting so many snags it's like...." He struggled to find a metaphor.

"A kitten playing with pantyhose?" I opened the door for him, then ushered him forward with my palm on his right butt cheek.

He laughed. "Yes. That many snags. I wish I'd never heard the phrases *facial recognition software, biometrics, principal component analysis,* or—and this is the worst—the *hidden Markov model* before."

"Sounds positively dreadful at the hack factory these days."

"I'm not a hacker," he said automatically.

"Potato, tomahto."

A zaftig woman grudgingly made room for us on a squishy modern couch in the Great Hall. As she scooted over, I became concerned the bounce of her ample bosom might give her a concussion. I was unapologetic about making her move, however, because from this vantage point I had a view of the outside door to the left and Ozzi could see the door to the right. I could also observe anyone heading down the hallway to baggage claim. I checked the time. "Where is that train?"

"Don't worry. It'll be here."

"Why couldn't he just fly in the night before, stay in a fancy hotel, then get himself to the workshop like a normal person?" I tapped a fingernail on my knee.

Ozzi placed his hand over mine to stop my tapping but as soon as he removed it, the tapping began again in earnest. I was barely aware of it.

"In every interview Lapaglia rants about his hatred of air travel, but says it's easy and relaxing to ride the train to Denver," Ozzi said. "Apparently, he does it quite a bit."

"It sure says something about his level of fame that he can get most anything to happen within a short train ride from Podunk, Nebraska. I bet he tried to get the Dark Dagger Awards relocated to Omaha." I laughed at the absurdity but Ozzi nodded.

"Yeah, I read about that. Had to fact-check it before I allowed it to be posted on his Wikipedia page."

"Seriously? He tried that?"

"He's kind of a recluse."

"Understatement of the year. But I guess even The Great and Powerful Rodolfo Lapaglia has to do stuff to sell books once in a while." I leaned close and whispered, "I hope he's not a complete jerk. It's kind of a smarmy move to come to town two hours before an important event like this."

"I wouldn't mind having his life," Ozzi said. "Getting to come and go as you please. Making crazy demands."

"Be careful what you wish for or you might accidentally turn into a jerk author."

My finger started tapping on my knee again. Clearly this event wasn't nearly as important to Lapaglia as it was to me. He just needed to show up and give whatever stump speech he normally gives to writers—a little encouragement, a little how-to, a lot of malarkey. He wasn't on the hook for the financials since I somehow got hoodwinked into signing all the contracts because I was local—the venue, the food, the wine and cheese for the book signing reception. It added up. Penn & Powell must have bought his train ticket and paid for his hotel after the workshop, so that was something. When I asked Stephanie Szabo about Penn & Powell fronting the money, she pooh-poohed the idea. "Charlee, this is a big event. It will definitely sell out. You won't lose money, only make it." I'm such a putz. If I didn't need the money so badly, maybe I would have fought harder. *He better not screw this up for me.*

I scooted away from Ozzi to see the door better. Ozzi had the good sense to leave his Lapaglia first edition in the car so I dug through my bag and pulled out the book jacket from his most recent bestseller. I studied the photo of him, refreshing my memory so I would be sure to recognize him. Handsome enough, I guess, with that distinguished-looking, but generic salt-and-pepper-at-the-temples hairstyle middle-aged men had going on. But certainly not swoon-worthy. He looked a little smug. Or sad. Or like he knew a secret nobody else was privy to. I was sure I'd recognize him. The full-figured gal next to me was craning her neck, staring at the photo. I refolded the book jacket and returned it to my purse, twisting slightly to keep her from eavesdropping any more than she already was.

"I tried to get him to come in last night," I told Ozzi in a quiet voice. "I mean, c'mon. This train is coming from where, Chicago? And stopping in every podunk town along the way? How could it ever be on time?" I checked the clock for the forty-leventh time.

The woman shot daggers at me then heaved herself from the couch. She turned, giving me one more once-over. So, a twice-over, I guess.

As she walked away, under my breath I said, "Geez, lady, I'm sorry if my perfectly modulated conversation disturbed you." I turned to Ozzi. "I was using my indoor voice, wasn't I?"

"Yes. You're imagining things. People are always stressed out when they travel." He rubbed my knee. "Let's talk about something else. Oh, have you heard about that teaching job?"

I brightened a bit. Teaching at the community college wasn't going to make me rich, but it would certainly ease my financial pain a bit. "Not yet, but I heard that I'm a shoo-in. I've already started working on the curriculum."

As I was telling him the books I wanted to teach, we were interrupted by a man walking up to us.

"Excuse me, can I have a minute?"

I looked up and saw Detective Ming-Like-The-Vase's extra slick hair. He was one of the detectives who questioned me in the murder of Melinda Walter. I immediately retraced the path of my whereabouts for the last few days. My pulse quickened at the memory of throwing a movie stub in the trash at the theater as we were leaving the other night. A perfectly good alibi, wasted. You'd think I'd learn.

"Detective Ming!" I spoke too loud and too fast.

He obviously didn't recognize me. I stood. "I'm Charlee Russo. You thought I killed my agent?" I stuck out my hand, hoping it wasn't dripping with guilty-level amounts of sweat.

"How could I forget?" he said, shaking my hand.

"And you remember Ozzi Rabbinowitz?" Ozzi stood and offered his hand.

"You're not after me for something else now, are you?" I regretted it as soon as I said it. Ming wasn't exactly known for his sense of humor.

He frowned. "Should I be?"

"No, of course not." I sat down then bounced back up. "Of course not."

Ming allowed a tiny inscrutable smile to twist the corners of his mouth. "Actually I'm here asking people if they recognize this woman." He handed me a photo of a woman in her 30s, maybe her 40s. I held it so Ozzi could see, too.

I knew this poor woman had to be missing. Or worse. I closed my eyes. Took a deep calming breath before studying her photo. "Doesn't look familiar to me," I said.

"Me either," Ozzi said.

"Are you here often?" Ming asked.

"Here? At the train station?" I asked.

Ming nodded. "Meeting this train."

"No, first time meeting the train," Ozzi said.

"We come down here to eat sometimes when we're downtown. The Sixteenth Street Mall shuttle comes down here." I babbled a string of words that ran together about restaurants we liked. *Will Ming always have this effect on me?* I forced myself to slow down. This was not about me. "Why? Who is she?"

"Her name is Tiffany Isaac. Murder victim. We have reason to believe she's met this train before. Just trying to find out if anyone knows or recognizes her."

"Oh, that's sad." I studied the photo again with this new information in mind, but I still didn't recognize her. "That's an interesting necklace she's wearing. If it was in one of my books it would be a clue."

"Why's that?" Ming asked.

"Because it's such an interesting, unique design. Look at those delicate curlicues. It looks like a flower."

Ozzi inspected it closer. "I see letters. Like a fancy monogram."

"Looks like a squiggle to me," Ming said.

"It's probably handmade. I bet if you find out who made it, you can find out more about your victim."

Ming seemed unimpressed by my logic. "Indeed." He held out his hand for the photo. "Thanks for your time." He moved on to a group of people nearby.

"He didn't seem like he wanted your help to crack his case," Ozzi said.

"I know, right? What's up with that?"

I checked the time and glanced toward the doors again. Still no train. My eyes wandered around the large room. "Look over there. Standing at the Terminal Bar. It's the King and Queen of Herzegovina. They're here on vacation."

Ozzi looked where I indicated a tall blond couple. "That's not the Royal Herzegovenes. That's the entire Herzegovinian summer Olympics team. She's a pole vaulter. He's—"

"Their water polo team."

Ozzi grinned.

"He's really good."

Ozzi searched the room to continue our game of "What's Their Story?" We played it whenever we had time to kill in public. He pointed to a woman with a huge pile of luggage and stepping stone kids—an infant, a toddler, a preschooler, and a first grader. "She's sending the older one off to Hogwarts."

"She'll need a luggage cart. And I don't see the right platform."

I pointed at a wiry old man with silver hair. It was shaved two-thirds up the sides of his head, but the top was left long. Really long. He wore it in a braid that fell halfway down his back.

Ozzi followed my pointing finger. "He's here to whack someone. They shouldn't have ratted him out after that shakedown."

He pretended to hide behind me as the man's eyes raked the room. "Oh no! Now he's seen us. We need Witness Protection."

"Fuggedaboutit." I feigned disinterest by cleaning my thumbnail. "He's not very big. I can take him. Don't you worry your pretty little head, Oz. But look over there." I indicated the buxom woman from earlier, leaning against the wall, staring at us.

"What? She's waiting for the train too."

"She's staring at us."

"No, she's not. She's staring at the door, just like we are, using the full force of her mind to get the train here faster."

I stared at her, trying not to be obvious about it. I couldn't put my finger on it, but that woman seemed full of power and confidence. She certainly exuded more than I did. "I think she must be Israeli special ops." I watched her reach into her purse and without even looking, pull out a pair of dark aviator glasses and slide them on her face in one deft movement. She didn't stab herself in the eye or anything. I reached for Ozzi's arm but he was too far away so I swatted the air between us. "Oz, did you see that? How cool was that ... just reaching in and finding what she needed in her purse without searching or pawing through geologic layers of crap? Wow. Definitely special ops. And she's cool enough to wear sunglasses indoors. Not many people can do that."

Ozzi put on his sunglasses.

"Like I said..."

"I don't look like special ops?"

"No. You look like a frat boy after a night of binge-drinking."

He pretended to guzzle from a bottle then took his sunglasses off.

"I wonder how people see us," I said.

"Political power couple." He sat up straight and smoothed his wavy brown hair. Then he gathered it up in a messy man-bun with his hand. "Or maybe college drop-outs here for the legal weed."

It was remarkable how he could go from buttoned-up to skuzzy so quickly. "You're a master of disguise, Mr. Rabbinowitz ... if that's your real name."

I studied the Great Hall, crowded with people, some waiting to travel, some waiting for travelers, some guests of the swanky hotel having their morning coffee, and some just sightseeing the historic old building. "Despite the fact nobody is interested in us and our activities, I'm sure, if they thought about it, they'd decide we were world famous sleuths only called in on the very toughest cases, like Sherlock Holmes or Hercule Poirot."

"Like the Case of the Very, Very Late Train from Nebraska."

"Exactly," I said. "Or the case of why I always have to pee so much."

"Oh, that's easy. Weak will, too much coffee, and lentil-sized bladder."

"You are an excellent sleuth. But now, if you'll excuse me and my tiny bladder." I hurried to the restroom.

As I was struggling with the soap dispenser, I felt a presence behind me. I looked up and in the reflection of the mirror saw the zaftig woman so close she might have been my shadow. She pinned me to the sink, her enormous boobs and belly squishy against my spine. She put her mouth next to my ear. "I don't know what kind of game you're playing, but stay away from my man."

I pushed her away and lunged for the paper towel dispenser. "Ozzi? He's your man? I don't think so." I quickly dried my hands while hurrying toward the exit. *How can there be nobody in the women's room right now?*

As if on cue, the door pushed open and a woman with two young girls came in. I scurried past them down the hallway back to the Great Hall, the buxom woman bouncing at my heels.

I kept moving toward the Great Hall, but said, over my shoulder, "Lady, Ozzi and I have been dating for more than three years. I think you're mistaken."

"I heard you talking about him. I'm just warning you. Stay away from him. He's mine."

Talking about him? Oh, good grief. She was talking about Lapaglia. That's why she was shooting daggers at me earlier. When I emerged from the hallway to the Great Hall, I was relieved to see the crowd surging. The train finally arrived and we could gather Lapaglia and get out of here. I kept one eye looking for Ozzi who wasn't on the couch any longer, and one eye on the crazy lady so she didn't sneak up behind me again. I saw her pull her phone from her back pocket and when she did, something fell to the floor. It looked like a business card holder. She pivoted away from me, talking on her phone. I rushed over and scooped up what she'd dropped. Wouldn't hurt to know who she was, just in case. I was right, it was a plastic case with a red-on-red raised logo on the front. I rubbed my thumb over it while I watched her fade into the crowd.

Should I ask Lapaglia about her? Not sure how I'd broach that subject, since he was married, but he should probably be warned that his girlfriend was accosting strangers. Or maybe she was a stalker and he didn't even know her. I glanced over my shoulder in the direction she'd gone.

I dropped the business card case in my bag while I searched the crowd for either Ozzi or Lapaglia. We had to get to our event. If we left in the next five minutes and I drove fast, we could still get there on time. But just barely.

Ozzi came up behind me and I jumped. "Oh! I thought you were that crazy lady again!"

"What crazy lady?" He craned his neck to see over the crowd.

"That Israeli special ops lady. Seems Lapaglia is a bigger jerk than I thought because she's claiming to be his girlfriend and warned me away from him."

"But he's married!" Ozzi looked like he did when he found out Red Velvet Cake was made with beet juice. The ultimate betrayal.

"I know. And she's not the lady I saw in the photos from when he won the Dark Dagger Award a few weeks ago."

"What photos?" he asked.

"Online. From the group that puts on the awards. I saw them when I was looking for info to write my introduction of him for today."

"I've heard rumors for months that their marriage was a disaster and I keep getting community edits on Lapaglia's Wikipedia page that his wife has this boyfriend, Thomas Percy—"

"You remember his name?"

"So many community edits," he moaned. "I kept deleting them but they kept popping up. I was forced to make an 'unconfirmed rumors' section and just let it stay there. I hope nobody sues me for defamation or whatever."

"Why do the fans of Lapaglia's thrillers care about the state of his marriage?"

"Same reason there are Peeping Toms, I guess."

Ozzi and I stood right in the stream of traffic as the crowd surged around us. Two boulders in a swirling confluence of humanity. People entered from the outside door as well as from the hallway where baggage claim was located. "Regardless of what we think, we have to find him, and soon, to get to this event." I stood on tiptoes trying to peer in every direction. A meerkat during a wildebeest migration.

Ozzi slowly rotated in the heavy foot traffic. We both searched for Lapaglia.

The crowd became thicker so I stood on a wooden bench against the wall. I scanned every man's face while I mentally kicked myself for not making a big sign to hold up with his name in large print AND for believing Ozzi when he assured me that he'd recognize him right away and that Lapaglia would hate seeing a big sign with his name on it.

The crowd thinned but still no sign of him. Ozzi indicated that he'd walk outside to the track to check out there. I stayed up on the bench. Now the crowd had ebbed to barely a trickle. I hopped from the bench and followed the hallway to baggage claim. Only a couple of people milled there by the big open window that served as the luggage pass-through. I stuck my head in so far that a burly railroad employee pulled me back into the hallway.

"I'll get your bags, ma'am."

"No, I'm looking for a passenger on the train."

"This is for baggage, lady, not people. They come in through the door. Sheesh."

"I know, but I—"

The employee busied himself with wrangling two oversized bags for a couple. I glanced through the window again but only saw three bags: one with purple flowers, one covered with the Denver Broncos logo, and one child-sized Curious George roller bag. I didn't think any of those were Lapaglia's. I returned to the Great Hall. It made sense that he wouldn't check a bag, since he was only staying overnight. He probably only had a small carry-on.

Ozzi had surely run into him outside by now so I went there. No Ozzi, no Lapaglia. Just the stragglers getting on the train so it could continue on its way to California, with people seeing them off.

I raced back indoors where I ran into Ozzi hurrying out.

"Did you find him?" We spoke at the same time. "No, did you? No, did you?"

I turned in a helpless circle in the Great Hall. Where was he?

"I'll go check the restroom," Ozzi said.

I walked in an aimless path around the flower stand and a coffee kiosk. I saw the National Railroad logo on a large window. I hurried around the corner to talk to the clerk. There were two people in front of me. One was finishing up a loud complaint about the cleanliness of the restroom on the train. The clerk calmed her down by promising to submit her complaint form to the proper person. The next person in line took so long asking about directions to the Brown Palace Hotel, I was ready to drive him there myself.

Eventually it was my turn. "Can you tell me if someone was definitely on that train that just got here?"

The clerk, a no-nonsense, no-neck kinda guy, looked at me suspiciously. "Why?"

"Because I was supposed to meet someone and he never got off the train."

"Are you sure he got *on* the train?"

Not really, but since that thought never crossed my mind, and carried the potential to send me into a full-fledged meltdown, I wasn't about to tell him that. "Absolutely sure."

He stared at me so long I felt a trickle of sweat sneak down my butt crack. Finally he said, "Name."

"Charlemagne Russo."

He typed. "Nobody by that name."

"Oh. That's my name. Your passenger is Rodolfo Lapaglia."

He rolled his eyes then typed again. "Yes, that ticket got lifted."

"Lifted?"

"He was on the train."

"But I never saw him get off."

"Not my problem, lady."

"Where could he be?" I knew the guy didn't care and that clearly we just missed him in the crowd. But that didn't make me any less whiny.

A woman cleared her throat. I turned and saw five impatient people behind me. "I'm sorry." I stepped out of line and made my way back to the Great Hall.

I dug the photo out of my purse again. Unfolding it, I showed it to the barista. "Did this guy buy coffee in the last half hour?"

"Nope. Sorry."

Half an hour ago I wouldn't have thought Lapaglia was the type to buy flowers, but now that I knew he had a girlfriend, I asked the teenage girl minding the flower kiosk if she'd seen him.

She barely looked at the photo. "Not likely."

"Are you sure?"

She waved an arm around the flowers. "You think I'm so busy I wouldn't notice a customer?"

"Thanks anyway."

"Whatev."

I saw Ozzi walking toward me. Alone.

"I checked the restroom and all the shops. No sign."

"He probably headed straight out to get a cab or went out to eat or something, even though he knew we were picking him up." My stomach rolled and I hugged myself. "I knew he was going to turn out to be a jerk. I just knew it."

TWO

"Take a breath. It'll be fine. I'm sure he either forgot or didn't know we were picking him up and went straight to the cab stand. We just didn't see him in the crowd."

"Probably." My phone rang and I checked the caller ID. "It's AmyJo. I hope she's got everything under control there." I answered. "Hey, Ames."

"Where are you? People are getting anxious."

"Little glitch, but don't worry. The train was late and we missed Lapaglia. We're thinking he hurried off to find a cab. Probably get there before we do. We're on our way."

It took us forty-eight minutes to jog to the car and speed down Interstate 25, merge on the tollway to the Parker Arts, Culture, and Events Center—commonly called the PACE Center—where I'd rented the space for today's event. I screeched up, parked where I shouldn't, and we ran inside.

AmyJo met us in the lobby. Her mascara had worked its way from her lashes to form dark half-moons under her eyes. She had either just taken a Zumba class or she was very, very nervous. We spoke in unison.

"He isn't here?"

"He isn't with you?"

"Oh, no!" I checked the time. It was after ten. Lapaglia was supposed to give a two-hour workshop beginning at nine o'clock. Then a box lunch Q&A period with us both from eleven until one, another workshop with Lapaglia from one until three, and then the public book signing, complete with wine and cheese reception, until five o'clock, the culmination of which was to be the highly anticipated live auction of five manuscript critiques from him.

I put my head in my hands and tried to wake myself up from this nightmare.

"Charlee, what do you want us to do?"

I heard AmyJo but didn't answer. Couldn't answer. My first instinct was to march into the room, and tell the two hundred angry people sitting in there what a jerk Rodolfo Lapaglia is, then give them their money back. But I couldn't do that because I didn't have their money. I signed all the contracts—for this place, breakfast pastries and coffee, the box lunches, the wine and cheese—and put all the deposits on my credit card. But all the registrations went through Lapaglia's website. He already had an online payment system set up because he sold downloads of his "How To Write" tutorials, as well as t-shirts and ugly trucker hats that say *Read More, Mob Less*.

Lapaglia has all the money and I have all the bills.

I started to hyperventilate. "I ... can't ... breathe!" I reached for Ozzi who walked me to a lobby chair, sat me down, and bent my head toward my feet.

"Deep breaths, Charlee. Iiiiiiin ..... oooooooout. Iiiiiin .....ooout. That's right. In .... and out. Just like that."

"Uh oh," AmyJo said.

I kept my elbows on my knees and raised only my head. Red-faced, curl-lipped, vein-twitching people were streaming from the event room. Right at me. The only thing missing from this scene were the pitchforks.

Ozzi held my upper arm and urged me to my feet. It took

some effort on his part because all I wanted to do was hide under the cushion and pretend this was all a dream.

I stood, but AmyJo, bless her midwestern heart, stepped between me and the angry horde.

"Listen up, people. I know you're mad, but we just can't seem to find Mr. Lapaglia at this exact moment. He's around somewhere, but his train was late, and now he seems to have gotten himself lost on the way to the suburbs." She offered them her normally infectious, corn-fed, orthodontist-approved smile, but this crowd was well beyond that.

She tried again. "Charlee, here," she gestured toward me, "has done everything in her power—"

"Except get him here!" someone in the back yelled.

"Or give us our money back!" another yelled.

"Yeah! Give us our money back!"

They all started chanting, "Money back, money back!"

I had to rescue AmyJo. I couldn't expect her to protect me any longer. I wanted her to, don't get me wrong, but it seemed selfish to expect it. I stepped in front of her and raised my hands. "Hang on, guys. Let me explain." When they quieted, I took a deep, cleansing breath. "I can teach the workshops in his place, or just the Q&A. Show of hands?" I remembered how much the participants loved my sessions at the Stumptown Writer's Conference in Portland a couple of months ago.

The crowd started up their chant again, but this time half of them chanted "Money back" and the other half chanted "Lapaglia." The difference in syllables made my head throb almost immediately. Well, that, and the whole angry mob thing.

I raised my hands again until they quieted. "Listen. I don't know what to tell you. Lapaglia isn't here. I don't know where he is—"

"Call him!"

"I don't have his number." *And he didn't have mine,* I thought with dismay.

"Likely story!"

It sounded lame to me, too. I asked him for his cell number several times for just this reason, but he ignored my request. He probably thought I'd sell it on the black market. *As God is my witness,* I thought, *if I had it, I would give it to every person in this room. For free.*

"I really don't have his number. I don't know where he is—"

A woman in front turned to the crowd and said, "Lapaglia never does appearances like this. Why would he come all the way to Denver to do this one and then not show up?"

A man standing next to her took up the gauntlet. "Yeah. You made this whole thing up. You manufactured this event to steal our money!"

The crowd started another chant. "Steal our money ... steal our money!" Since it faded away fairly quickly, they must have realized it didn't sound like the demand they wanted.

Ozzi stepped forward when the crowd began to surge. "Stop right there. Charlee Russo didn't steal your money and she didn't try to hoodwink you in any way. She's just as much a victim as you are. Now, she's trying to make it right by doing the workshops you paid to hear—"

"We PAID for Lapaglia!"

They started up the "Lapaglia" chant again. I wasn't sure if they wanted him to actually teach now, or if they were so riled up they wanted his head on a pike instead. I preferred the pike, that's for sure. Did he do all this on purpose to steal money from them? Is he purposely leaving me to hold the bag? Surely he's rich, though, with all those bestsellers in print.

My head throbbed and I was weak with resignation. Why did stuff like this keep happening to me?

A refrigerator-sized man stepped forward and loomed

over me before Ozzi could insert himself between us. He towered over Ozzi, too. "If you don't refund our money right now, I'm going to call Archie Cruz." He performed a quick-draw on his phone that made Ozzi and I both duck.

The crowd mumbled their approval for Archie Cruz. A few in the back even started chanting his name.

"Archie Cruz? Who's that?" Ozzi whispered, straightening himself in that nonchalant way you do after you stumble over a shadow on the sidewalk.

"He's that guy on the local news who does the *Your Advocate* segments. Little bit gossip, little bit consumer help for people who think they've been wronged somehow." I kept my eye on Godzilla.

"Exactly." Godzilla held out his phone to show me he was already on Archie Cruz's website.

I took a deep breath. "For the last time, I don't have your money. Rodolfo Lapaglia does." Brainstorm like a thunderbolt shot through me. "Oh! We can start the bidding on the manuscript critiques Lapaglia was going to auction off!" I beamed at Godzilla who refused to beam back. "Then I can start reimbursing everyone!"

"What did she say?" a voice from the back called.

Godzilla turned. "She said she's NOT giving us our MONEY back, but suggests we can give her MORE money for those manuscript critiques."

The voice called, "You mean those manuscript critiques from someone who never even bothered to show up here? The ones we're not likely to see in our short, sad lifetimes? *Those* manuscript critiques?"

Godzilla nodded. "Yep. The very same."

"Well, when you put it like that ..." It had seemed like a good idea at the time.

The crowd began murmuring again, but this time they began to move apart. Some headed back to their seats to pick up notebooks and computers that wouldn't be used today, except, perhaps, for composing furious missives soon to be posted on Archie Cruz's website, and every social media platform known to humanity.

HashtagI'mScrewed.

As they filed past me, glaring or muttering under their breath or outright cursing me, I said, "Listen ... I'm sorry! This isn't my fault! But I'll figure it out and get you your refunds as soon as possible. Expect to hear from me with good news! Soon! Very soon." I knew they didn't believe me. I didn't really believe myself either.

The caterers had wheeled in carts stacked with the box lunches. Many in the crowd veered toward them to grab a lunch, sometimes two, on their way out. The caterers had no idea what was happening, but pasted on their happy server smiles and said over and over until I wanted to throttle them, "Enjoy ... hope your event is going great ... enjoy ... have a great day!"

I heard more than one participant say, after grabbing a box, "Pretty expensive turkey sandwich!" But most of them said stuff I wouldn't want my mother to hear.

THREE

After they were all gone, Ozzi, AmyJo, and I plopped into chairs. They both wore dazed expressions, so I could only imagine how I looked. The caterers seemed confused by the fact everyone had streamed out the doors but they still had a hundred or so box lunches left over on their carts.

"Um, Miss Russo?" one of them said. "What should we do with these?" She gestured to the remaining boxes.

I stared at the still sizable stacks of boxes, turkey or ham or veggie sandwiches with chips and a dill pickle spear nestled inside. I bought all those. How long would it take me to eat them? Could I even finish them before they went bad? How much room did I have in my fridge? How fat would I get and how long would it take? Of course, I'd give some to Ozzi and AmyJo. And the rest of the members of my critique group. And anyone else I could think of.

"I could start my own deli." I snorted. "Wait. I *could* start my own deli! Will you guys help me?" I turned away from the box lunches and back toward Ozzi and AmyJo.

"In for a penny, in for a pound," AmyJo said with a shrug.

"Whatever you need, babe."

"Could you wheel a couple of these carts and try to sell these lunches at the park or someplace? At least I can start to recoup some of the money to reimburse everyone."

"Sure."

After promising the caterers that they'd get the carts back within an hour, AmyJo and Ozzi consolidated most of the boxes onto two of the rolling carts. Two of the catering staff, who were locals, pointed AmyJo toward the Parker Library where there was always a crowd of families playing in the splash fountain. Then they pointed Ozzi in the opposite direction, toward apartments, the three-block shopping district, and the park.

I held the doors for them as they left. "Thanks for doing this, guys. I owe you."

"You'd do it for us," AmyJo said.

"Neither of you would ever find yourself in a mess like this," I said.

"But if we did, you would." AmyJo bumped her cart over the threshold.

"I absolutely would."

"Be back in a jiffy with pockets of cash." Ozzi gave me a kiss I didn't deserve. "What are you going to be doing?"

"Trying to find Lapaglia."

He bumped over the threshold behind AmyJo and disappeared down the street.

I went back to the comfortable lobby chairs and collapsed into one. The catering staff stacked the remaining box lunches on the nearby table AmyJo had used for registration this morning. Was that only a few hours ago? Sitting there, I tried to organize my thoughts enough to figure out what to do. I was furious, anxious, exhausted, worried, and confused. I was the mulligatawny of stress.

And suddenly starving. I opened one of the lunches and removed the top slice of bread to see what I'd be eating. Figures. Veggie. I was going to eat it anyway when I realized I had, what, thirty lunches to choose from? I opened boxes until I found a ham sandwich and a turkey. I removed the smoked turkey from its nest of lettuce and bread and loaded it onto the top of the honey ham to make it a Charlee Russo Special. Took a bite. I didn't know if it was dry because it didn't have enough mayo or mustard, or if I was only tasting my anxiety.

I dropped the double decker sandwich back in the box, gave the pickle a half-hearted lick, then shoved it all away.

With no plan in mind, other than calling for help, I picked up my phone. Before I could dial, the pop-up bookstore staff of three rounded the corner. Two twenty-something men carried boxes. The other, the owner, pushed a fully loaded handcart. She looked as angry as her struggle bun, which defiantly clung to her head, albeit sliding down, with most of the hair hung in disarray around it.

"There you are," she said to me. The men stopped too, but she waved them away. "Go get that truck loaded. I need to have a little chat with Miss Russo here."

"Take a sandwich if you're hungry," I called after them. I waved my hand toward the box lunches. "Are you hungry, Dee?"

"No, I'm not hungry." Dee's voice had an edge I'd never heard before. Probably because I'd never before made her spend hours setting up a pop-up bookstore, only to drive away every single potential customer.

"Dee, listen, I'm—"

"Yeah, sorry, I'm sure. But that doesn't change the fact I'm out a day's wages for those two, I missed my kid's baseball game, I had to set all this up and then immediately tear it down ..." She grabbed the handle of her handcart and gave it an angry shake.

I knew she really wanted to do that to me.

"Are you sure you don't want a—"

"No!"

"Dee, I promise I'll make this up to you. I don't know what to say. Lapaglia didn't show up. I don't know where he is. I don't have his number. But as soon as all this is straightened out, I'll come down to the store and do a huge book signing party. I'll invite everyone I know, get all my author friends to sign too. You'll make a ton of money."

"Do what you want. But nobody will find your books in my store ever again." She pulled back on her handcart and started for the doors. "Ever. Again." When she got there she turned back, "And you can tell your publisher to expect returns of all your books I have in stock."

Tears welled in my eyes but I blinked them away. I would not let her see me cry. But this was simply too much. I knew she and her staff would be wheeling back and forth past me through the lobby, so I grabbed my bag and found a quiet corner in the event room. I turned a folding chair with my back to the door so even if she came in here I wouldn't have to see her. I still didn't have much of a plan, since it was Saturday and I knew my editor wouldn't be at her desk. I called anyway and when her voicemail came up I said, "Stephanie ... Steph ... listen. I'm in trouble here. I went to pick up Lapaglia from the train station and he wasn't there and when I got here, everyone demanded a refund that I don't have because Lapaglia has all the money and they threatened me with this news guy who I KNOW will ambush me when I'm stress-eating an entire box of doughnuts or something and Dee from the bookstore won't carry my books anymore and I just bought a new car I can't really afford and I had to pay for all this stuff and you TOLD me I wouldn't LOSE any money only MAKE it and ... and ... so many sandwiches!" What little composure I had disappeared like a dandelion puff in a tornado and the message cut off mid-sob. I didn't bother to call her back. I'm sure she understood.

I took some deep breaths and eventually stopped crying. I dialed my agent, Piper O'Shaughnessy, the only other person who might possibly help me. Of course, it was still Saturday and she didn't answer her phone either. I didn't bother to leave a message. I'd only sob through my pitiful story anyway. Besides, what could Piper do about it? She was in New York and Lapaglia wasn't even a client of hers.

I sat and felt sorry for myself for eight more minutes but then snapped out of it. I didn't want Ozzi and AmyJo to see me sniveling away like this while they were actually out trying to help me.

From my bag, I removed the notepad I expected to use to take copious notes of Lapaglia's words of writerly wisdom. I started scribbling some math instead. On the left side of the page I wrote the number of registered attendees and the registration amount they paid. On the right side, my costs. Venue, advertising, breakfast pastries and coffee, box lunches, wine and cheese—

Wine and cheese! I jumped up and ran to find the caterer. She was putting a box into her van.

"Charlee, I was just going to find you. Since whatever happened here ... happened ... what do you want me to do with the wine for tonight?"

"That's what I wanted to ask you about. Can you pretend I never ordered it or the cheese?"

She tilted her head and narrowed her eyes, studying me for an uncomfortably long time.

"Please?"

"Sure. Never happened. I'll take it all to the wedding I'm doing tomorrow."

"Seriously? You will?" I wanted to hug her but I knew if I did I'd probably pop her like a tick. That's how happy she made me.

"Yeah. I didn't open it. No harm, no foul. Besides, you look like you need a little good news."

"Ohmygawd, I DO! Thank you so much!"

"But I'm still charging your credit card on file for everything else."

"I figured, but this means a lot. It really does."

She waved me away like a pesky gnat. Probably sensed I might hug her.

After awarding her a deep and deeply ridiculous bow from the waist, complete with prayer hands that neither of us wanted to see, I went back to my notepad.

I crossed off *wine and cheese,* which only left me on the hook for this venue, advertising, breakfast pastries and coffee, and the box lunches. I estimated the costs based on my memory, added in the registrations if I had to reimburse them, and groaned at the number. I didn't have that kind of money. That was almost the cost of my car! Which I also owe! I began hyperventilating again and put my head between my knees.

"Charlee? You okay?"

I opened my eyes to see Ozzi's shoes in front of me. I sat up. "Did you guys sell all those sandwiches?"

"Um ..." Clearly, Ozzi didn't want to tell me.

"We sold a bunch of sandwiches!" AmyJo was too perky even for her so I knew she was lying.

"How many?"

"Sooo many!"

"How many?"

"Almost all of them."

"AmyJo, just tell her," Ozzi said.

"I sold ten and Ozzi sold three." She saw me looking around for the carts. "We loaded the rest into your car and my truck and gave the carts back to the caterer."

I pulled my notepad toward me. "So how much did you sell them for? How much did we make?"

"Fourteen dollars." AmyJo wrinkled her face, as if that would keep the bad news in.

"Fourteen dollars." I tried to wrap my brain around the

math, but couldn't. I raised my hands in a *what-the-what* manner.

"I sold two at five bucks each to a couple at the park, but they had a kid with them and they said he'd hardly eat any of his," Ozzi said.

"So?"

"So I sold them his for a dollar. And then the restaurants down there found out what I was up to and chased me off."

I looked at AmyJo. "So that's eleven bucks. You sold ten box lunches for three dollars?"

"They were kids. Hungry kids. Kids don't have any money when they're playing in a splash pool. No pockets. No wallets."

"Okay. Fourteen dollars down, fourteen billion to go." I plastered on my rah-rah cheerleader face, despite feeling like a just-sacked quarterback. "I have to do what I can to find Lapaglia, so let's drop these sandwiches off somewhere. Then I can concentrate on salvaging my reputation and my bank account before the angry mob sics Archie Cruz on me and I have to see myself on the evening news."

"Pish," AmyJo said. "That's not going to happen. He's after bigger fish than you." She cringed. "Not that you're a fish at all. Why would he go after you? You're just a penny-ante—" She wrinkled up her face.

"Thanks, Ames. I think."

We each grabbed an armful of the box lunches remaining on the table. I handed off two more to the bookstore employees as they passed. When I saw Dee pushing her handcart toward the side doors, I hurried the opposite direction toward the restrooms.

When I finished in the restroom, the venue was practically deserted. The caterer had sent her staff away, closed up her truck, and driven off. Dee and her bookstore staff were finishing up loading their van. Ozzi and AmyJo were already in the parking lot making sure their loads were evenly balanced and they could see out the rearview mirrors. The lone janitor was happy to see the back of me because it must have meant he got the rest of the day off. As I handed him a box lunch and thanked him while hurrying out the door, I saw a man with a silver braid duck around the corner.

When I got to the car, I asked Ozzi, "Did you see that guy with the long braid?"

He looked around then returned to his task. "What guy?"

"He looked just like the guy from the train station we pretended was in the mob."

Ozzi snapped his head up. "Could it have been Lapaglia?"

"No. Too small and skinny. Don't you remember him from the station? It was just a couple hours ago."

"Sorry."

"It was probably just one of the janitors anyway." I glanced over my shoulder but didn't see anyone. A slight uneasiness pricked at me. Was it possible Lapaglia wasn't just being a jerk? Could something have actually happened to him? It seemed unlikely. I brushed it from my mind.

AmyJo took her truckload of sandwiches to the food bank attached to her mega-church while Ozzi drove my car to Samaritan House to unload. When we finished I asked if he'd drive home too, so I could make some phone calls while on the road. I didn't know if it would help, but I felt like I had to do *something*.

As he drove back to our apartment complex I placed several calls, none of which were answered. I left increasingly frantic, and often duplicate, messages explaining that Lapaglia was missing and asking for any information about his whereabouts or his contact information. I started with my agent, then moved down practically the entire contact list at Penn & Powell Publishing. I began at the top with the publisher himself, the contracts department, the editorial director, my editor, her assistant, the publicity guy, both his part-time assistants, and the sales department, just for good measure. If I knew who scrubbed the corporate toilets I'd probably have called them, too.

By the time I finished, we were home. As Ozzi pulled into my parking space, I dug around my bag for my house keys. I felt something I couldn't identify and pulled it out. It was the business card holder that woman at the train station dropped a thousand years ago this morning. I opened it and saw five identical business cards. The logo on the cards matched the one on the plastic case. I read the name. Martina McCarthy, Marketing Expert. That must be her name. Nobody carries around multiple copies of someone else's business card.

I studied the familiar-looking red-on-red logo but couldn't decide if it was really familiar, or just familiar because I saw the case at the train station. I held it out to Ozzi. "Look at this logo. Is it familiar to you?"

It took him all of two seconds to respond. "Yeah," he said, matter-of-factly. "It's the same design as that necklace on the dead girl in the photo Detective Ming showed us."

FOUR

Sleep had eluded me and I waited in bed for the sun to make an appearance, signifying an appropriate time to get out of bed. I had checked my phone obsessively the rest of the day and all night to see if there was any word from Lapaglia or anyone from Penn & Powell. Nothing. Unless you count the angry emails and social media posts from people asking me for their money back from the workshop. I sent them all the same message. *I'm sorry. This is frustrating for everyone. I'm trying to fix it.*

There wasn't even anything from my agent, who I was fairly certain remained tethered to her phone most of the time. I splayed my legs out from under the sheets, then pulled them back under again. I didn't know what to do about my situation or my personal comfort.

Ozzi woke up, pulled me close and nuzzled my neck. I got that familiar tingle, but couldn't sustain it. "Sorry. My mind is elsewhere."

"Not after your mind." He licked my ear.

The tingle rushed back, but again, sadly, faded. I sat up and sighed. "Raincheck?"

"Always." He knelt behind me and rubbed my neck. "Did

you sleep?"

"Not really." I turned toward him. "I'm worried about Lapaglia. It seems weird he hasn't called anyone at Penn & Powell yet. And last night, late, I called the hotel Steph booked for him and they said he hadn't checked in."

"Agreed. Very weird. But I'm sure he's fine and this is all just a misunderstanding. Maybe he got the dates mixed up."

"Maybe." I sighed. "I feel bad being so worried about something as mundane as money when maybe something really bad happened to him."

"Nothing happened to him. And it's normal to worry about this. It's a lot of money!"

"I just don't know what to do. I can't afford any of this right now, even when I get that teaching job."

He kissed my shoulder. "I know how you could save some money."

"How?"

"Move in with me."

"What?" His apartment was on the third floor of Building JJ in the back of the complex, mine was on the ground floor of Building D in the front of the complex. We watched the sun rise from his bed and watched it set from mine. We both liked this arrangement, or so I thought. Together, but with some elbow room. "You love having your own place."

"But I love you more."

"Ohferpetesake, you're killin' me with adorableness here!" I planted one right on his mouth, tongue and everything. "I love you more than grilled cheese sandwiches, and you know how much I love grilled cheese sandwiches"—he nodded —"but I can't let you do that. First, because you don't really want to live with me—" He tried to protest but I put one finger on his lips. "Right now. And besides, it still wouldn't be enough money. Not soon enough, anyway."

The relief on his face would have made a lesser woman angry, but I found it endearing. Because I felt the same way. I had no doubt we'd move in together at some point—some future point in the future a long time in the future—but for now, this arrangement was perfect. We were perfect. And I wasn't going to let this fiasco screw it up for us.

"No. I've got to figure this out, find Lapaglia, and get him to reimburse me and all those participants. But thank you for the offer. You are a true gentleman." I slipped him some more tongue. "But how 'bout we go get some breakfast, then visit Miss Martina McCarthy at the address on her business card?"

"It's Sunday. She's probably not there."

"I know. But I have to do something or I'm going to go crazy."

Ozzi stepped into the shower with me and my engine revved. We got a little dirty before we got clean, but in short order were presentable enough to make our way to Espresso Yourself, our favorite coffee shop slash bookstore across the street from our apartment complex. I glanced up as I always did and smiled at the handmade wooden sign painted in bright, cheerful colors with their tagline, *for when you have a latte on your mind*.

We were up and at 'em a bit earlier than usual on a Sunday so the crowd was sparse. We were greeted by the forty-pound strawberry-blonde canine hostess, Nova. I bent to rub her velvety ears and kiss her in the middle of the white blaze on her snout. "Hello, sweet girl. Got a table for us today?"

She accepted my love, waited for some sort of benediction from Ozzi, and after she got a chin chuff and a couple of loving thumps on her side, led us to a table in the corner. She curled up, nose to tail, on the floor next to me. She and I had an unbreakable bond since I was the one who rescued her from a bitterly cold snowstorm over the winter and introduced her to Lavar and Tuttle, the owners here. They cleaned her up and got her a check-up with the vet who also checked her for a microchip. When he found none, Lavar and Tuttle kept her while performing their due diligence to find her owners. They put up posters, put photos and notes all over social media and the neighborhood online group, but nobody claimed her. They named her Nova because that's the sudden appearance of a bright new star. And she was.

Tuttle came out of the kitchen wiping his hands on a towel, which he then flipped over one shoulder. It looked tiny compared to his bulging pec and bicep. He'd retired from the Marines several years earlier, but he was still the poster boy for Uncle Sam's muscular fighting machine. He brought two mugs and the coffeepot. "Hey, you two lovebirds. Want your regular?"

"Hi, Tut. I do," I said, while he poured our coffee. "And throw in a mini bacon quiche for my little friend."

"I don't want a mini bacon quiche," Ozzi said, confused.

"Not you. Nova!" At the sound of her name, she lifted her head. I bent to pet her. "Who's a hungry girl?"

Ozzi said, "I doubt she's hungry, cleaning up all the dropped food around here."

Tuttle's free hand fluttered to his throat. "Sugar honey ice tea, boy!" A Marine who cursed in code always made me laugh. "That dog wouldn't deign eat a crumb from the floor. She patrols all day, and if she sees some spill, she stands at attention near it until we clean it up. Improvise, adapt, and overcome."

Ozzi laughed. "Are you sure she's really a dog? Maybe she's actually an oversized cat."

At the word, Nova scrambled to her feet and raced around the cafe.

"Nova. Stand down," Tuttle commanded.

Nova glared at Ozzi then sat at Tuttle's feet, staring up at him. If she could talk she would have said, "Why are you discussing the lowest species of the animal kingdom if there isn't one to dispatch?"

"Sorry, sweets. False alarm." Tuttle rubbed her head. "She

doesn't like F-E-L-I-N-E-S or their owners. If a F-E-L-I-N-E owner comes in, she'll sit near and watch them till they leave. Like security guards watch me in department stores." Tuttle flashed his ultra-white teeth.

"Who are you calling Sweets?" Lavar came up behind Tuttle, wrapped his arms around his abs, and kissed his cheek. Tuttle might have been chiseled from obsidian, but Lavar was molded in bronze. Not quite as big, but it was clear they both loved their free weights. And their free weights loved them back. And arms. And chest. "Hey, Oz. Hey, gorgeous." He stepped from behind Tuttle, sat at our table, and kissed my hand.

"Hey, yourself," I said. "You look mighty spiffy this morning." I indicated his teal-on-pink paisley bowtie over his pink Oxford.

"Just came from church. That congreeegation was on fire! Praise Jesus! Sermon was all about—"

"Uhn uhn uh." Tuttle waggled his finger at him. "You know the rules. You can't preach about Jesus in here unless I can preach about—"

"I know," Lavar said good-naturedly. "The Flying Spaghetti Monster."

"I was going to say 'science,' but okay. Now give me a kiss so I can go get these fine and deserving customers their breakfast."

Ozzi and I shared a smile at their antics and sipped our coffee.

After Tuttle returned to the kitchen, Lavar said, "So what brings you two in so early on the Lord's day, I mean Sunday?" He grinned.

"I couldn't sleep so I made my perfect boyfriend get up with me." I flashed a silly grin at Ozzi.

"Something worrying you?" Tuttle asked.

"Um, yeah. If by *worry* you mean scaring the bejeebers out of me."

Lavar leaned toward me, wrapped his huge hands around mine. "Talk to me."

I told him everything.

"So, this Lapaglia is missing? Have you told your brother?"

Ozzi put down his coffee cup. "That's a good idea."

I shrugged. I leaned on Lance's police expertise for research purposes, and lately, all too often for personal problems. On more than one occasion, most recently in Portland, he had lectured me that adults enjoyed free will and just because we couldn't locate them when we wanted, it didn't mean they were technically missing persons. "He's doing some sort of firearms training this weekend, but I was going to call him later. I know what he'll say, though." I mimicked his voice. "It's no crime to ditch out of an author event."

Ozzi shook his head. "That's a terrible impression."

"Don't sound a thing like him," Lavar agreed. "Tell me more about this Lapaglia fellow."

"Nothing more to tell, in case I forgot to mention that Rodolfo Lapaglia might be a world-class dillhole if he's doing this on purpose." At that last part, my voice got loud and screechy. I couldn't help it. And it made me feel like a dillhole when I considered again that something might have happened to him.

Lavar flashed his gap-toothed smile to reassure the other customers who turned toward my ruckus that all was well and to continue with their pastries and coffee.

"Charlee," Ozzi said. "I really think you should quit using his name so loudly and so ... so ... angrily. Everything you say might be slanderous and you can't afford any more trouble right now. We don't know what happened and until we do—"

"He's right. Y'all better pipe down or you may get lit up by someone."

I glanced at one, then the other and sighed, even though I wasn't sure what *getting lit up* might entail. Didn't sound good, though. "You're right." I dug around for Lapaglia's book jacket in my bag and yanked it out, perhaps a little too roughly, because it tore. I finished the job, leaving just the ragged margins around his face on the author photo. I held it out to Lavar. "Here's his picture."

Lavar put his finger on his chin and went full gay. "Ooh, gurl! He a purty one! Mm mm mmmm."

I rolled my eyes so hard it hurt my neck. "My mom always said pretty is as pretty does and right now I have no idea if what he's doing is anywhere near pretty." A guilty twinge rankled me when I again wondered whether he might actually be in trouble somewhere. I wadded up the scraps from the book jacket and threw them away in the big trashcan near the front door. I saw a familiar silver braid outside in front of Espresso Yourself. I hurtled myself out the door with a hysterical, "Who ARE you? Are you following me? What do you want?" But by the time I got there, he was gone. I ran to the corner near the alley but didn't see him. When I got back to Espresso Yourself, Lavar and Ozzi both stood on the sidewalk poised for trouble.

"What's going on?" Ozzi was in a slight crouch, ready to spring.

"That guy with the braid. I think I saw him again."

Lavar set his jaw and planted his feet in a wider stance. "Should I get Betty?" He kept his voice low.

"No! You keep that thing locked up," I said.

"Who's Betty?" Ozzi asked.

"My gun."

Ozzi wrapped his arm around my shoulder and steered me back to our table. Lavar followed, telling customers everything was fine.

"I think you should call Lance," Ozzi said. "It does no good to have a brother on the police force if you won't let him know what's going on. You have a disappearance, perhaps theft or embezzlement or whatever they'd call it, and now some guy might be following you? Call Lance."

"Gotta agree with the bf on this one, Charlee. Make the call. I'll go help Tut."

Lavar ducked into their office between the front counter and the kitchen. When he came out I saw he was untucking his shirt. He caught me looking and shrugged. Ex-combat Marines always felt safer with a gun.

I dialed Lance's number. As it rang, I said to Ozzi, "He won't answer. He has that training—Oh. You answered. I thought you were in a class or something."

"On a break. Why'd you call if you knew I was busy?"

"Ozzi made me."

Even through my cellphone I knew Lance had tensed. "What's up, but make it quick."

I told him about Lapaglia. When I finished Ozzi whispered, "Don't forget about the guy you keep seeing." I shushed him.

"Charlee, it's no crime for the guy not to show up at your event."

"I KNEW you'd say that." I bugged my eyes at Ozzi, feeling vindicated even though Oz hadn't heard a word Lance said. But I'd tell him. You could be sure I'd tell him. "But should I report him as missing?"

"What did the train people say?"

"That he got on the train."

"And where did he get off?"

"I didn't ask specifically. I just assumed—"

"That's why you'd never make a good cop."

Brothers were infuriating sometimes. "Should I report him as missing?" I asked again, this time putting dramatic pauses between each word.

"No. Is he married? Call his wife and get her to do it."

"I don't know his wife."

"I'm sure you'll figure it out. What would a character in one of your books do?"

"She'd ask her helpful contact at the police department to help her."

Lance laughed. "You always say fiction is easier than real life. Here's another example."

"Thanks a lot."

"You're welcome, Space Case. I gotta go."

Lance hung up before I could even say goodbye. But my alert rang with a text from him. "Be careful. Let me know if you need anything." Then he added a couple of poop emojis.

I responded with a thumbs-up, an okay sign, and kissy lips.

Brothers were infuriating, but I knew this one had my back.

I put my phone away.

Ozzi said, "Why didn't you tell him about the braid guy?"

"Because it would just worry him." I thought for a moment. "I don't even know if that's who I saw. Maybe it's just my imagination. I need to concentrate on problems I *know* I have. Like Lapag—the Author Who Shall Not Be Named."

Lavar brought out our food and poured us more coffee. I noticed he kept his back to the wall and his head on a swivel. I didn't know if that made me feel protected or more anxious. I decided the best course of action was to ignore Lavar's gun and instead, placed the bacon quiche on a paper napkin on the floor next to Nova. She graciously thanked me with a dainty lick to my fingers, then very delicately nibbled it with her tiny front teeth. Such a lady.

While Ozzi and I ate, I considered my options. "The more I think about it, the more I'm sure that Martina woman with the business cards must be involved in this somehow. Otherwise why would she be at the station? Maybe she whisked him away right from under our noses."

"Or maybe they had a secret place to meet up, if they were

having an affair like she said. Maybe he got off the train and never even came in the building. They could have met out on Wynkoop or he could have taken the light rail someplace."

I couldn't remember if she had hurried outside after accosting me in the restroom. I pictured where people got off the train. Union Station was straight across the plaza, but if they veered to the right, they'd go around the building and be on Wynkoop Street, full of shops and restaurants to duck into. And if they'd doubled back, away from Union Station, they'd be able to catch a light rail train anywhere.

I pulled out one of the business cards and placed it on the table between us, then typed in the URL of the website listed. "Under construction. Great." I performed a search for her name. She didn't seem to have the accent to be a realtor in Dublin, the address to be a Hollywood hair stylist, or the body type to be an Olympic sprinter. "I don't have time to plow through 5,660,000 hits on her name. I have to talk to Martina McCarthy."

"What if she turns out to be a stalker?"

"I doubt she's going to tell us that."

"Probably not."

We finished breakfast staring at the card in the middle of the table. I willed it to talk to me and tell me everything I needed to know about Martina McCarthy. It remained silent.

FIVE

We drove in Ozzi's Prius to the address on the card. It was in the Cherry Creek shopping district in the middle of a block flanked by a nail salon and boutique on one side, and a pet store and frozen yogurt place on the other. They all appeared to be open, since parking was scarce. We circled the block and parked.

We walked past FroYolo and saw an employee writing flavors of the day on a chalkboard out front. The Furry Fiesta Pet Store was having a sale on puppies and puppy supplies and it was mobbed with excited kids and harried adults.

"Nine hundred bucks for a puppy? Why don't they go to the shelter and put those puppy mills out of business?" I grumbled, veering toward the door.

Ozzi caught my hand and pulled me back. "Oh no you don't. Only one crusade per day and you have a mystery to solve. Focus on Martina."

"Fine." I dodged two adults with two little boys and a surly teenager heading past us toward the pet store. "But people should adopt dogs instead of buying them from pet stores!" I raised my voice so the family would be sure to hear.

The teenager stopped on the sidewalk and stomped her

foot. "See, Dad? I TOLD you this is bogus. We HAVE to go to the animal shelter. It's a matter of LIFE and DEATH!"

Nobody did drama better than a teenage girl on a mission. I stopped to watch.

Her father clamped her on the shoulder and tried to steer her into the pet store. She wouldn't budge. He gritted his teeth. "The boys have their hearts set on a pug puppy. And this store has three pug puppies. On sale. Right here. Where we are." She still didn't budge. The rest of the family entered the store. He pointed his finger at her. "Wait right here until we're done."

"Done ruining the world, you mean." She put her hands on her hips, clearly a pose her weary father had seen before. The girl looked at me. "What are ya gonna do? People refuse to be reasonable."

"Yes, they do," I said. "But I will say, pugs have a certain charm. I have one in my life. He's a mess. Can barely breathe since his face is so squished in, but his wheezing is second only to his capacity for unconditional love. You want my advice?"

"Why not," she said.

"Whatever dog they get, love it with your whole heart, but keep working on your folks to adopt the next one. They'll come around."

"I don't know. They had three kids. I don't think they're very smart." She leaned against the brick wall, one foot planted flat behind her. Cool as only a teenager could be.

Ozzi and I both laughed. "Good luck to you."

"Whatev." She turned her head, signaling the end of our encounter.

Ozzi held his hand on the door of Martina's business address but didn't open it. "Are you ready for this?"

"You mean do I have a plan?"

"*Do* you have a plan?"

"No." I crooked my finger at him. "Give me a minute." He

let go of the door and followed me back to the brick wall. I leaned against it. The teenage girl gave a loud "hmph" before moving away from us. I knew she kinda wanted to go in the pet store, but she couldn't very well do so now, after her outburst. She sat on the curb instead.

"What's my plan ... what's my plan," I murmured, flicking the business card back and forth. It made a pleasing little *fwoop* sound between my fingers. The card *fwooped* right out of my hand. When I stooped to pick it up, I frowned. I walked toward the curb in front of the building and looked up at the sign. I looked at the card again. Ozzi joined me at the curb.

"What?"

"Look at the logos." I handed him the card then nudged my chin skyward at the sign on the building. "They're completely different." The curlicue logo on Martina's card did not match the stylized lettering spelling out Pandora's Mail Box on the sign above us.

"You're right," Ozzi said. "I was just looking at the address on the building."

"This must not be the right place." I crossed the sidewalk and pulled open the door.

We stood in the lobby surrounded by freestanding kiosks of packages of stationery and shipping supplies. Lining the walls were mailboxes, large and small. I had a flashback to where we picked up our mail in college, mostly scary stuff like financial aid notices, but sometimes cookies from home. In the rear of the store was a long counter with one employee helping a customer package up a box.

"Oz, this isn't her business. It's just where she gets her mail." I moved toward the counter in the back, waiting to speak with the employee. I watched her work. Her thin, mousey hair hung limply in her face. She didn't even bother to brush it back or tuck it behind an ear. Like she and her hair had a fight and she'd lost. Badly.

"Packing peanuts or craft paper?" she asked the customer in a voice that reminded me of Eeyore.

"What's the difference?" he asked.

She didn't look up. Just shrugged without answering. And they say customer service is dead.

"Packing peanuts, I guess."

She maneuvered a huge, flexible tube over the man's box, pulled the lever and held it as Styrofoam pellets poured into the box. By the time she'd let go of the lever, an equal number had poured onto the counter. She brushed them to the floor. Every time she moved I heard them squelch and crack under her feet.

"Plastic, filament, or gummed tape?" Eeyore asked.

The man laughed. "No idea. Which would you choose?"

Again, she didn't look up, just shrugged.

The man looked at us for help.

Ozzi said, "I'd go with plastic."

"Definitely plastic," I said.

"Plastic it is, then," he told Eeyore.

She taped his box, but their interaction was so painful I couldn't watch anymore. I inspected the packages of stationary until the man left. Then I said to Eeyore, whose nametag I could see now and showed REGINA, "I'm looking for someone." I held Martina's business card out to her.

Eeyo—Regina simply stared at me through her curtain of hair.

I tried again. "Martina McCarthy? She has a box here?"

"Yeah?"

"Yeah, she does? Or yeah, continue with your question?"

She didn't respond so I showed her I could win a staring contest with a bored employee any day of the week. The key was to sing *Twinkle, Twinkle Little Star* over and over in your head.

Finally she indicated the business card. "You know as much as I do." The effort seemed to exhaust her and she had to brace herself by bending over the counter and resting her head on her arms.

I shot Ozzi a *will you get a load of this* look. He clearly could not get a load of it either.

"Regina, luv"—I don't know why I thought channeling my inner Vera Stanhope would help—"I know this is hard on a wee bairn such as yourself, but I need you to answer my questions."

She raised her head, tucking her hair behind her ears. Vera Stanhope comes through again!

"Luv, do you know Martina McCarthy?"

"Seen her once or twice. Gets packages sometimes."

"Atta girl. Does she pick up her mail at a regular time every day?"

"Shouldn't say. Privacy stuff."

I felt as exhausted as she looked so I was happy to conclude this conversation, or whatever it was. "Thanks, luv, you've been a big help." I kind of meant it, too. I feel like this was the longest, deepest, most intimate interaction she'd had in a very long time.

As Ozzi and I left, I made note of the hours posted on the front door. We held hands as we walked back to the car.

"I'm coming back here before they open tomorrow. I need to talk to this Martina McCarthy."

"Charlee, didn't she threaten you at the train station?"

"I suppose. But only to keep me away from Lapaglia. Obviously I've done that."

"Obviously." He dropped my hand so he could slip his hand around my waist and pull me close. "I really think you should stay away from her. Wait until you can talk to Penn & Powell."

I nodded. "I'll call them first thing tomorrow. Since they're in New York, I can call really early. But I doubt they're going to help."

"But they might. Or maybe they've already heard from him."

"Maybe. But don't get your hopes up." We walked a little further. "I have to find him. I need that money, despite any vague threat from her."

"Just do me a favor and don't do anything until you talk to your editor."

"That's my plan. But if they can't or won't help, I'll be waiting for Martina McCarthy starting at eight o'clock tomorrow morning. I'll wait there as long as I have to." I saw the look on his face. "You can come with me if you want."

"I can't. I have that presentation tomorrow." Ozzi stopped walking as a cocky grin spread across his face. "But I have an idea." He led me across the street and zigzagged through the short blocks of the shopping district until we got to a huge toy store.

"This is your idea? Buying a game?" I gave him a sidelong glance. "Do you think I'll be bored on my stake out?"

"No, but I think you might not be safe." He opened the door for me. "They sell costumes here. Let's look for disguises. If I can't be there with you, I'd feel better if I knew you might not be recognized."

"I'm going to talk to her, Oz. Pretty sure she'll recognize me. And don't you think she'd turn and run if she saw a naughty nurse coming at her?" I didn't say anything about that mob guy, because I didn't want to worry Ozzi any more than he already was, but I wouldn't mind being incognito if he really was skulking around after me and not just a figment of my imagination.

We got upstairs to the costume department and the first one I saw was the naughty nurse outfit. I held it up. The dress barely covered my lady bits. "Like this?"

Ozzi leered. "Let's hold on to that one."

"Not."

"Aww."

"Isn't the idea to blend in? Not be noticed?"

"I suppose." He pulled a melodramatic sad face.

We shopped for more than two hours, having fun but also collecting some solid disguises—hats, wigs, dowdy housecoat, a baker's outfit that made me look like Lucy Ricardo at the chocolate factory (or maybe Ethel Mertz; it was pretty dowdy), and my favorite ... a pregnancy suit. Ozzi pulled out his credit card. He laughed and nodded at the rhinestone cat-eye glasses and a huge tangerine-colored drag wig I had donned. Sure, they were more noticeable, but lordy, they were fun to wear.

In fact, I wore the glasses and drag wig home while Ozzi wore my new Farrah Fawcett wig. I didn't know if it was the innate politeness and tolerance of the populace of Colorado, but nobody even looked twice at us.

Maybe this disguise thing really was a good idea.

SIX

At six on the dot Monday morning, I dialed Stephanie Szabo's number at the New York offices of Penn & Powell Publishing. I knew she'd be at her desk an hour before everyone else got there. I was miffed she hadn't responded to my frantic messages over the weekend, but she once told me she could get half a manuscript edited in that hour before her day really began, which was probably what she was trying to do today. Tough luck.

"Charlee! I was just getting ready to call you, but I didn't know if you'd be up this early."

"Hey, Steph. So you got my messages?"

"Yes, but just a few minutes ago. I turned my phone off. My sisters and nieces were here for the weekend. I feel just awful!"

Now I felt awful for thinking she was ignoring me. It's hard to remember some people have actual lives that didn't revolve around my drama. "No, it's fine, but I need to find Lapaglia. Have you heard from him?"

"No. I called him and left a message but he hasn't called back. Still never showed up at the hotel. I don't know what else to do."

"What would really help me is if you could reimburse the money all those participants paid for his workshop, and the money I fronted for all the costs."

"Me personally?"

"No. Penn & Powell. It was your idea, after all. You said it would be good for my career. And his."

Steph was silent long enough for me to wonder if the call dropped.

"Are you there?"

"Charlee, I can't do that. I don't have the authority and I know my boss wouldn't agree to it."

"But it was your idea!"

"I know. And I feel terrible."

"Well, that doesn't help me in the least." I was trying to keep my anger and frustration in check. I didn't need to lose another editor.

"I know! What can I do to help?"

"Front the money."

I heard her take a deep breath and whoosh it out. "Here's the thing. I didn't run this workshop event of yours up the chain of command here. Nobody signed off on it because nobody knew."

"But didn't you guys pay for his train ticket and hotel?"

"No. I told him I'd try to submit it afterward … because I knew they wouldn't go for it. I figured he'd forget about it because the event would go so well."

"Steph!"

"I know, I know. But I really thought it was a slam-dunk, that nothing could go wrong."

A series of squeaky frustration noises escaped from my mouth before I could control myself. "Stuff went wrong. Stuff went very wrong."

"I know. And I feel terrible."

"So I've heard." I didn't really have a Plan B for Steph so I wracked my brain. How else could she help? "What you have to do, then, is find Lapaglia, and pronto. Give me his cell number. And do you have his home number in Nebraska?"

"Um ... Charlee, I can't give you his number."

"Why?"

"Client confidentiality. I signed a paper."

I couldn't believe what I was hearing. "You SIGNED a PAPER? What about all the papers I signed? You know, the ones that promised to pay a gazillion dollars THAT I DON'T HAVE?"

"I'm sorry!"

I took a deep breath to control my temper and my tremor. Luckily these days it only showed up under extreme duress. Like when I'd exhausted all options and my cause seemed lost. "Okay. Can you give me his agent's info?"

"Um—"

"You have GOT to be kidding me!"

"I can call Lapaglia's agent and explain the situation. We have a working relationship so maybe I can get through to Lapaglia that way. I doubt his agent would talk to you anyway."

She was probably right. "Okay, fine. You keep trying to call Lapaglia and his agent and get my money back. And let me know the minute you find out anything."

"You know I will, Charlee. And believe me, I feel just awful."

Fat lot of good that does me. "I know, Steph. Just get me my money."

"I'll do my best."

I hung up, had a good cry, then called my agent.

Her assistant answered. "Piper O'Shaughnessy's office."

"Hey Tina. Is she in? It's Charlee Russo."

"Oh, Charlee." Tina's voice changed in a way that made my stomach lurch. "She's in the middle of a conference call—"

"Can you give her a message?"

"No, she told me to interrupt if you called. Hang on."

That did not sound good. But at least I knew she got my messages.

"Hey, Charlee, I just have a minute."

"Thanks for taking my call, Piper."

"I just wish I had better news for you."

"What—"

"I can't do anything to help except maybe lean on Penn & Powell to reimburse you. I'm calling them as soon as this conference call is over."

My heart sunk even lower, if that was possible.

"Don't bother. I just talked to Stephanie. She won't help." I had a brainstorm. "Hey, you wouldn't happen to represent Rodolfo Lapaglia, would you?"

"No. Sorry."

Maybe less of a brainstorm and more of a drizzle. "Do you know who does?"

"No, but I can try to find out." I heard fuzzy mumbling, like she'd covered the phone to talk to someone. "Charlee, I've got to go. I'll be in touch."

She was gone and I was on my own to solve this.

Looked like I had to talk to Martina McCarthy after all.

SEVEN

We forgot to bring the bags of disguises up from Ozzi's trunk yesterday so I headed to his apartment to borrow his keys. I got three-quarters of the way there and saw his empty parking space. He must have left early for his big presentation. I toyed with the idea of not using a disguise, but Ozzi would be mad, and truth be told, a disguise probably was a good idea.

I returned to my apartment and donned the rhinestone cat-eye glasses and tangerine-colored drag wig. I followed the intricate steps the salesclerk gave me to properly attach the wig, since it threatened to fall off so many times yesterday, even when it was wedged between my head and the ceiling in Ozzi's car.

After it was properly pinned and secured, I gave a yank on the tendril that hung over the front of my left shoulder. The enormous updo didn't budge. I placed the rhinestone glasses on my face and studied my new look in the mirror. Striking a pose, I spoke to the vamp in the mirror. "I'm not invisible, but I sure don't look like I did on Saturday." Let's hope nobody paid any attention to me today either, including the mob guy. I had second thoughts about the rhinestone glasses and tossed them in my bag instead. No reason to go over the top.

I waved goodbye to my reflection and headed for my stakeout of Martina McCarthy.

I slid into my car, but my hair barely fit. I lowered the seat and scrunched down to drive. I got there before the shops had opened, and scored Hollywood parking, right on the street in front of the mailbox store. I shut off the engine, rolled down my window for some air, and sat in my car, waiting.

I checked the time. My car heated up fast on this summer morning even with the window open, and I had to pee. Only eight minutes had passed. Ten more minutes until the place even opened. This was going to be a long day.

A woman shoved a key in the lock on the glass door, twisted it, and went inside. It wasn't Eeyore Regina, who, I suspect, must be weekend help. If "help" was the right word. An hour and fifteen minutes passed. I lost count of how many people entered Pandora's Mail Box who weren't Martina. Where was she? My bladder couldn't wait much longer. Sweat trickled down my temples. How did people wear wigs? These things were hot.

I couldn't take it anymore and went inside to ask if I could use their restroom. The woman behind the counter was weighing boxes and adding shipping labels. She looked up when I neared and blinked twice. "Can I help you?" She was easily four thousand times perkier than Regina. And she definitely noticed my wig.

"Can I use your restroom?"

"Sorry. Employees only."

"Really? It's kind of an emergency."

"Try the pet store next door."

I hurried out the door and into the pet store. I didn't break stride, but figured it was toward the back. "Restroom?" I wasn't about to take no for an answer. Situation dire.

The man cleaning the fish tanks just pointed in the direction I was already heading.

When I finished, I grabbed a plush toy for Peter O'Drool as my thanks for the use of the facilities. The man never took his eyes off my tangerine updo, but while he rang me up told me his daughter made the rainbow-colored flamingo in my hand. He squeaked it at me as I handed him my credit card. "One of a kind." I wasn't sure if he meant me or the toy.

On my way back to my car, I peeked in Pandora's Mail Box in case Martina had snuck in while I was otherwise preoccupied. All clear. Just as I finished wrangling my wig into the car, I caught a glimpse of a woman walking away from me halfway down the street. She was poured into the tightest polyester dress I'd ever seen. So tight you could probably read the washing instructions on her undies. I squinted. Was it? I stepped out of my car and strained my neck. I think it was! Martina had come and gone while I was piddling. Damn my lentil-sized bladder.

Dodging gaping shoppers and tourists, I sprinted down the sidewalk after her, trying to finalize what I wanted to say to her. For a large woman, she sure hustled. Martina had crossed the street, but I missed the light and waited impatiently at the crosswalk. I didn't take my eyes off her. She was not going to get away from me before I could ask what she knew about Rodolfo Lapaglia and his whereabouts.

The light changed and I jogged across the street. The wig felt like thirty pounds of concrete slamming my spine with each step. I was more than a block away, but I saw her red dress bobbing in the crowd. She turned a corner. I hurried to catch up.

When I rounded the corner I saw the neighborhood had changed from shopping to office buildings and there were very few pedestrians. I was only about half a block behind Martina. An impossibly tiny woman with long black hair wearing one of those colorful Indian-looking outfits, kind of a cross between a sari and a pantsuit, walked toward Martina, about half a block from her. The woman looked up, adjusted her glasses, and abruptly pivoted away from Martina. It was plain she was trying to avoid running into Martina, but her short legs were no match for Martina's long strides.

Martina caught up with her in no time at all. I could see Martina talking and gesturing, but couldn't make out any words. I debated whether to get closer to them, but I was intimidated, drag wig notwithstanding. I pulled out my phone and got ready to dial 911 if things turned violent. I crept closer, trying to hear what Martina was saying.

The tiny woman wasn't doing any talking, just listening to Martina. I couldn't see Martina's face anymore, but even from behind, her body language showed she was angry. Even her red dress seemed angry. Fingers jabbed, legs firmly planted, boobs and belly almost touching the woman. The woman was clearly frightened. She leaned backward at every jab, the exact inverse of Martina's posture toward her. Behind her glasses, her eyes were wide, and her mouth hung slack.

But just like that, Martina finished her tirade. She brushed past the woman, walked a short distance, then heaved herself into a pickup truck parked at the curb. The woman and I both watched Martina drive away. Then the woman came toward me, continuing on her journey. I waited for her, intent on asking about Martina when she reached me, but she veered into one of the buildings before she got to where I waited on the sidewalk.

I debated whether or not to follow her in but ultimately decided I had to know what the altercation was about. Since my plan of confronting Martina had been thwarted, I wanted at least some kind of information for all my trouble this morning.

Before the first set of automatic doors whooshed open, I saw "Steele Street Library" and their hours posted in vinyl letters on the door. I paused in the irregular polygon-shaped vestibule between the two sets of doors. I stepped to the larger area on the side, probably built to encourage people to take phone calls outside the main part of the library. I used the space to take a moment out of the way to allow my eyes to adjust from the bright sunshine and to think about what I might say to her. I needed to play it cool, try not to alarm her. She already had one scare this morning.

After the second set of automatic doors whooshed closed behind me, shutting out the glare of the sun, I glanced around but couldn't find her. I wandered the library, past the new fiction section, the computers for book check out, the DVDs and music CDs, ending at the children's section in the back, where I found her adjusting a nametag on her top.

She was even tinier than I thought, not much bigger than the kids pulling books off the shelves and stepping on the alphabetical carpet squares making up an enormous dragon on the floor. Up close I saw she was wearing eyeglasses painted to look like a ladybug, complete with little antennas over the bridge of her nose.

"Cute glasses," I said.

"Thanks." She cut her eyes at my wig, tilting her head to see the very top.

It occurred to me that she was so tiny, she probably had to shop in the children's section at the optometrist.

She didn't look at me and continued fiddling with her nametag. I saw that her hands were shaking the teensiest bit.

I peered at her nametag. "Lakshmi, I couldn't help but notice that lady yelling at you outside."

"Yes. She does that." She had a quiet, high-pitched voice. Like a cartoon pixie.

"So, you know her?"

"I have to get ready for story time." I watched as she arranged cookies and apple juice boxes on a table near a comfy-looking wooden rocking chair.

I followed her over, but before I could ask anything else,

one of her co-workers intercepted her and said, "Lakshmi, as soon as you're done with story time, I need you to re-shelve nonfiction."

Lakshmi replied so quietly I could barely hear her. "The volunteers are doing that."

The woman waved a hand at Lakshmi like she was a pesky mosquito. "I need them for something else," she said, then turned with a flounce, giving me and my wig a very judgmental once-over.

"Bosses can be awful," I said after the woman was out of earshot.

Lakshmi looked at my feet. "She's not my boss."

A stylish woman in a business suit marched up holding a toddler's hand. "I'll be back in a couple of hours." She transferred the boy's hand to Lakshmi's hand. "Be a dear and watch Edwin until I get back." The woman addressed Edwin before leaving. "Behave yourself. Tell Miss Lakshmi if you need anything."

After she left, Edwin looked up at Lakshmi. "Give cookie. And juice."

Lakshmi did.

Wow. Could anyone be more passive? I felt bad that she might not want to talk to me, but I had to do what I had to do. I came around the back of the table and helped her by removing the remaining juice boxes from a cooler and placing them on the table while she arranged cookies on a plate.

I felt a tug on the hem of my jean skirt. I looked down to see Edwin staring up at me. He pointed at a juice box.

"You already have one." I pointed at his hand.

He offered me the juice box in his hand.

I took it and jiggled it. "Half full." I attempted to hand it back but he wasn't falling for that. He kept a steady finger pointing at a box of juice on the table. I glanced at Lakshmi who shrugged. I handed Edwin a new juice box. He solemnly shook his head, continuing to point.

"This one?"

He shook his head.

"This one?"

He shook his head again.

I handed back his half full juice box. "Listen, Edwin, darling. If you want juice, you'll drink this one. Now go away."

He took his old juice box from me, a stunned look on his face as he toddled away. Seems I was the only person in Edwin's short life to tell him what's what.

She acknowledged my help with a tiny smile and an almost imperceptible nod.

I accepted this as an invitation to speak to her. "Lakshmi, that woman out on the sidewalk. I'm looking for any information about her or about—" I remembered Ozzi's admonition not to slander Lapaglia, which seemed like good advice since he was a bestselling author and I was in a library. I pulled his photo from my bag. "This man."

She glanced at the photo and sighed. "You're another one."

"I'm another what?"

Lakshmi continued placing vanilla wafers in a circular pattern on a plate. She spoke in her quiet, breathless voice. "I haven't seen Rodney in a while, but maybe Cecilia has."

It sounded like she said Rodney instead of Rodolfo, but I didn't correct her. "Cecilia?"

"Cecilia Lindstrom. I introduced them a while back."

"Where can I find her?"

"She's a graphic designer at a print shop a few blocks away."

As she described the directions, I realized it was near the place where we bought the disguises. I stuffed the photo back in my bag. "Thanks, Lakshmi. Good luck with story time." As I left, Edwin sucked his thumb while giving me the stink-eye.

I walked to the print shop and spoke to an older woman

with spiky hair sitting at a computer. "I'm looking for Cecilia Lindstrom. Would that be you?"

I swear I saw her hair get spikier as her eyes widened. Without a word, she went through the door that separated the lobby of the print shop from the production area and closed it behind her. Was my wig that scary? It hadn't seemed to bother Lakshmi or even Edwin. I waited, baffled, alone in the middle of the lobby for several minutes. I started for the door to the production area but there was an angry, all caps "Employees Only" sign on it. I stepped back. I stepped toward it again. Back again. Forward. Back. I did this weird print shop waltz for a long time. Finally, I had my hand on the knob. It turned from the other side and a man emerged.

"Please leave before I call the cops."

"But—"

"Please."

"But—"

"Listen ...." He paused and studied my enormous drag wig. "Lady." He shrugged. "We don't want any trouble. Just leave."

"But—"

"I'm asking nicely. Now go." He strode to the front door and opened it. "Please."

I wondered what the spiky-hair lady told him. That I was going to rob a print shop in broad daylight in this wig? Did she think I had a weapon tucked up under that beehive? Was there anything to steal from a print shop anyway? I slipped one of their business cards out of a holder on the counter, keeping as much distance from the man as I could while I slunk out the door.

A couple steps past the shop I stopped and patted my wig. It took the full length of my arms to reach the top. When I lowered them, I stroked the tendril hanging over my shoulder. This couldn't have anything to do with a drag wig. It's simply too ridiculous. If that spiky-haired lady was Cecilia

Lindstrom and she knew Lapaglia, and Lakshmi knew them both AND Martina, I was sure this had something to do with Lapaglia.

My wig and I trooped back to the library.

The story time kids were running amok in the children's area. Lakshmi half-heartedly tried to control them using her tiny voice. It did not appear to be working. This was probably how story time always played out because Lakshmi didn't look too upset. But was that cause or effect?

I gently maneuvered two boys fighting over a book away from where Lakshmi stood so I could talk to her more privately. I told her about what happened at the print shop. "Why was she being so weird?"

Lakshmi shrugged. "Maybe she's nervous about Tiffany."

"Tiffany who?"

"Tiffany Isaac."

That name sounded familiar. Tiffany Isaac. Isaac Hayes. Theme from Shaft. I heard the synthesized keyboard riff. Shaft was a detective. Detective Ming! "That girl who was murdered?"

"Miss Lakshmi, I have to go potty." Lakshmi took the hand of a young girl and led her to the restroom. "Watch the kids," she told me.

The two boys who had been fighting over the book now stood before me staring at my wig. When they saw me looking at them, the floodgate of questions opened — "Can I touch that?" ... "Does that hurt?" ... "Do birds live in there?" ... "Why is your hair so big?" ... "Do you want to color with me?" ... "I don't like apple juice. Will you get me root beer?" ... "Who's your favorite Transformer?" — and didn't stop until Lakshmi got back. How did parents and teachers do this all day, every day?

The other children started to close in on me, trapping me like I was a wounded sparrow and they were a pack of feral cats. I handed the plate of cookies to the nearest one and took my chance to flee. "Hey, can I get your cell number so I don't have to bother you at work in case I have questions?" I asked Lakshmi.

She didn't seem the least bit surprised by my request; she simply wrote her number on a sticky note for me.

I detoured to the mystery section and looked to see if they had any of my books on the shelf. I grinned when I saw one copy each of my first three titles sandwiched between Nancy Picard and Dorothy L. Sayers. It always made me ridiculously happy to see my books on a store or library shelf, but it was silly because that meant nobody had bought or borrowed them. It *should* make me happy when my books *weren't* on the shelf, but when that actually happened it hurt my feelings, proving once again what oddballs authors are.

I snapped a picture of my books to post on social media. While my phone was out, I entered Lakshmi's number and the print shop number into my contacts list, then dropped the sticky note and the business card into the trash.

As I walked through the library I puzzled over the altercation between Martina and Lakshmi, Cecilia Lindstrom's odd behavior at the print shop, and Lakshmi's cryptic comment about the murdered woman, Tiffany Isaac. I toyed with the idea of returning to the children's section to discuss it with her, but decided instead to call her later when it would be easier for us to talk.

I also took a moment debating with myself whether to visit the card catalog to see if the copies of my other books were checked out or if the library never bought them. Sheesh. Writers. So needy. I was oddly proud of myself for not succumbing to the temptation. No good ever comes of that.

The interior set of automatic doors whooshed open to release me from the library. I stepped into the vestibule between the two sets of doors. As soon as it whooshed shut behind me, I felt a hand grab the shank of synthetic hair that hung over my shoulder.

EIGHT

My head yanked backward. "Ow!" Instinctively I reached both hands on either side of my wig. I was immediately sorry I took the costumers advice about proper wig attachment. If they yanked hard enough, they might come away with not only the wig, but all of my real hair pinned underneath.

Using my wig as their lever, my assailant spun me around until we were face to face.

The mob guy from Union Station!

He was wedged in the corner facing out and maneuvered me so that my back was to the area between the two automatic doors. He was even shorter than I thought. I had at least thirty pounds on him, and a couple of inches. My hair, however, towered over him by more than a foot. If anyone came in from the street, I'm not sure they'd even see him behind me.

I struggled to get away, but it was difficult since I was afraid to let go of my wig, lest he rip all my hair out. He might have been smaller than me, but he was wiry and strong and had the benefit of surprise.

I managed to get one hand on his thin, gray braid and yanked it hard.

"Ow!" He released the arm he'd used to encircle my shoulders and brought it up to the side of his head.

We were now mirror images of each other, clutching shanks of hair and pulling each other round and round in the foyer, grunting and yelling.

"Where is Lapaglia?" He spoke in a New Jersey accent that I may or may not have imagined.

"No idea!"

"Do not lie. You must know since you did that event with him. Everyone knows he does not do public stuff like that."

We'd come full circle again in our little corner. He yanked my hair harder, which I didn't think possible, and his mouth was millimeters from my nose. He'd had garlic recently. I yanked his braid harder and forced him and his breath away from my nose.

"I don't know anything about Lapaglia. I'm looking for him myself."

"You tell him Square Face wants to chat with him. Or else." He narrowed his eyes and looked at me from the weird angle I'd held his head. "Are you shaking him down?"

"Blackmailing Lapaglia? Why would I do that?"

"I bet you write those books. You know what he knows." His sudden insight made him momentarily relax his grip.

My complete bafflement rendered me unable to take advantage of his loosened grip. Instead, I relaxed *my* grip on *his* braid. "I must know what he knows about what?"

"Everything. Me. My boss. The Family." He didn't miss the opportunity to take advantage of my relaxed grip. He yanked my hair so far I had to bend sideways at the waist. I watched his peacock blue alligator half-boots slip on the carpet, causing him to yank harder. I shrieked and he covered my mouth with the hand he'd been holding over mine on his braid. "I need to know how you know so much about us and our ... activities. Start with everything you know about my boss."

"Awf mrt een naw yu kwe fat mrch layth yaw boff!"

He pulled his hand from my mouth. "What?"

"I SAID, I don't even know YOU, Square Face, much less your boss!"

His eyes bulged and he seemed incapable of blinking. He let go of the handful of my hair completely. He whispered, like there were spies everywhere, "I am not Square Face!"

I took the advantage this time and yanked his braid harder, so *he* had to bend at the waist and stare at *my* shoes. "What IS your name then, dillhole?"

He flailed his arms to either grab my hair again or to get me to let go of his, but I used my superior height and weight, and his slick-soled shoes, to keep him off-balance. I saw someone round the corner to exit the library. I awkwardly held the Braid at bay and watched the woman walk toward us. I carefully timed the opening of the automatic door, or hoped I did, anyway.

As soon as the door whooshed open, the woman gaped at us, planting herself directly in the path of the laser beam controlling the door. She tried to make sense of the scene in front of her. Drag queen beating up a tiny old man. I pulled the woman forward out of the way of the continuously opening and closing door and told her to run. As soon as she did, I kneed the Braid in the groin and pushed him inside the library where he sprawled on his back. The door whooshed closed and I ran out the second door.

The woman raised her hand like she was going to take a picture on her phone. I shook my head at her. She made the right decision and lowered her phone. The last thing I needed was to get anyone else involved in whatever this was I was involved in.

"You really need to get out of here," I said, dragging her

away. "That guy? He's committing a hate crime against me." I pointed to my wig. "But I have it under control."

She got a righteously woke look on her face and fist-bumped me. "You are the best drag queen I've seen in a long time. You go ... girl!" She hurried away from the library with her fist raised over her head, Angela Davis-style.

I was glad nobody else had witnessed anything. The last thing I needed was a curious crowd.

I hugged the side of the building, picking my way around blooming potentilla bushes that scratched my legs, peering carefully into the library windows as I went. I'd expected the Braid to race right out of the double doors after me, but he hadn't. What was he doing in there?

I got all the way to the end of the building with only a couple of people on the sidewalk staring at the drag queen sneaking through the bushes. Nobody inside seemed to have noticed me. I went to the very last window and cupped my hands so I could see inside better. The story time kids were even wilder than before, gobbling cookies and having juice squirting contests. I wondered where Lakshmi was.

My heart vaulted into my throat when I saw her talking to the Braid away from the story time area. Lakshmi had her arms wrapped protectively around herself. He stood much too close, but didn't seem to be touching her. The Braid must be involved in Lapaglia's disappearance, despite his earlier questions of me. It must have been a ruse, some sort of scheme I didn't yet understand. Clearly, the Braid had more information than he let on, if he was talking to Lakshmi.

I emerged from the potentillas, brushing off their tiny yellow flowers clinging to my jean skirt. I zipped away from the library, scared that the Braid would come after me again and now more worried about Lapaglia. If there was foul play and the Braid was after Lapaglia, I had to redouble my efforts to find him. I simply wanted to get him to pay me back, but it seemed the Braid had more drastic, perhaps permanent, ideas for him.

As I hurried back toward my car, I pulled out Martina McCarthy's business card and called her. She had to be at the center of this. Voice mail. I decided not to leave a message she could easily ignore, instead veering toward the Pandora's Mail Box.

Eeyore Regina was working behind the counter again, but I didn't care since I didn't need her assistance today. I felt sorry for the line of customers who did need her assistance, though. I wanted to shout, "Run! Save yourselves!" but refrained. Instead, I pulled a small notebook and pen from my bag and with a shaky hand, scribbled a note. *Please call me. I'm the woman you met at the train station.* I signed it and added my number. I folded it in half and rechecked the address on Martina's business card.

I was attempting to shove it in her mailbox when the woman I saw unlocking the door earlier slapped my hand aside.

"Just what do you think you're doing?"

"I'm ... uh ... leaving this note for one of your ... mailboxees."

"You can't just shove mail in without a stamp."

"Then I'll buy a stamp." I glanced at the door, fully expecting the Braid to find me here. My heart raced, thumping so hard I couldn't believe this woman didn't hear it.

"You'll need an envelope, too."

I caught on to the manager's upselling game. She was going to nickel and dime me to death. Maybe literally. Normally I would be happy to play Thwart a Power-Hungry

Employee, but I was in a bit of a hurry. "Then I'll also buy an envelope."

"You can't just buy one envelope."

"Then I'll buy a box of envelopes."

She pointed to a display. "Five hundred or a thousand?"

"I just need one!"

She shrugged.

I walked to the display of stationary I'd perused when I was here with Ozzi on Sunday and plucked off the package closest to me, a mod hippie design with the ironic message *Thinking of You*. I tore it open, placed my note in one of the matching envelopes, and handed the stationary package back to her. "This and a postage stamp, please."

"We don't sell individual stamps. Smallest I have is a book of twenty."

"Fine. Ring up this stationary and a book of stamps."

She went to the register. "Cash or credit?"

"Credit." I handed her my card, glancing nervously at the door. At least she didn't make me wait at the end of Eeyore Regina's line.

She swiped it through her credit card reader, frowned, swiped it again.

I gulped. Had they locked my account since I was over my limit? *Was* I over my limit? Had all those event charges gone through?

She wiped the magnetic strip with her finger and tried again. She shook her head and handed my card back. "Isn't working."

Blushing, I pulled my last thirty dollars from my wallet. Why was it when your credit card didn't work—through no fault of your own—you're made to feel like a criminal?

She finished with the transaction and handed me back a measly amount of change. I thanked her, trying to keep the sarcasm from my voice. Returning to Martina's mailbox with my note inside an officially stamped and licked envelope, I again attempted to shove it in. The manager reappeared next to me. I pulled my hand back before she could slap it.

"You can't do that."

"You told me I needed an envelope and a stamp. Which, you might remember, I just bought." My voice veered into *shrill* range.

"And now it needs to be mailed." She gestured toward the letter drop nearby.

"How long will that take?"

"Two days. You're not special."

"Let me get this straight. I need to drop this"—I waved the envelope at her—"into that letter drop and you'll collect it out of there, send it off to some processing center, and then it will come right back here, where you'll put it in this"—I banged on it for effect—"mailbox?"

"You need to address it first. Otherwise it'll come back *Undeliverable*."

I had the feeling Eeyore Regina wouldn't have been as strict as this lady. I took a deep breath and tried not to let frustration and panic overwhelm me. Pasting a fake, Miss Congeniality smile on my face, I said, "Can I give you five bucks to drop this into Miss McCarthy's mailbox without going through this rigmarole? It's important she gets it soon."

"Are you bribing a postal employee?"

Defeated by bureaucracy, I wrote Martina's address on the envelope and dropped it in the letter drop under the withering scrutiny of the manager.

"Two days?"

"Give or take," she said.

"But you said—"

"Is there anything else I can help you with today?"

I wanted to say she hadn't helped me at all. But I didn't. "No, nothing else. I'm good. Thanks." I turned toward the door in time to see what I'd been dreading through this entire transaction—the Braid heading this way. I pivoted and wrenched open the door with the Employees Only sign. I'd seen an alley behind this block of buildings so I knew there had to be a back door.

"You can't go through there!"

"Lady, I'm going through this door and out your back door," I called over my shoulder. "You can watch me do it, if you like, but that's what I'll be doing."

She followed me through and chased me all the way down the corridor to the back door. I started running down the alley, sandals slapping the pavement, and she took a few steps after me. I heard the door bang shut, then an angry, "Dammit!" I turned and saw her tugging on the handle to get back in.

I hated to revel in the *schadenfreude* of the moment, but I kinda did. If she'd only let me shove my note in Martina's mailbox in the first place, none of this would have happened. She wouldn't have to walk all the way around the block to get back to work, and I wouldn't have to hoof it down this disgusting alley. It was probably best that she would be delayed getting back to work. The Braid might even be gone before she did so. I wondered if he was looking for me or if he was there to ask questions about Martina like I had. If so, I hoped he waited in Eeyore Regina's line and didn't speak to the manager about me. All he'd have to do is ask, "Seen a lady in a huge orange wig come in here?"

I hurried toward my car, hoping they weren't going to have that conversation. Or, frankly, any conversation.

All I wanted to do was go home, dive under my covers, and stay there for a thousand years. But I knew I couldn't. Lakshmi was in danger, perhaps because of me. I was certainly in danger and maybe Lapaglia was too. Until I figured out what was going on, I couldn't be sure. I was almost to my car, but I changed direction and headed to the costume shop.

I race-walked while trying to unattach my wig from my

head. Easier said than done. I didn't know if it would have been better or worse for the Braid to have yanked it off as I was leaving the library. Maybe then I would have been able to run away immediately. Unless keeping me at the library in our hair-pulling contest kept me safe. Perhaps it was better not to know.

Even though people on the street didn't really react to me properly wearing a tangerine drag wig, they did tend to gape at me wearing a tangerine drag wig sliding down the side of my head. I couldn't quite get all the pins out. Darn that costume guy and his excellent instructions.

I gave up about half a block from the shop, knowing I would be demanding immediate help from the first employee I saw. The wig bounced just over my ear as I hurried along. I couldn't even imagine what I looked like. Wait. Yes, I could. I looked like an arrow on one of those neon signs along a country highway, my hair pointing the way to a roadside honky tonk or a diner serving all-you-can-eat biscuits and gravy.

I had to get to the store before the Braid saw me and before my beehive poked out someone's eye.

NINE

Bursting into the costume shop, I didn't even wait for my eyes to adjust to the darker interior. Just barreled toward the stairs where I knew the costumes were. I only stopped when I ran into the concave chest of the employee who helped us on Sunday.

"Hey, hey, hey. What happened here?" He gestured to my collapsing hair.

"Get me out of this thing. Please."

He marched me toward his desk tucked in the far corner and sat me in his swivel chair. He began plucking out pins. It felt like I was being attacked by crows.

"You didn't answer me. What happened to you?"

"I thought it would be easier to get off than it was so I started on it as I was walking."

"Why didn't you wait until you got home?" Pluck, peck, pluck.

I knew I couldn't tell him the complete truth, so I told him a different truth. "Because I'm an idiot."

He swung my chair around and squatted so he was right in my face. "You are NOT an idiot. Now, quit talking nonsense."

I knew he was simply worried about my self-esteem, but it was hard to explain to people that I really didn't think I was an idiot when I called myself an idiot. It was just shorthand for when I did something stupid. Although, really, was it technically stupid that I was trying to un-disguise myself?

"You're absolutely right. I'm not an idiot. But I probably could have thought this through a little bit better."

He peck-pluck-pecked me until I was finally freed. I rolled my neck, which felt a thousand pounds lighter.

"Thanks ... I don't even know your name and I feel like we've just had an intimate moment."

He laughed. "Harland."

"I'm Charlee. Happy to officially meet my new best friend." I ran my fingers through my temples until they met in the back and massaged my scalp. Practically orgasmic. I stopped before I embarrassed myself. "But now, Harland, I need another disguise."

He raised an eyebrow. "Disguise?"

"Costume," I corrected, even though we both knew I hadn't misspoken.

"What about all those you bought the other day?"

"They're locked in my boyfriend's car and he's at work—"

"And you're running from someone."

I didn't want to confirm the obvious. "Don't be silly. I'm going to a ... costume party."

"On a Monday afternoon." I must have made a face because he added, "Not that I don't believe you. But no matter. It's none of my beeswax." He walked over to the six-foot-tall rack of costumes and started flipping through them. I liked a stylish carnation pink flight attendant outfit that reminded me of one my Barbie had. It matched her sporty pink convertible.

"Can I change into it now?"

"Sure. I'll ring it up so you can skeedaddle on your way."

The top was a little too small and the bottom a little too big, but so was I, so who was I to complain?

I handed Harland my credit card and kept my fingers crossed behind my back. My hopes sank as he pulled it out of the reader and tried to swipe it. He rubbed it on his shirt and tried to swipe it again. He gave me a weak smile and spoke gently. "Sorry. Declined. Do you have another card?" He handed it back.

"I have a library card and a loyalty card from the hot dog place on Colfax. Will you take either one of them?" I slid the useless card back in my wallet then dug in my cash pocket. I glanced at the register, then rifled through my bills. "Not enough." I sighed, then went back to change out of the Barbie outfit.

When I came out in my t-shirt and jean skirt, I handed him the suit neatly draped on the hanger. He handed me a flowing caftan on a hanger and a puddle of multi-colored fabric I assumed might be some kind of hat. "Try this," he said.

I stuck my hand in the puddle of soft fabric and a turban with a huge bow on the front sprung to life. I wondered how many people had been treated for lice either before or after wearing this. "I don't think I can afford it."

"Yes, you can. This was a rental that came back to us in pretty bad shape. I never even put it back on the rack. Try it." He must have seen the revulsion on my face because he added, "Don't be a ninny. It's been washed. Perfectly clean."

With only a small shudder that I tried to keep hidden, I tucked my hair up into the turban and threw the roomy caftan on over my clothes. "Ugly, but it might do. How much?"

"How much you got?"

I fanned my bills in my hand. "Eight dollars."

Harland plucked out the three ones, leaving the five with me.

"Are you sure?"

"It's three more bucks than we ever would have gotten for this." He pointed out stains and tears in the caftan. "And that turban is butt-ugly. I never liked having it in the store."

"It's been a pleasure doing business with you, Harland. I'll send everyone here for their costuming needs."

"Thanks. Wear it in good health." He cocked his head. "Be careful out there, Charlee."

"I will." I felt better knowing I still had work to do and the Braid would be looking for a towering head of tangerine hair —if the Braid was looking for me at all. I hoped that wasn't the case, but I felt more confident in my ugly turban and stained caftan.

I knew I had to try once more to talk to Cecilia at the print shop. I just hoped she wouldn't hide from me again.

As I was walking, Ozzi called. "I just have a quick minute before I need to get back, but I wanted to know how it went with Martina."

"I missed her, but found more of his girlfriends."

"Plural? Geez, I misjudged this guy."

"I'm on my way to talk to one of them right now."

"Are you driving?" He had a thing about cellphone use in the car.

"Nope. Hoofing it. You should know me better than that."

"I do. I guess I'm just braindead from this project. I'll make it up to you later."

I made some yummy noises. "Promise?"

"Absolutely. But now I've gotta go."

"How's your thing going?"

"Jury's still out. Love you."

"Love you, too."

I reached the print shop and saw Cecilia through the window loading paper into a copier. I took a deep breath and pulled open the door. At the bell, she turned to greet me.

"Hi! How can I help you today?" She sounded very pleasant and enthusiastic. Clearly, she hadn't recognized me.

"You're Cecilia, right?" She nodded so I continued. "I need to ask you about Rodol—" I remembered Ozzi's admonition about slander. I dug in my purse and pulled out Lapaglia's photo. "I need to ask you about this guy."

I expected her to bolt, but she didn't. She sounded a tad less enthusiastic, though.

"What about him?" She suddenly narrowed her eyes and stared closer at my face. "You were here earlier."

I nodded.

"Okay. So what do you want?"

This conversation was not going how I expected. At all. My curiosity got the better of me. "Why did you hide from me before?"

She finished loading the paper and closed the doors of the copier. She glanced around the empty shop, as if she expected someone to have miraculously appeared. She put her fingers to her lips then pointed at Lapaglia's photo. "We're having an affair," she whispered. "I'm married and so is he."

That didn't explain it. "But why—"

"I don't know what his wife looks like. He said she had long hair, I don't know. But I know for a fact she wouldn't be caught dead in *that* outfit." She waved a hand up and down at me. I decided not to take offense.

"So, earlier you thought I was his"—I waggled the photo —"wife?"

She nodded. "Scared the sh—scared me a lot. He says she's the jealous type. Has a temper."

"What about Martina and Lakshmi?"

"Don't know any Martina." She raised her eyebrows. "Is Lakshmi involved with him too?"

"I don't—"

"Never mind. I don't care. I'd prefer it if he had another girlfriend. Lots of them, in fact. It would keep him from getting too attached to me. My husband isn't the most ... understanding man." She touched the side of her face but just as quickly lowered her hand when she noticed me staring. "Lakshmi, though. That kind of surprises me."

"But you'd be okay with that?" This was a very weird conversation.

"Absolutely. The more, the merrier. You, me, Lakshmi, this Martina you mentioned, Tiffany. Velvet's mafia is alive and well." Cecelia barked out a laugh.

I tried not to react to her gay slur, thinking the pejorative phrase for the "gay agenda" had been retired long ago. She hadn't even used the *Velvet Mafia* idiom correctly.

Cecelia was still talking. "—an hour or two away from my husband every so often, be with a man who doesn't smack me around, and he'd"—she gestured at the photo—"get away from his shrew of a wife." She must have seen judgment on my face. "Everyone deserves to be happy, you know."

"Of course they do," I said, wanting to retort she should include LGBTQ people in the pool of folks deserving of happiness. I held my tongue, though. I was curious about who she meant. None of my business, not really. But maybe. "For the record, I am definitely NOT having an affair with him. I need to find him about some business we had together. And just so I'm clear, you don't know Martina McCarthy?" She shook her head. "And this Tiffany you mentioned—"

"So sad. Total computer geek. I introduced Ron and Tiff. She and I were taking a computer class together in the evening to learn how to create ebooks. Formatting and designing book covers and stuff. I didn't really understand the formatting stuff, but she caught on real fast. I refer customers to her all the time." Cecilia corrected herself. "Referred. She died recently. Some kind of accident, I heard. Like I said, sad."

"Very." I didn't want to be the one to tell her that Tiffany was murdered, but what if Lapaglia was somehow involved and Cecilia was in danger? Or maybe Cecilia had more current information and Detective Ming's investigation showed it was an accident? I made a mental note to call him when I got home. If it was still a murder investigation, I could just tell him I met someone who knew Tiffany and then he could talk to Cecilia himself. And if it was an accident, then maybe I could quit thinking I'd stumbled into yet another murder situation. Win-win for me either way.

I decided to change the subject and get more information about Lapaglia, since Cecilia was happy to talk to me. "How often do you see him?"

"I don't know. Every six weeks or so?"

"When was the last time?"

"Maybe a month ago. He brought in some of his work. I like it well enough. Little simplistic. But I've only seen a couple of signatures."

I didn't know what his signature had to do with anything, but I'd never heard his thrillers called simplistic. The ones I had read seemed to weave in lots of story threads. But to each his own, I guess. That's why there were so many books in the world. I felt more than a little nosy, but if she was going to keep answering my questions, I was going to keep asking them. "So if it's not his work that drew you to him, then what?"

She got a wistful, dreamy, somewhat sad smile on her face. "He's interested in me. It's fun. I feel I can relax around him. He always asks about my job, what I'm working on."

"Which is?"

Cecilia explained a bit about what she does as a graphic designer at a print shop, then her voice took on a hard edge. "My husband doesn't know or care how good I am at matching my PMS book, or setting up bleeds, or how I just learned to die cut. Nor would he even listen to an explanation, unless I tied him to a chair and held a gun to his head."

I tried not to be too judgmental about the violent imagery, but I guess I could understand her attraction to Lapaglia.

Contrasted with Cecilia's husband, he sounded like the perfect man.

The tinkly bell chimed and a customer entered the shop, requiring Cecilia's attention.

"Thanks for the info, Cecilia, but I'll let you get back to work now." I started to leave, but turned around. "Hey. Could I get your direct number in case I have more questions?"

She selected a business card from the plastic holder on the front counter and scribbled a number on the back. "That's my cell."

While I walked to my car, I called Detective Ming and left a message linking Cecilia to Tiffany. "But, please, don't tell her you got the info from me, okay?" I didn't know if he would or not, but decided it would ultimately be fine either way. I mean, I was potentially keeping her safe from a murderer. Whether that was a valid reason for her abusive husband maybe finding out she was having an affair was a bridge to cross another day. "And there's something else I want to report. This skinny guy with a long gray braid attacked me and maybe followed me around Cherry Creek this morn—" My phone beeped and I looked to see who was calling ... Detective Ming. "Gosh, that was quick," I said.

"You were attacked?"

"Yeah. He grabbed me at a library."

"Where?"

"By my hair."

"No, where is this library?"

"Oh. Steele Street in Cherry Creek."

"Are you hurt?"

"No."

"Was he?"

"I'd like to think so, but probably not. Maybe his feelings, getting beat up by a girl."

"Got a description?"

"Like I said. Skinny. Wiry. Long gray braid. Hair shaved up the sides. Peacock blue alligator half-boots."

"Random or targeted?"

"Targeted. Definitely. He was talking nonsense about this author I know, Rodolfo Lapaglia and the mob. This braid guy wants me to tell him where he is. And he thinks I'm blackmailing him."

"Are you?"

"What? No." It seemed like Ming was just humoring me now, not actually taking any kind of report. "Oh! And the Braid was at Union Station on Saturday. You might have seen him yourself."

"Hmm."

I wondered what that *hmm* might mean.

"Any witnesses to the altercation?"

"No. Wait, a lady saw us right before I kneed him in the ... groin."

"Did you get her name?"

I regretted telling her to lower her phone. In retrospect, a picture might have been a good idea. "No. And I don't think it would do any good anyway."

"Why?"

"Because I think her attention was completely focused on me."

"And why would that be?"

"Because I was wearing a four-foot-tall wig in Ronald McDonald orange."

He paused exactly as I knew he would. "Of course you were."

"I can explain—"

"I'm sure you can. Instead, just call 911 if you see him again."

"That's it? Wait until he attacks me again?"

"Miss Russo, this all sounds a bit far-fetched. A member of the mob is after you while you're in costume—" He said the word like it was coated in olive oil.

"Disguise."

"Either way, there's not much to go on."

"Not much!"

"Let me rephrase. There's certainly a lot going on *with your story,* but not much that the Denver PD can take action on."

"I'm not making this up."

After a pause—or maybe a standoff—he said, "I'll send it down to have patrol keep an eye out for a ... skinny guy with a long gray braid."

"And I'll call 911 if I see him again." *Fat lot of good that will do me, sounds like.*

"You do that."

I meandered around the upscale business district wondering if Ming would actually tell the cops to watch out for the Braid, or if he really was just humoring me. And why would he have to humor me anyway? We have a history. I'm not some crazy, hysterical—I remembered the tone of his voice when he mentioned my disguise. Screw him.

When I finally remembered where I parked my car, I was never so happy to see it in all its olive red glory. It was blazing hot inside, though, so I turned on the AC full blast and sat there with the windows down until I could touch the steering wheel and gearshift without blistering my hands.

I mulled over everything I knew about these girlfriends of Lapaglia's. It made sense that Martina was harboring Lapaglia, giving him a safe place to hide out, but from what? Me? His wife? The Braid? The other girlfriends? Cecilia didn't know about Martina, but Lakshmi did. And Cecilia and Lakshmi both knew Tiffany. But so what? What did that mean?

What if Martina wasn't harboring Lapaglia? What if she was holding him hostage? There could be a million reasons for that. Jealousy. Ransom. In cahoots with the Braid. Maybe Martina was a mob moll. No, that couldn't be, because then the Braid would know where Lapaglia was and wouldn't be chasing me.

Maybe Martina was just plain pissed off that he had all these other girlfriends. Maybe Martina just found out about them. Leading her on, playing her for a fool, taking advantage of her. Could she be involved with Tiffany's death AND Lapaglia's disappearance? Extreme jealousy would certainly explain Martina's altercation at the train station with me and on the street with Lakshmi earlier.

And what about Lakshmi? She knew Martina, Cecilia, and Tiffany and seemed perfectly fine with the other women. But she's such a doormat, maybe someone forced her to do something she didn't want to do. Or maybe she just got tired of being a doormat and snapped. She definitely had that defeated *whatever* sort of demeanor.

Cecilia? With all that violent imagery? She seemed fairly forthcoming with me but maybe she was hiding something. Years of spousal abuse might twist you up in ways I probably couldn't even imagine.

I spent the rest of the drive home trying to figure out how I'd explain the motivation of these women in one of my mysteries. Which would I choose as my villain?

When I pulled into my parking spot, I saw Don Singer from upstairs struggling to step over the knee-high decorative fence bordering the grassy area where Peter O'Drool liked to poop. I pulled out the plush rainbow-colored flamingo dog toy I bought earlier to give to Peter.

"Hey, Don, need some help?"

He turned. "Oh, hi, Charlee. I got all the way over here, climbed the fence, and realized I forgot a poop bag. Gotta head back up for one."

"Want me to get it for you?"

"Nah. Barb always says I need more exercise." He accepted my hand to steady his balance over the short fence. "She also says I always forget the poop bags."

"She's not wrong."

"I know, gosh darn it." He climbed the outside staircase to his apartment. "Interesting outfit, by the way. Love the hat."

I placed a hand on the top of my head. Oh, yeah. The turban. I kicked at the caftan and let it billow. "You should try something like this. Very comfy. Forgot I was even wearing it." Unlike a drag wig.

Don walked toward the stairs and I heard him say hello. I looked up to see a woman walking past him. I stifled a giggle because she was swaddled in a loud print scarf and oversized sunglasses, looking like Gloria Swanson on the set of *Sunset Boulevard*. Two of us in extreme outfits in one apartment complex.

I turned back to Peter O'Drool and squeaked the flamingo. "Hey, Pete. I brought you a present." I waved it at him.

The pug burst out from under a juniper at the same moment a rabbit did. Peter ran straight at me, sailing over the decorative fence. The rabbit took off in the opposite direction. *What goes on under that juniper?* I wondered if this was a game Peter and the bunnies liked to play or if they really were mortal enemies.

Peter danced around my feet, huffing and wheezing from the effort. I squeaked the toy again then tossed it to him. It bounced off his face and landed on the sidewalk between us. It was almost as long as he was. He scooped it up, biting it to make the squeaky noise. He dropped it on the sidewalk, did a little do-si-do of joy, then picked it up again, squeaking it over and over, perhaps keeping time to a song only he could hear.

While I watched Peter play, a pair of peacock blue alligator half-boots appeared on either side of Peter O'Drool. I watched while two hands scooped up Peter from the sidewalk. The Braid!

Peter happily chomped his toy, snuggled in the Braid's arms. I saw the sneer on his face and froze.

"You better find me Lapaglia before the cops do. Or you will be sorry." The Braid made a knife action across Peter's throat. "And let us keep this between you and me. No need to get others involved." Pete let go of his toy and it dropped into the Braid's arms, just long enough for him to lick the Braid's face.

The Braid ran with Peter O'Drool and his squeaky flamingo between the buildings and through the complex, disappearing while I remained rooted to the sidewalk, stunned into paralysis. I heard an engine roar to life from a parking lot in the back.

Peter O'Drool had been dognapped!

TEN

"Sorry that took so long," Don said. "I had to wait until Barb stopped laughing at me to help me find the new stash of poop bags." Don frowned when he saw my face. "What's the matter?"

My throat worked up and down, but no sound came out.

"Charlee?" When I couldn't answer, Don called up to his balcony. "Barb! Something's wrong with Charlee!"

Barb called over the railing. "What's all the ruckus?"

I looked from Barb to Don to the direction the Braid had gone with Peter. While Don and Barb discussed whether they should call Ozzi or my brother or the paramedics, I forced my brain into gear. "No, I'm fine. But Peter ... it happened so fast ... I didn't know what to ... I'm so sorry!"

"What happened, Charlee?" Don's voice was sharp.

Using my entire arm, I pointed in the direction the Braid had run. He'd told me not to tell anyone, but surely that couldn't mean Don and Barb. "Peter just got dognapped!"

"What? What are you talking about?" Barb hurried down the stairs to Don. "What is she talking about?"

I covered my face with both hands and took a long shaky

breath. "I don't exactly know, but that author I was doing the workshop with on Saturday—"

"He stole Peter?" Barb's eyes went wide.

"No, no, no. He writes these books about the mob—"

"Rodolfo Lapaglia. Yes, I've read all his books. What does this have to do with Pete?" Don's words were clipped.

"I'm not explaining this well." I looked around frantically, hoping to see Peter and learn this was all just a joke.

Don grabbed both my biceps. "Charlee. Where is Peter?"

"Dognapped."

Barb gasped. Don ran his hands through the thin hair on top of his head.

"Let me start at the beginning—"

"But they're getting away!" Barb wailed.

I remembered the sound of the engine roaring away. "They're already gone, Barb. Listen." I wasn't sure I was doing the right thing by telling them, but they had a right to know, despite the Braid's threat. "I think the guy who took Pete has something to do with the mob that Lapaglia writes about. He stole Pete to force me to find Lapaglia. But he said he might hurt Pete if I told anyone, so you can't do anything."

"But we have to call the police!" Barb's nest of curls bounced with the force of her words.

Don stared at me, then gently put an arm around his wife's shoulders. "We can't, Barb. We'll handle this ourselves. You, me, and Charlee." He looked at me. "You in?"

"Completely! It's my fault Peter's gone!" I couldn't hold it together any longer and the three of us huddled together there on the sidewalk, tears falling freely.

I was glad Don didn't want to call the police. Besides, what kind of priority would they give a dognapping? Low, I'm sure. Detective Ming barely cared about the Braid assaulting me. And if they didn't care about a human kidnapping when I was in Portland, they sure weren't going to care about a dognapping in Denver. Plus, I already knew who did it.

I pulled away from our group hug and put my mind into cop-mode. What would they do, assuming they cared? If it was a kid snatched off the street they'd canvas the neighborhood for witnesses.

Barb and Don continued to cry and console each other.

"Don't you worry," I told them. "We'll find him. I promise. I'm going to go follow the direction they went."

I ran off between the buildings. I stopped everyone I saw, asking if they'd seen a short, skinny man with a long gray ponytail carrying a pug.

Nobody had seen anything. I was about to give up when I saw a man walking an Irish setter on the opposite side of the parking lot. I hurried over to him and described the Braid.

"Yeah, I saw him. The dog had a toy he was squeaking. That's what made me look up. They got in a black El Camino. Went that way." He pointed.

"Are you sure?" I felt a surge of hope.

"Absolutely. This one here investigates every blade of grass twice a day, don't you, King?" At the sound of his name, King raised his eyes while keeping his nose buried in the grass. "I have plenty of time to watch the world go by. Plus, you don't see many classic El Caminos these days. Especially with matte paint."

"Did you get a license plate number?"

"Nah, I was looking at the car. My buddy in high school had one. A bunch of us would sit in the bed while he and his girlfriend canoodled inside. This one time—"

"I'd love to chat, but I have to find that guy." Unlike him, I did not have plenty of time to watch the world go by.

When I got back, Barb and Don had disappeared from the sidewalk, so I hurried inside my apartment and called my brother. I'd keep it vague. If Lance said the cops couldn't help, I didn't want any whiff that I'd called them to get back to the Braid. But if they *could* help....

When Lance answered I asked, "What do you know about dognapping?"

"Who got dognapped? A show dog? One of those dogs you met in Portland?" I didn't actually answer, just made some noncommittal noises, so he continued. "Dogs are stolen for the reward money, especially show dogs. Huge rewards for those. Racing greyhounds, too. Dalmatians are stolen for their fur. Famous case some years back."

Lance laughed at his little joke. I did not. "Not funny."

"Whatev. Some dogs are stolen for medical research. And for dogfighting."

I gasped. If the Braid even thought about .... Tears sprang to my eyes and I angrily wiped them away. "What if they're microchipped?"

"That's important, but only if you find the dog to reunite it with its owner. It's not a GPS tracker."

"Will cops ever get involved?"

"In a stolen dog? Rarely. It's considered a property crime, and as much as someone loves their family pet, it's not worth much." I started to protest but he interrupted. "I know, I know. But sentimental value is different. And, Charlee, more than two million pets are stolen every year. That's a seventy percent increase in the last few years. People could keep their pets safe if they'd quit letting them go off-leash or tying them to bike racks or lamp posts outside coffee shops and beer gardens. These are almost always crimes of opportunity." He paused a beat. "Gives new meaning to the term hot dog, eh?"

Again, he laughed, but I knew he wouldn't if he realized we were talking about Peter O'Drool. I desperately wanted to tell Lance the whole truth, but he already said the police couldn't do anything. And what if the Braid found out somehow? I could never forgive myself if my actions caused him to hurt Peter.

I returned to what Lance was saying. "I had a case once where someone stole a service dog. Heartbreaking. We never found it."

"What if someone saw the car the dognapper was driving?"

I heard the shrug in Lance's voice. "If it's a slow day they might broadcast the description and tell patrol to be on the lookout for it. But we don't have many slow days these days. Why do you want to know? Researching a book?"

I couldn't bear any more information about dognapping. And I couldn't shake the image of the Braid miming slitting Peter's throat if I didn't find Lapaglia before the cops did. "Never mind. No more dogs."

"You hear from your disappearing author yet?" he asked.

"No, but I've been talking to all his Denver girlfriends. Or at least all the ones I know about. I don't even know how many there are."

"You already know this, but it's not a crime for a married man to disappear or to have girlfriends. And you don't really know that anything happened to this guy. If the ticket guy told you somebody used his train ticket, there's no reason to think it wasn't him. The only crime I see is your embezzlement of funds."

"Not funny, dude. What about Lapaglia stiffing me on all this stuff? I could barely buy stamps this morning." Ugh. On top of everything else, I needed to call my credit card company. Maybe I could get them to raise my limit.

"I probably already know the answer to this, but did you and this Lapaglia guy have a contract of any kind?"

"Are you *trying* to make me cry?"

"Well, even if you did, it would only be civil anyway. No cops involved." Quieter, he added, "Wish I could help more, Space Case. Do you need money? If you do, just say the word."

"Thanks, but I'm okay. I think. But when I lose everything, I reserve the right to camp in your living room."

"Give me some warning so I can change the locks."

"Will do. Oh, and I don't need to tell you not to tell Mom about any of this, right?"

"About any of what?"

"Exactly. See you, Lance. Thanks."

For all the obvious reasons, I was in serious need of a grilled cheese sandwich. I slathered butter on two pieces of bread and sliced enough cheddar and jack cheese for three sandwiches. Then I proceeded to pile it all on top of the piece of bread I dropped in the pan. I turned the burner to medium low, the perfect temperature for optimum melting without the chance of burning. I carefully balanced the other piece of bread butter-side-up and pressed the sandwich with a spatula. I placed a lid on top to assist with the optimum melting, then leaned against the counter while it warmed.

I was glad I hadn't blurted to Lance that it was Peter who'd been nabbed because then I would have had to tell him about the Braid. Lance couldn't do anything and he'd only worry about me. That's what brothers did. Plus, I didn't want him to get tangled up in the mob, if that's even what this was. Maybe it's not even related to the mob. Maybe it's just a squabble between the Braid and Lapaglia about something stupid that I inadvertently stepped in the middle of. I kind of have a history of doing that. Regardless, whatever it was, as soon as I find Lapaglia, it would all be over and I'd get Peter O'Drool back. I hoped.

I checked the melt factor on my sandwich. Coming along nicely. I replaced the lid for a bit longer. Timing was important. Too long and the bread wouldn't crisp and if that happened, I may as well toss it in the trash. Like that would ever happen. I grabbed a handful of chips from the bag while I waited. As I munched them, I mulled over everything Lance said about dognapping. I thought about Lavar and Tuttle's stray, Nova. She looked kind of like a greyhound, with her long legs and sleek snout. *I hope nobody thinks they stole her.* They did everything imaginable to find her owners, starting with looking for that microchip. I knew Peter was chipped, but like Lance said, a microchip isn't a GPS tracker. Wouldn't that be great, though? To be able to dial up a Dog Find app and track Pete wherever he was? Why the nerds built Twitter instead of that was beyond me.

My sandwich was grilled to perfection, golden and crisp on the outside, melty and soft on the inside. I cut it diagonally because I'm fancy like that, and cheese flowed out like lava. I ate it too fast to truly enjoy it. But I was used to that, seemed to be my modus operandi, especially when I was stressed. A defining characteristic, if I was sketching out a character in a book. That's a laugh ... me, an interesting character in a book. Ha!

As I finished up my chips, I made a quick brainstorming list of the things Lavar and Tuttle did to find Nova's owners. I'd do the same to try and find Peter just in case the Braid released him somewhere. Craigslist, social media, our neighborhood online group, flyers.

I wiped my greasy fingers on the kitchen towel and scanned through the photos on my phone for a good representative one of Peter. I downloaded it then designed a quick "Dog Lost" flyer on my computer. While I waited for my printer, I changed into a pair of shorts and a clean t-shirt. I added an oversized pair of sunglasses and tucked my hair into a baseball cap. I really wanted to lay low in my apartment, because I was scared of another run-in with the Braid, but I had to do something to find Peter. Besides, the Braid already knew where I live. I felt my forehead wrinkle. *How in the world did he find out where I live, anyway?*

What was going on? The Universe seemed to enjoy messing with me lately. First, my agent's murder, then that crazy kidnapping at the conference in Portland, and now this? What had I done to cause my easy, boring life to go so haywire? I thought about all the chaos I created for the heroes in my books and felt momentary guilt. But they really were heroes. They leaped to answer their call to action. They wanted to save the world and solve the mystery. I, on the other hand, was a textbook "reluctant hero." To me, "call to action" was what happened when AmyJo wanted to go to a movie or when Ozzi wanted to go out to dinner. They call, and I spring into action.

But this was too much. Too much action. Too much calling.

I fiddled with my sunglasses. Didn't seem like I had much choice, though. Pete's life might be in danger, all because of me. I couldn't rely on dumb luck or risk mistakes.

Why couldn't I outline my life like I outlined my books?

I did formulate a plan, though. I'd go everywhere I'd ever seen the Braid, putting up flyers along the way. I started with our apartment complex, but I saw that Don and Barb beat me to it. Every surface that could hold a flyer had a big picture of Peter O'Drool smiling back.

I walked across the street to Espresso Yourself and told Lavar and Tuttle that Peter was missing. I picked their brain about everything they did when they were trying to reunite Nova with her owners, hoping I was forgetting something obvious. No such luck.

Nova greeted me while I'd been talking. She stood nearby and when I hadn't taken the time to pet her, she nudged my thigh with her snout. I genuflected, resting one knee on the floor, nuzzling and rubbing her while the men and I talked. When I straightened, she wagged her tail softly then nudged me again before walking away. It seemed to be her way of thanking me, maybe the doggie version of *See ya later* or *Have a nice day*.

When they'd told me everything they could think of,

Lavar pressed a streusel-topped blueberry muffin into my hand. "It's all I can do, Boo."

"What about one of those prayer bombs?"

He raised his arms in praise. "Let the grace of our Lord rain down upon you!"

"Wait. Was that it? I thought there was more."

"Recession must have hit the church." Tuttle winked at me behind Lavar's back.

"Don't you get all up in my face about the chur—" He saw the grin on Tuttle's face and pulled back his wagging finger. "You're going straight to hell, Tut. You mark my words."

"You'll miss me."

"You'll miss both of us," I said.

"Get on wit your bad selves." Lavar hugged me. "And in answer to your question, no, that wasn't your prayer bomb. I'll submit the request to the congreeeegation first thing in the morning. Maybe we can get it scheduled for tomorrow."

"That would be great. Would they do one for Peter, too?"

"If it's good enough for St Francis of Assisi, it's good enough for me. I'll get it done most ricky tick."

I took that to be Marine for *right away*. I wasn't entirely sure I believed that a congregation full of churchgoers could help deliver Peter O'Drool back safely to us simply by the force of their prayers, but I also wasn't entirely sure they couldn't. And maybe it was enough that Lavar believed.

"Thanks, both of you." I walked over to where Nova had curled up on the floor and rubbed her velvety ear. "And goodbye to you, sweet girl." I lingered over her, hoping I'd be able to rub Peter's ear soon.

I returned to the apartment complex, grabbed the stack of flyers and a roll of packing tape, and got in my car. I geared up to go to all the places I'd seen the Braid. It was the only thing I could think to do. I kept an eye out for his black matte El Camino while I drove.

The Cherry Creek shopping district was crowded with

people taking advantage of the gorgeous summer day, winding down to meet friends for drinks or dinner, or to browse the high-end shops. Finally, though, I found street parking and headed for the library. Even though this was far from our apartment complex, the Braid had been here and might be back with Peter. I put up flyers wherever I could find space.

When I got to the library, they told me Lakshmi had gone for the day. Pulling my baseball cap lower, I took a spin around the stacks. I didn't really think the Braid would be in a comfy nook reading the latest bestseller, but since I didn't understand anything that was going on, I certainly couldn't rule it out.

I walked over to the print shop, placing flyers as I went. When I got there, I saw it was closed for the day.

No further plan came to mind, so I made my way back home. I trudged up the stairs to Don and Barb's apartment and knocked lightly. Barb immediately threw the door open like she'd been waiting for someone. She looked so hopeful it broke my heart.

I had no words, only managing a stiff shake of my head. She pulled me into a hug and we stood there, wrapped together.

"I'm so, so sorry," I said, my head buried in her shoulder. "I didn't mean for this to happen."

"Of course you didn't, dear. It's not your fault."

"It's completely my fault."

"Now you stop talking like that this minute. I won't hear another word." Barb pulled a tissue from her sleeve to wipe her eyes and dab at her nose. We let go of each other and I sat down on their couch.

Barb walked over to the recliner where Don sat and placed a gentle hand on his shoulder. He reached up and covered her hand with his. When he raised his hand, I saw one of Lapaglia's books on his lap.

We sat in silence for a while. Before I left, I heated up some soup for their dinner. I forced them to sit at the table and eat it, along with some crackers and jam I'd set out. I didn't make it two steps before Barb handed me a plastic wrapped loaf of zucchini bread.

"For you and your beau," she said.

I nodded. This was the only time in the history of our friendship that I didn't want to devour her sweet treat immediately. My heart just wasn't in it.

Downstairs I called Ozzi and he came over.

"How'd the rest of your day go, babe?" He pulled me in tight.

I immediately started crying. I couldn't help it.

He pulled back to look me in the face. "What? What happened?"

"Peter ... Peter was ..." I was crying so hard I struggled to get the words out. "Dognapped!"

"What? When?"

"This ... afternoon... a few hours ago." I buried my face in his chest and he let me stand there until I was done. When I pulled away, there was a wet patch on his shirt. I wiped it ineffectively with my hand. "Sorry." It almost made me start bawling again, but he just smiled at me.

"I've had worse things spilled on me." He led me to the couch. "Sit here. I'm getting you something to eat and then I want to hear everything."

I didn't tell him about the grilled cheese earlier because I knew he was probably hungry. And just like me feeding Don and Barb, he wanted to nurture me. It's what people do in times of crisis.

He came out a few minutes later with some sliced gouda on a plate, along with some crackers, a few dill pickle spears, a handful of baby carrots, and the tin of chocolate covered almonds.

I was surprised when my stomach rumbled. "You always

know just what I need." I crunched a carrot while I placed cheese on a cracker.

Ozzi returned to the kitchen where I heard the distinctive *pfft* of bottles of craft brew being opened. He handed me a chocolate stout.

I took a swig. "Mmm." Some nibbles, some quaffs, and my man made everything a little easier to bear.

He sat down next to me and I recounted my day. I toyed with the idea of not telling him about the Braid accosting me at the library, but decided I needed to. I was right on the button that he immediately became upset and worried. I tried to make light of it, for his sake, but maybe my own as well.

"I gave as good as I got. Don't worry about me."

"But—"

"He doesn't want to hurt me. If he did, I'd be hurt right now."

"But—"

"He needs me to help him find Lapaglia."

"And then what will he do?"

"I don't know, Oz. But I can take care of myself."

"I think you should talk to Lance about everything."

"I already talked to him about dognapping. There's not a thing the police can do."

Ozzi stared at me, not fooled for a minute. "I said, you should talk to him about *everything*. That includes the Braid."

"I told Ming. He's on it."

"And now you should tell Lance."

"Tell him what? I don't even know what's going on. I'll be fine. I just need to figure out about all these girlfriends. What was Lapaglia thinking? As soon as I find him, I'll get Peter back. Whatever beef he has with the Braid is between them."

ELEVEN

As soon as the alarm rang the next morning Ozzi resumed his personal quest to persuade me to tell Lance about the Braid. Once again I refused.

"I'm not getting my brother mixed up in all this when I don't even know what *this* is." I kissed him and swung my legs over the edge of the bed. "But if you're so worried about me, I wouldn't mind your company today. I'm going to go stake out Martina's mailbox place again and see if I can talk to her and/or maybe follow her. I can't help but think she's hiding Lapaglia."

Ozzi slipped his arms around my waist and pulled me back to bed. "I wish I could, babe, but—"

"I know, I know. Your big project." I pretended to pout. "You love your facial recognition project more than you love me."

"Yes, of course I do," he murmured, nibbling my ear. "My project never says girly nonsense like that."

"Mmm ... maybe you should do this more often." An inadvertent moan escaped my lips.

Ozzi pulled back with mock horror on his face. "What? And make my project jealous?"

I hit him with a pillow and we dissolved into sexual chaos for a few moments until he groaned and struggled from my bed. "I've got to take a shower. Come with?"

I knew that would add at least half an hour to our morning, which neither of us could afford. "Sorry, love. But I'll make coffee and slice some of that zucchini bread Barb gave me."

He pretended to weigh the options in his hands. "Soaped up Charlee or zucchini bread ... soaped up Charlee or zucchini bread." He knew which way the wind was blowing this morning so his scales tipped heavier on the zucchini bread side. "Fine. Make me some breakfast, woman."

I hit him with the pillow again with feigned indignation before I left the room. But I wasn't so indignant that I didn't turn to watch his marvelous backside walking into the bathroom.

As the coffee brewed and I scrambled some eggs to go with our breakfast cake, I thought about my plan for the day. I'll get to the mailbox place early, like I did yesterday, and watch for Martina. But instead of speaking to her, I'm just going to follow her, and hope she goes to her house or wherever she works. Then I won't have to get up at the crack of early to go on any more stakeouts.

We ate quickly and Ozzi rushed to work, but not before pulling me close. "You know I'd rather be with you than at work, right?"

"Yep. I was just teasing you. I know this project is important to you and you need to focus on it. Don't worry about me."

"I'll call you when I can."

"Don't get freaked out if I don't answer. Remember I'll be on stake out. Undercover. Incognito. Very hush-hush."

"I never get freaked out."

That was true. He never did. Not outwardly anyway.

"That's why I love you. Now skeedaddle off to work, you technological wizard, you."

He grabbed another piece of zucchini bread on his way, blowing me a kiss full of crumbs.

I reached for another piece as well, but startled and dropped it when the apartment door banged open. Ozzi heaved the bag of costumes on the couch. "Don't forget to wear one of these." He pointed a finger at me. "No excuses."

"No, sir!" After a snappy salute, I locked the door behind him, then went to take a shower. As I stood, naked, waiting for the hot water to make an appearance, my phone rang. I turned off the water and crossed to my nightstand to see who it was. My editor from Penn & Powell.

"Steph? Have you found Lapaglia? Where is he?"

"No. Sorry."

"Well in that case, hold on a sec." I put the phone down and wrapped a towel around myself. "Okay, I'm back. What's up then?"

"You're gonna hate me."

"Never." *But perhaps.*

"I tried to get upper management to reimburse that money for the event on Saturday, but they won't budge."

"Can they just float me a loan or something? I'm sure Lapaglia will reimburse me just as soon as we find him." I wasn't at all sure of that, but I was desperate.

"That's what I said, but they refused."

"Will they reimburse the participants?" If they weren't worried about me and my finances, maybe they'd worry about the reading public.

Steph was quiet a long time. "I'm sorry. There's nothing I can do."

"Nothing? Really?"

"I don't know where he is, Charlee."

"Can you give me his home phone number in Nebraska? I can try calling there. Maybe talk to his wife?"

"I called her yesterday, but she never returned my call."

"Steph, I need to do something. I have to find him and it sounds like nobody wants to help me."

Another long silence stretched between us. I knew she was still there, though, because I heard her breathing. Then I heard what sounded like a file cabinet slamming.

"I shouldn't do this because of privacy issues, but I'm going to give you Lapaglia's home number. You can talk to Annamaria yourself. But don't tell her I gave you the number, okay?"

"Okay."

"I mean it, Charlee. This could mean my job."

"If anyone asks, I'll just say I'm a Google ninja."

I wrote down the number and disconnected. This wasn't a call I wanted to make naked so I took a shower in record time and put on shorts and a t-shirt before I dialed.

When a woman answered I said, "Is this Annamaria Lapaglia?"

"Yes."

"My name is Charlee Rus—"

"Whatever it is you're selling, I don't want it."

"Ma'am, I'm the author in Denver who was going to do that author event on Saturday with your husband."

"*Was going to do*? Didn't you do it? What are you talking about?"

"Mrs. Lapaglia, have you talked to your husband recently?"

"Not since he left for the train station."

"So you don't know."

"Don't know what?"

"Um ..." It didn't seem right that I was the one to give her this information.

"Please tell me."

"Your husband never showed up in Denver. He missed the event."

"Where is he?"

"Mrs Lapag—"

"Call me Annamaria. Where is he?"

"Annamaria, I'm sorry, but I don't know where he is. I was hoping you could tell me."

"Why are you so concerned?"

I paused. Her husband was missing and she hadn't heard anything yet. I needed to tread lightly. "That event we were doing? Well, there were some ... costs involved. I put the food and the venue and the advertising on my credit card, but he took in all the money for the registrations."

"Sounds like something he'd do. He's very ... generous."

That was the opposite of what I'd been thinking, but okay, if she said so. "I'm hoping you can get into his online payment system and release those funds to me so I can pay the bills and reimburse the participants."

"No."

"No?"

"Yes, no."

"But ..."

"Listen. I'm sure you're another nice person that Rod met during one of his many trips to Denver. But I'm sure he has a good reason for not doing that event with you. And I'm sorry, but I don't know anything about any online payment system—"

"It's the one on his website where he sells his tutorials and stuff. Maybe he has a place where he keeps his passwords?"

"I must say, I find this very suspicious. *You* tell me my husband is missing—not the police—and now you're asking me for money? This seems quite irregular." Her voice was flat, calm. "Are you trying to blackmail me? Shake me down? If so, you are barking up the wrong tree."

Wow. Who *was* this woman? She didn't even sound like she cared that her husband was missing. Maybe he disappeared a lot.

I tried a different approach. "I'm absolutely not trying to shake you down. The money that he collected was to pay for the things we agreed to pay for."

"Do you have a contract with Lapaglia—my husband?"

"We had a ... gentleman's agreement. Can you at least confirm that your husband was on his way to our event in Denver when he got on the train? Is it possible he forgot?"

"Anything is possible, Miss ..."

"Russo. Charlemagne Russo."

"And you're another author?"

"Yes."

She sighed. "Let me see if I understand you correctly. You're telling me that my husband had some sort of rendezvous with you in Denver, and that he has a secret bank account? That's very painful to hear, since I've done most of the work on his books. It would seem I deserve that money. Not him, and certainly not you. So, if you'll excuse me, I have things to attend to. Oh, and if you hear from him, please tell him to call home immediately."

My head spun. I remembered something the Braid said when we were pulling hair. Something about how I should know where Lapaglia was because I probably wrote those books with him. But now Annamaria was saying she did most of the work on the books? What did she mean, anyway ... transcribing? Editing? Is she actually the author of these books? Lots of time women feel they must disguise their names under the notion, often too true, that men won't read thrillers written by a woman. Did she agree to have her husband's name on the books? Does the Braid know this? Maybe not, if he's after Lapaglia.

"Wait, Annamaria, one more question. Do you know an older man, kinda short and wiry, with a long gray ponytail?"

"Listen. If he's going to come after my money like you are, just tell him to stay away. Don't call here again."

She hung up and I realized she never answered my question. Did she or did she not know the Braid?

~

I sat at my kitchen table tapping one fingernail, trying to make sense out of everything Annamaria told me. Her concern for her husband didn't quite ring true. If someone told me Ozzi hadn't shown up like that, I'd be beside myself with worry. Maybe the rumors about her having a boyfriend were true.

I logged into Rodolfo Lapaglia's Wikipedia page and saw the 'unconfirmed rumors' section Ozzi had mentioned detailing Annamaria's alleged affair with Thomas Percy. I clicked on his name and the embedded link took me to his Facebook profile. He listed his employment as Trainee Conductor with National Railroad. He worked for the railroad? Did the two of them kill Lapaglia to get him out of the picture? Would Annamaria have spoken with me at all if she had recently killed her husband? Maybe Thomas Percy took matters into his own hands. Was he on the train with Lapaglia on Saturday?

I looked up the National Railroad website and found the number for customer service. I asked for the human resources department and was put right through.

"This is Mavis. How may I help you?"

Mavis sounded like she hadn't had enough coffee yet, so I was extra perky on her behalf, hoping it might rub off on her. "Good morning, Mavis. I'm trying to find one of your employees—"

"What's his extension? I'll put you through. Next time just dial it direct."

"That's what I was trying to tell you. I don't know—"

"If you don't know his number, how am I supposed to connect you?"

After interacting with Eeyore Regina and Mavis, maybe we *should* be planning a funeral for customer service. It might really be irrevocably dead. "I don't know where exactly he works, but his name is Thomas Percy. I need to know if he was working on Saturday, on the train coming from Nebraska into Denver."

"What's his name?"

"Thomas Percy."

"Last name?"

"I'm confused."

"Then what do you think I can do? Do you know how many people work for National Railroad?"

"A lot? And I'm trying to find out if one of them was working on Saturday." I tried to rein in my irritation but wasn't succeeding. Mavis was stealing my perkiness. I felt it ebbing away, like I was a pen losing its ink, each letter getting fainter and fainter until it becomes simply an indentation on the paper.

"Why?" she asked suspiciously.

This was going nowhere. Time for a little creativity. "Because ... because my elderly mother had a little accident on the train coming into Denver Saturday morn—"

"What's the accident report number?"

"I don't think one was taken."

"Why not? What happened? If you're calling for a settlement, you'll need to speak to our attorneys AND have the accident report number."

"No, nothing like that. There was no injury, but this Thomas Percy was very helpful and I wanted to show our gratitude, maybe mention the incident to the newspaper, perhaps a reward of some—"

"In that case, let me take a look. I remember hearing about that. I was the one called the doctor for your momma. Is she okay, by the way?"

"Yes, my mother is fine." Not technically a lie. Unlike what Mavis said.

"That's so good to hear. Can I put you on hold for the teensiest bit, hon?"

Either Mavis' coffee kicked in or the idea of a citation and possible reward greased her wheels just enough so that some human decency could ooze out. I felt a renewed injection of ink in my pen.

"Okay, I'm back. You still with me, hon?"

"Yes. Still here."

"I found one Thomas working that route between Omaha and Denver on Saturday. Last name is Percy."

Like I said earlier.

"You can mention my name too. It's Mavis, M-A-V—"

I hung up on her. "Sorry Mavis. You were snotty to me. No fake reward for you." It irked me that she'd try to take credit for something she wasn't even involved in, especially a completely fabricated story.

She did confirm, though, that Thomas Percy was on that train with Rodolfo Lapaglia. But was Thomas Percy really the secret paramour to Annamaria Lapaglia? And if so, did he have anything to do with Lapaglia's disappearance? Was I just being paranoid?

Occam's razor says that the simplest explanation is usually the right one. The more assumptions you had to make, the more unlikely the explanation. And with Thomas Percy, there were a lot of assumptions and explanations to make.

What if Lapaglia disappeared himself? That was a much simpler explanation. He'd stated on record in more than one interview that it's really hard to be him, to go out in public, always whining that he was too famous. Barf. But maybe he got tired of it all, decided to use me and our event to chuck it all for a new life in Denver with his girlfriend. Or girlfriends, plural.

Which led me right back to Martina McCarthy. I checked the time. Still early enough to get down to the mailbox place before it opened. Maybe today I'd be luckier.

I pawed through the bags of costumes Ozzi brought up from his car. "Aha!" I remembered being denied toilet access on my stake out yesterday and pulled out the silicone and foam 9-month pregnancy bodysuit. "Nobody would deny a pregnant lady a bathroom." And I couldn't bear the thought of having to buy another squeaky dog toy at the pet store as thanks for the use of the facilities.

I also remembered what happened with the Braid yesterday and called AmyJo. "Are you working today?"

"Not until three. Why?"

"Want to help me do something?"

"I'll be there in twenty."

While I waited for AmyJo, I wiggled into the suit, which was surprisingly comfy, and pulled on a blond bob wig. I learned my lesson from the drag wig and didn't pin this one on, just tucked my hair up into it. I gave it a final tug, arranging it convincingly enough. If the Braid accosted me again, I would be more than happy to have it come off in his hand while I ran away, much like a gecko escaping a snake.

I pulled the caftan over my head and tried to smooth it over my new belly. No can-do. It wasn't quite big enough, which seemed unnecessarily discriminatory to pregnant ladies. Even fake ones. I struggled out of it and stood before my open closet door, assessing my options. I flung each hanger to the side until I was in the no-man's-land of dusty clothes I hadn't seen in ages.

"Score!" I brushed the dust off the shoulders of a tea length rose-colored sateen bridesmaid dress with an empire waist, flaring the skirt right under the bust. I threw it on over my body suit and looked in the mirror. It was not the effect Constance Duggan was going for when she picked it out for us to wear in her wedding, but it would do perfectly today. It was a little snug across the middle, and the fabric didn't flow like it had the last time I wore it. I swayed and gave a little twirl. Hm. The fabric was less *flow* and more *thunk* today. I added a pair of canvas sneakers without socks and I was ready to go.

I thought about calling the phone number on Martina's business card before going all the way over there, but what would I say? Better to surprise her. Get the drop on her. Meet her face-to-face. Or belly-to-belly, as the case may be. She's got to be hiding Lapaglia. Why else would she have been at the train station to meet him? People don't just up and disappear. They up and move in with their girlfriends.

The sooner I found him and delivered him to the Braid, the sooner I'd get Peter back. I'd happily give up my quest for reimbursement if only I could get Peter back to Barb and Don.

When AmyJo arrived she gaped at my enormous pregnant belly. "Does your mom know about this? And Ozzi? Wait. It is Ozzi's, right?"

"Very funny." I handed her the dowdy housecoat and Farrah Fawcett wig.

Her eyes lit up and she bounced up and down. "Are we going on another stakeout?"

The excitement in her voice made me laugh out loud.

"That's why I like you, Ames. Always up for adventure."

"Who is it this time? Is somebody breaking into Espresso Yourself again? Do Lavar and Tuttle know?" Her eyes widened. "Did they *hire* us?"

"Nope. I'm trying to talk to that lady who dropped the business card holder and threatened me at the train station. We're going to surprise her when she picks up her mail."

AmyJo shrugged off her disappointment.

It was later than I expected and I had to park two blocks from the mailbox store. AmyJo detoured into a deli for fortifications while I hurried around the corner. When I got there I saw the sidewalk was closed due to construction. The detour took me through an area where scaffolding and plywood rose up around the sidewalk. I emerged from that a few steps before reaching an alley. I was three-quarters of the way across when I heard an oily voice in my ear.

"Do not make a sound or the pooch gets it." The Braid grabbed my upper arm from the back and steered me down the alley, away from the oblivious crowd on the street. Away from AmyJo. He stopped near a chain link fence.

"Look! It's Lapaglia!" I shouted. When he turned to look at my fake-out, I shinnied up the fence.

When it was clear there was no Lapaglia, he turned back and saw me struggling on the fence, fingers and sneakers scrambling for purchase halfway up.

I squealed and almost fell when I saw he had Peter O'Drool tucked under one arm. With his other arm, he grabbed at my midsection, which was now higher than his head. All he could do was grab a handful of rose-colored sateen, along with my silicone and foam belly. I held on like a Cirque de Soleil trapeze artist. He couldn't pull me down with one hand, no matter how hard he tried.

"Give me Peter O'Drool," I demanded, aching fingers entwined in the wire fencing.

"Give me Lapaglia," he countered.

Stalemate.

My fingers were on fire. I didn't know whether to go the rest of the way up and over the top and get away, or to come back down into the alley and try to wrest Peter from his arms. I also didn't know if I could do either of those things. All I knew was I had to get him to let go of my foam belly. No, I knew something else. AmyJo didn't know where I was.

I had to stall until she got here. "How'd you recognize me?"

"That car of yours is an eyesore," he grunted.

"*Distinctive* is the word you're looking for." My arms quivered with effort, but I couldn't shake his grasp. I jammed my sneakers into the chain link openings, stepping and maneuvering until I had rotated and was perpendicular to the ground.

He was on his tiptoes, clutching me at a weird angle. He still squeezed Peter, but Pete didn't seem to be in any distress. In fact, he looked like he enjoyed this game. At one point he licked the Braid's face and my leg in one deft motion. The tickle sent my feet scrambling even higher on the fence. I was prone, sprawled sideways across the fence, my head now a bit lower than my feet.

"If you keep doing this, how am I supposed to find Lapaglia?" I yelled.

The Braid only grunted.

I held on, feeling like my fingers might slice right off my hands and be left dangling on this sad alleyway construction fence. My abs quivered but hung in there and I silently offered up thanks to Marcy, my occasional yoga instructor for all those planks and chaturangas.

Still only two directions I could go. Up and over the fence without Peter, or back down to the alley, with maybe a chance of grabbing Peter.

I had decided to take my chances in the alley and tried to figure out how to get down without falling when I felt the Braid let go of me.

"What's going on here?" A man's voice boomed down the alley.

"This man stole my dog! Grab him!" I yelled.

The Braid took off down the alley, still clutching Peter. The man hurried over, tool belt jangling, and helped me down.

"No, no! Go get my dog! I'm fine!"

"Lady, you're pregnant. Let me help you."

"I'm not! Go get Peter!" I dropped the rest of the way to my feet. My legs buckled and the man helped me up.

"See? You're not fine. What's Peter's number?" He pulled out his phone while continuing to hold my arm.

"I don't need an ambulance. I'm not pregnant, this is fake!" I poked myself in the belly.

AmyJo hurried over, carrying a bag in one hand and a cardboard tray with two cups in the other. "What's going on here?" She swung the bag at him. "Let go of her!"

The man dropped my arm and stepped back from AmyJo who continued to pummel him with the bag of food.

"I'm calling the cops," he said to AmyJo.

"No! *I'm* calling the cops. Hold my bagels." She slapped the bag into my belly and thrust the coffees toward me.

I took them from her. "It's okay, Ames. This guy was trying to help me."

Keeping a wary eye on AmyJo, he explained to the 911 dispatcher what had happened, answered some questions, relayed my name, then listened. He rolled his eyes then said, "Well, if they ever decide to show up, I'm at the big Liberty job site. Ask for Larry."

"Doubt they'll come," he said to me after he disconnected. "See something, say something, right? But when you do ...."

"Listen, Larry. You did exactly the right thing. You saw someone in trouble and you took action."

"And I'm sorry about the bagels," AmyJo said. "Here, you take them. Peace offering."

He shook his head and took another step back from her. "Did that guy really steal your dog?"

I nodded.

"Bummer." He pocketed his phone. "And you're not really pregnant?"

"Nope."

"And you're not hurt?"

"Promise."

"I'm sorry I didn't chase the guy. Not gonna lie, I was a bit rattled. Nothing like this ever happened to me before." Larry blotted his forehead with his arm.

"Me neither," I said.

"Me neither." AmyJo offered the bagels again.

Larry shook his head. "If the cops show up I'll tell them everything."

"I'll call them, too."

Larry only agreed to return to his job after insisting on walking us back to my car. I figured the Braid was still around here someplace, so it seemed prudent to allow an escort to my car.

After Larry left, I explained everything to AmyJo. "It's probably not a good idea to wait around in front of the mailbox place all day for Martina with the Braid on my tail. Maybe she'll respond to that note I sent her."

We got in and locked all the doors even though it was stifling. I didn't want to be surprised if the Braid was still lurking around. I blasted the air conditioning while AmyJo rooted around the bag of bagels.

"Sesame or blueberry?" she asked.

Accepting the blueberry with a grateful nod I said, "Sesame seeds always get stuck in my teeth." I took a bite then a swig of coffee. I settled the bagel on one knee and set the cup in the console. "I think I should call Detective Ming. Keep an eye out."

"For what?"

"Guy with a long silver braid carrying Peter O'Drool. Or, you know, anything else that seems weird."

"On it."

AmyJo swiveled all directions in her seat, then rearranged the mirrors for best advantage while I dialed Ming.

His voicemail came up. I rambled my message, buying time because I assumed he'd call me while I was leaving it like he had before. But he didn't. Now he'd have to listen to my long, rambling message about how the Braid chased me up a fence. I had the feeling he wouldn't take my call very seriously.

I had been so happy to see that Peter was safe, but now

kicked myself for not trying harder to get him away from the Braid. I should have just belly-flopped down off the fence and landed—splat—right on top of the Braid, squishing him and his stupid hair flat as a pancake. But then I would have risked hurting Peter, too. For now, I guess I had to be happy with the knowledge that Peter was safe and seemed happy and taken care of. But I hated myself for losing him again.

I readjusted the mirrors and pulled away from the curb. I had to quit thinking about Pete because it was hard to drive when my eyes swam with tears. I wanted to quit thinking about everything, so I dropped AmyJo at her truck in the parking lot of the apartment complex without inviting her in, telling her I had some errands to run.

"Liquor store?"

"You know me too well." I smiled at her. "Thanks for going with me today, Ames. You wield a mean bagel." I finished mine.

"I could kick myself for not getting there in time. If only I hadn't ordered those bagels—"

"You couldn't have known. Besides, nothing bad happened." At her skeptical look I added, "Nothing *really* bad, at least."

She popped the last bite of bagel in her mouth while she pulled off the Farrah Fawcett wig. She dropped it on the seat as she stepped out and removed the housecoat which she tossed on top to the wig. "Call me later? I'm off at nine."

I nodded and watched her climb into her truck. I waved as I headed to the liquor store.

It was actually a liquor superstore—a refurbished grocery store—and I pushed a cart up and down the aisles. I couldn't seem to make any decisions. Beer? Mix-and-match local craft beer? Guinness? Something Japanese? Something on sale? Wine? Red or white? Australian? French? Italian? Colorado organic? I slowly and aimlessly wandered up and down, back and forth. People stared like they'd never seen anyone indecisive about their alcohol purchases.

After an excruciatingly long time, I filled two mix-and-match craft beer six-packs with two different brands each of red ales, chocolate porters, summer lagers, IPAs, stouts, and a couple of hard ciders — the ultimate in non-decision making.

I trudged up the sidewalk toward my apartment, six-pack in each hand. For a split-second, I expected to be ambushed by Peter O'Drool racing toward me like he had so many times in the past, tail wagging so hard his hind legs lifted off the ground. But just as quickly I remembered.

Instead, I was ambushed by two men, one with a huge camera on his shoulder, the other with a huge microphone which he shoved in my face.

"Are you Charlemagne Russo?"

"Uh ..." He looked familiar, but I couldn't quite place him. He fell in step beside me as I continued toward my apartment. He kept the microphone thrust in my face, but it had turned and I now saw the Channel 29 logo. Ugh. Archie Cruz from the consumer *Your Advocate* segments. I picked up my pace.

He did too. "Why did you steal all those people's money from the event you held on Saturday? Was Rodolfo Lapaglia ever actually scheduled to appear? Was it some sort of bait-and-switch scam? False advertising? Embezzlement plot?"

I stopped, dumbfounded by his allegations. I should have sprinted for my door without a backward glance. Instead, I allowed the cameraman to frame up the shot perfectly, probably with Archie Cruz centered next to me, microphone shoved in my face at a practiced angle which did not, unfortunately, obscure it. Cruz looked pompous and indignant on behalf of whoever had tipped him off to the fiasco on Saturday.

I should have smiled enigmatically and sauntered away, impervious to his false allegations and insinuations.

However, I chose a different strategy. "I never .... I didn't .... You can't just .... I have no idea ...."

My statement was probably verbatim what all of his ambushees muttered, so he didn't miss a beat. "Clearly, you have something to hide, Ms. Russo. Why are you wearing a disguise?"

I looked down and saw my pregnant belly. Suddenly all the stares at the liquor store made perfect sense. But nothing else did. I looked up at Archie Cruz. I looked at the camera. I looked back at my belly. I looked at the six-packs in my hands. I looked at Archie. Camera. Belly. Beer. Camera. Beer. Belly. Archie.

Then I did what any sensible, innocent person would do when confronted by a local TV news bully like Archie Cruz. I ran to my apartment, fumbled with my beer so I could find my keys, then slammed the door behind me.

TWELVE

I left the beer on the floor by the front door, then thought better of it and placed the six packs in the refrigerator. Warm ale would never cure what ailed me now. I shimmied out of the pregnancy bodysuit, flung it across my bedroom, and stood under the hot, steamy pulse of the shower, silently begging it to wash away the memory of this morning.

But it didn't. All it did was crystallize all the things I should have calmly said to Archie Cruz and his cameraman. "No, Mr. Cruz, there was absolutely no bait-and-switch or any misappropriation of any funds for the writer's event I was supposed to hold with Mr. Lapaglia on Saturday. The fact is, Mr. Lapaglia never showed up, something that worries me and our joint publisher very much, and should worry his fans. Your time would be better spent trying to help us locate him so we can find out what happened and offer reimbursement to everyone who signed up. And while this pregnancy suit and short blonde wig might be a disguise in the broadest of terms, it is not an attempt to dodge creditors, if that's what you're insinuating. Now, if you'll excuse me, I have no further comment. Good day to you, sir." And then if he tried speaking again, I'd simply hold up my hand and say, *"I said good day.*" And then I'd glide serenely to my door where it would magically open so I wouldn't have to fumble with the beer or my keys.

I let the hot water try to massage the memory from my neck and shoulders, knowing full well that memory was etched there, perhaps forever. I consoled myself that it was just a brutal interview with only two witnesses, Archie Cruz and the cameraman. Since I didn't really say anything, it wasn't very compelling footage. Surely they wouldn't actually run something so boring on the news.

Feeling better after that insight and my shower, I went upstairs to tell Don and Barb that I saw Peter and he seemed safe and happy.

They sat me down, offering tea and Barb's homemade frosted sugar cookies. The TV was on in the background. Don lowered the sound.

I told them what had happened. They were happy to hear about Peter, but worried about me, even though I downplayed the confrontation. I left out the fence completely.

"Please don't worry about me."

"And you called the police?" Don asked.

"Yes. I left a message with the detective I'd spoken to about the Braid before." That seemed to placate them. I didn't have the heart to tell them that Ming thought I was a dingbat and probably didn't even listen to the entirety of my message.

Barb said, "Don had a good idea."

"What's that?" I asked.

"He's rereading all of the Rodolfo Lapaglia books, looking for some kind of clue." She looked at Don with soft eyes. "He's a genius."

He blushed. "Well, everybody knows that these books are thinly-veiled true stories about the mob. If this braid guy is involved somehow, maybe I can find some kind of reference and use it to track him down."

I stared at Don. "That's kind of brilliant. You could be a detective. Have you found anything yet?"

"Maybe. There's a recurring character, I forget his name, but he has this mohawk haircut—"

"And our guy has a long mohawk braid!"

Don shuffled through the pile of books on the table next to him. "He's mostly just a background character, but in this book"—he pulled one out and handed it to me—"they carry the subplot. I haven't read it in awhile, but it was something about him screwing up. Mohawk needs to make things right with the mob, but his girlfriend, Taffeta, double crosses him."

"The character's name is Taffeta?" I sat up straighter and flipped through the pages, remembering my conversation with Cecelia. "I heard someone mention velvet recently. Do you think that's a name? Could it be our Taffeta?"

Don shrugged. "Maybe. In the book Taffeta is killed."

"Oh. There goes that theory, admittedly not much of one." I thought for a minute then slapped my palm on the open book. "Maybe the fictional Taffeta is our real Tiffany. Maybe the Braid killed Tiffany because she double crossed him somehow!" I felt my heart rate quicken.

Barb blanched. "Do you really think the man who has our Peter is a killer for the mob?"

"Now, dear, don't get yourself all worked up," Don said in a soothing voice.

"Yeah, Barb, it's just a theory." Although I thought it was a pretty exciting one. "We need to cover all bases." Even though I wanted to explore this further with Don, I saw that it upset Barb so I let it drop for now. I knew Don would keep at it.

The conversation hit a lull. We all stared at the TV, listening to the quiet hum of the news anchor. My eyes glassed over while I munched a cookie and worried about Peter. Suddenly I snapped into focus when on the screen I saw the same photo of Tiffany Isaac that Detective Ming showed us at Union Station. I lunged for the remote and turned up the volume.

"Denver PD continues to search for leads in the murder of Tiffany Isaac. If you have any information, you're urged to call the number below. It's also listed on our website."

I exchanged a glance with Don.

The image faded and was replaced by Archie Cruz's face and the *Your Advocate* logo. That was replaced by an even more disturbing image—me, a hunk of blueberry between my two front teeth, looking like a pregnant alcoholic and guilty as hell. The three of us watched the entire clip with mouths agape. I couldn't process all of it, due to the way my brain squeezed down to a pinprick of computing power, but the gist appeared to be that he was looking into my "suspicious behavior" and offering to help "all those affected by the cancelled event." Presumably that did not include me.

When the segment was over and they'd cut to commercial, Barb said, "Well, at least it was just a short segment on the 4:00 news. Only us old people watch that."

Even though I had ditched the pregnancy suit, Don pointed to my belly. "Anything you need to tell us, dear?"

I blushed and shook my head. "No, nothing like that. Just ... um ... research for a book." My standard excuse when caught doing something anyone might think was weird.

"Then why didn't you tell Archie Cruz that?"

I stared at Don and let his perfectly reasonable question hang in the air.

"I have absolutely no idea."

~

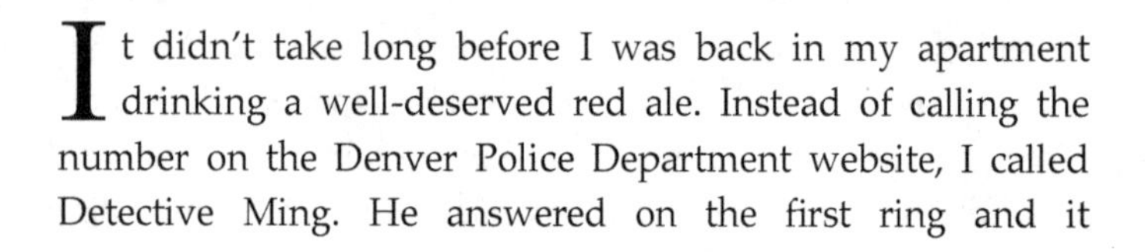

It didn't take long before I was back in my apartment drinking a well-deserved red ale. Instead of calling the number on the Denver Police Department website, I called Detective Ming. He answered on the first ring and it surprised me so much I blurted, "My braid guy might have murdered Tiffany Isaac."

"Who is this?"

"Oh, I'm sorry. It's Charlee Russo."

"Of course it is. Who else would I know who has a 'braid guy' and wants to tell me about a murder?"

Ming never joked, but this sounded kind of like a joke, so I was confused. "Let me start over."

"Be my guest."

"Rodolfo Lapaglia writes fiction about the mob. Have you read any of his books?"

"No."

"Well, they're eerily current. Like, the opposite of 'ripped from the headlines.' He writes stuff and then almost as soon as the book is out, the same stuff starts happening."

"Copycats. So?"

"My point is, they're very true to life. And a friend of mine has been rereading his collection of these books and he found this subplot in one of them with two characters—get this—one with a crazy mohawk hairdo, and the other, his girlfriend named Taffeta who he kills because she double crossed him!"

"Now I don't have to read it."

"It's not a spoiler. It's just like the Braid who has been bothering me, and I think his double crossing girlfriend is ... was ... Tiffany Isaac."

Ming was quiet long enough for me to become uncomfortable. But then he said, "Let me get this straight. You think Rodolfo Lapaglia wrote a book, however long ago, with a plot that follows real life within the last couple of weeks."

When he put it like that, no. No, I did not. "But there's no other explanation!" I knew I sounded petulant, but if the shoe fit ....

"Of course there is. Authors don't put real life events, especially true crime, in their fiction. That's just ridiculous. Never happens."

Was he kidding? "Always happens. Authors mine their own lives for all kinds of stuff."

"So, in your next book there will be a scene with a fake pregnant lady stuck in a fence at a construction site?"

"You heard about that."

"I did."

"I can explain—"

"I'm sure you can, because you have a very nimble imagination, but I don't want to hear your stories. Around here we deal in facts and proof and evidence. Let me know when you have some of that. Goodbye, Ms Russo."

As soon as he hung up, my phone lit up with phone calls and texts.

The first call was from AmyJo. "Any publicity is good publicity, eh?"

"What are you talking about?"

"Oh. You haven't checked social media."

A little piece of me died. "What." I said it like a thud, not a question.

"Apparently you were on the four o'clock news."

"*That* I knew."

"The clip is all over Facebook, probably Twitter and Instagram, too."

Another little piece of me died. "Who posted it?" I scrambled for my computer.

"Let's see ... nobody I know ... nine, ten, eleven ... people—"

"Eleven people posted it? On my page?" Every few seconds my phone beeped with an incoming call or text. This was bad. So very bad. Everyone I knew was going to see this. Friends, colleagues, fans. Ohmygosh, my mom!

"Let's see ... nope, fourteen, fifteen ... and they're getting comments. *Hiding something ... bait-and-switch ... stealing our money ... financial shenanigans*. They all seem to be from people angry about the event on Saturday. Eighteen, nineteen, twenty. Geez, Charlee, didn't you give anyone their money back yet?"

I felt a tightness across my chest and had trouble breathing. "I don't have any money, AmyJo. And I can't find Lapaglia, and Penn & Powell won't help and ... and ..." I took big gulping breaths, trying to jumpstart my lungs.

"Hey, I didn't mean to spring this on you. I assumed you would have seen it already. Get off the phone and start deleting those posts. You've got to do some damage control. I'll see what I can do on my end."

I knew there wasn't a thing AmyJo could do, but I thanked her and hung up. She was right. I needed to do some damage control. I scrolled on my computer, deleting what Facebook posts and comments I could, but they kept popping up faster and faster. I realized I had to lock down my profile, kept public to remain accessible to my fans. Look what that got me. Nobody was sticking up for me. Before I switched pages to change all my privacy settings, my stomach dropped through my shoes. So many of those posts had already been shared—eight times in five minutes—once by a prominent and prolific blogger with a huge following in the mystery community.

There was no way to get this genie back in the bottle.

I silenced my phone and finished locking down my personal Facebook profile and my author page, then moved on to my Twitter, Instagram, and Pinterest pages. Next I disabled all comments on my website pages and posts. And finally I shut down everything I could think of on my Goodreads account, short of deleting it completely. I knew it was only a matter of time, though, before the various online communities would start seeing posts and sharing them directly. Locking down my accounts was busy work, completely ineffective to contain the damage.

Goodbye funny videos and hilariously snarky memes my friends and fans sent me. Goodbye inspirational quotes about writing and life in general. Goodbye adorable pictures of babies and animals. Goodbye book reviews. Goodbye photos of my books in the wild sent to me by fans. Goodbye links to interesting articles. Goodbye delicious recipes I'll never make.

Goodbye digital life.

I peeked at the calls and texts on my phone. My heart sank and I wanted to turn it off completely but couldn't because like an excessively helpful dummy, I put my phone number on the Lost Dog flyers instead of Barb and Don's. I had to listen to each message from complete strangers to make sure they weren't calling about Peter. I also expected Martina McCarthy to call me when she got the note I sent her. And what if Lapaglia or my editor at Penn & Powell called? Or my agent?

I listened to and blocked at least thirty voice mails and texts. None were about Peter. How were these crazy people getting my number?

I needed some friendly words of encouragement, so I read texts and listened to voicemails from my friends.

First, Heinrich Gottlieb from my critique group. I pressed play and heard him take a big drag from his cigar. His words traveled through the smoke, something I'd seen in person a million times. "*Ach, liebling*. Don't let the *idioten* get you down."

Next I listened to Cordelia Hollister-Fiske, also one of my critique partners. "Charlee, I don't know if you're aware, but people are saying all sorts of things about you online. Call me if you'd like details."

Thanks, Cordelia, but I have all the details I need. I switched over to text messages.

From AmyJo, "I'm deleting everything I can and the rest I'm telling people none of this is true and to Snopes it. Lock your accounts down!" Then she added the Scream face emoji.

Exactly how I feel too, Ames.

From Jenica Jahns a simple, "People suck."

More scream emojis from AmyJo.

None of this was helping.

Just as I considered flinging my phone across the room, a call from my mom popped up. I grabbed it before it could go to voice mail. "I'm not pregnant, Mom!" I yelped.

"I figured. I have faith that you would have told me before you were ready to pop. What was with that outfit, anyway? Research?"

"Something like that."

"What's all this I've been seeing on Facebook about you?"

"Oh, Mom." I honestly didn't know where to start so I kept it simple. "You know that big event I was doing last Saturday with that author, Rodolfo Lapaglia?"

"Yeah."

"He never showed up."

"Oh no! What happened to him?"

"That's what I want to know. He kept all the money, but I put all the costs on my credit card and—"

"Do you need money, Bug?"

"No. Yes. Maybe. I don't know, Mom. I'm still trying to figure out what's going on. But since that smarmy Archie Cruz ambushed me and put me on the news, I'm really going to have to figure it out."

"How?"

"Good question." I snuggled into the corner of the couch. Mom's voice had relaxed me a teensy bit. "Even if I come up with the money, I don't even know who I should give reimbursement to. Everyone who signed up just brought their receipt as their ticket to show AmyJo to get in. I thought I had everyone's email address, but now I don't think I do. The registrations went through Lapaglia and I don't think AmyJo kept any of the confirmations from people." I started having trouble breathing again. "Mom, I honestly don't know what to do."

"Give me your bank account number. I'm transferring money right now."

I knew she couldn't afford to do that. "No, Mom. I'll figure something out."

"But—"

"I'll tell you if I get desperate."

"Charlee, call your brother. He'll help."

"I've already talked to him. He's on it." I didn't have the heart to tell her there wasn't one darn thing he could do, however. "But, Mom, don't call him. I don't want to pressure him. He's got so many other things on his plate." Which was an absolutely true statement; it just didn't have anything to do with me and this fiasco.

I could hear the uncertainty in her voice. "If you think so, Bug."

"Absolutely. Listen, Mom, I've got to go." I let her assume it was because I had so much to do, not because I was on the verge of hyperventilating and bawling my eyes out. I said goodbye and clicked away, cutting off the *I love you, Bug* I knew she'd add.

I closed my eyes and tried to control my breath.

When I could breathe halfway normally again, I stuffed my phone in the couch cushion and stood, vowing to do something normal. Then sat back down. Normal wasn't a thing anymore, was it? What was normal anyway? It used to involve answering my phone and going on social media. Playing with Peter O'Drool. Using my credit card.

I had a sudden thought. I hadn't checked my mail since Friday. Maybe there was a letter from the college offering me that teaching job. That would help put a dent in my debt.

I grabbed the mailbox key and opened my door inch by inch, ready to slam it shut the second I saw someone from the news with a camera or microphone. I peered around corners. No Archie Cruz. No Braid either. No angry mob with pitchforks and torches. I raced to the bank of mailboxes, relieved nobody was there. Small talk with neighbors seemed beyond my capabilities at the moment.

I collected up all the mail in my box without looking at it, and raced back to my apartment. I skidded around the corner where I saw someone standing at my apartment door. Stringy hair tucked behind her ears, making them stick out. Baggy scrubs. Suzanne from next door.

I groaned inwardly, knowing she was half-a-second from insinuating herself in my apartment.

She heard me and turned. "There you are! I brought you something."

Suzanne had been thanking me for getting her that part-time job on the bookstore side at Espresso Yourself. Putting in a good word with Lavar and Tuttle was all it took. No real effort on my part, but I felt I owed her after getting her into trouble a while back. A couple of those blueberry butter braids would have sufficed, but it seemed every time I saw her she had a new book for me or another butter braid. The books I often slipped back on to the shelves at Espresso Yourself, because I never felt confident that Suzanne hadn't swiped them, based on her history with petty theft and her casual relationship with the truth. The butter braids, however, I always kept. That was just gracious manners.

This time, though, she didn't have books or pastries. Instead, she held out some envelopes. "Got these in my mail by mistake."

"Thanks." I took them from her, but made no attempt to open my door. I knew she'd wedge herself in like a matchbook under a wobbly table leg.

"Two look like junk, but I don't like to presume. What do I know, maybe you're in need of laser hair removal or a new credit union. But one looks important. From a college."

I stepped past her and shoved my key in the lock. I tried to block the door, but somehow she got inside before I did. I'd have to figure out her trick. Then and only then could I thwart her overzealous neighborliness.

As I ripped open the envelope from the college, she asked, "What is it? Is it important? It looks important."

I pulled out the single piece of paper and dangled the envelope toward her. She grabbed it from me, even though I knew for a fact she had memorized everything typed on it.

I scanned the page, picking out words and phrases I didn't want to see. *Regret to inform ... very sorry ... the Board of Review ....*

My stomach flopped and the letter fluttered to the ground. Suzanne snatched it before it landed and read it.

"Those idiots don't know what they're doing." She shoved the letter back in the envelope, twisting and folding it until it fit. Kind of.

I didn't particularly want to share this moment with Suzanne, but it felt nice for a change to have someone on my side. "Thanks." Maybe it wasn't so bad that she shoved her way in. I could use a pal right now.

"Oh! Almost forgot. I have something else for you." She went next door, leaving my door wide open.

I hoped with all my might it was a blueberry butter braid. That's exactly what I needed. A little sugar salve for my wounds. Barb's leftover zucchini bread seemed much too healthy for this situation.

Suzanne came back with another envelope, larger and covered with the telltale green-and-white stickers signifying a certified letter. "I signed for it this morning while you were out." She handed it to me.

The return address was a four-name attorney's office in Denver. Four names. That seemed important. And scary. I pushed the envelope back toward Suzanne who pushed it back.

She frowned. "What do you think it is?"

"I don't know, but it can't be good."

"Want me to open it?"

"Yes."

She took it from me.

"No." I took it back.

I changed my mind again. "Yes, you open it." And again I took it back.

"Give it here, you wuss." She yanked it from my hand and ripped it open. She barely read it. "You're gonna be sued. Probably by someone married to one of these weasels." She pointed at the four names.

"What?" I yelped, grabbing the papers from her.

"No big whoop. Just small claims court."

"No big whoop?" I glared at her. "Huge whoop." I read the first page. Halfway down I had to blink because the words began to swim. My arm swung limply to my side, packet of papers grasped tight. "I'm being sued for *malfeasance with money* because of that Lapaglia event." I spoke out loud, not to tell Suzanne, but to try to make sense of it for myself.

"Like I said, big whoop. Besides, didn't you know this was going to happen when you stole all that money?"

"Stole that money? I didn't steal anybody's money! Where did you hear that?"

She shrugged. "It's all over my Facebook feed. Bunch of people and at least four weasel attorneys think you did."

"But I didn't." My legs turned to rubber and I plopped on my couch.

"Tell it to the judge."

Under normal circumstances, Suzanne's flippancy would amuse me. These were not normal circumstances, however, and I was not amused. I shook my head like an Etch-A-Sketch. I could sit here like a victim, or I could fight back. I clenched my fists until my nails dug into my palms. This was the moment I had to choose. Be a man or a mouse. Pull up my big-girl undies. Fight back or take it on the chin. I'd been yelled at, unfairly accused, pushed around, bullied, ambushed, made a social media pariah, had my credit ruined, AND had my hair pulled.

What was I going to do, fight back or take it?

I opened my fist and saw my white palms with red half-moons gouged into them.

I studied the place where I shoved my phone between the couch cushions.

I narrowed my eyes at the letter from the attorney's office.

I slowly raised my eyes to meet hers.

"Do you have a butter braid I can have?"

THIRTEEN

I didn't feel good about wanting to wallow in self-pity, but after I sent Suzanne away, with an "I'm just joking" lie, I came very close to crawling into bed and burrowing under the covers. I knew that wouldn't fix anything, but I was equally sure I didn't know what *would* fix anything.

I read the attorney's letter more carefully. I wasn't being sued. I was being *threatened* with being sued. That was a big difference. Suzanne was probably right. Somebody is married to, or friends with, this attorney writing the letter. It's a threat to show they're serious about wanting their money back. If only they knew I was equally serious about getting their money back to them. I wished I could tell them, but decided not to respond. At least not right now.

I think everyone involved wished it had never happened.

I thought about Ozzi saying he wouldn't mind having Lapaglia's life. At the time I told him to be careful what he wished for, but at this moment, I'd be thrilled to have anyone else's life. But whose?

I didn't have to contemplate the hypothetical for long because I heard the actual *meep-meep* of Ozzi's Prius. He had the habit of honking when he got home from work and drove past my apartment. That *meep-meep* was the sweetest sound I could imagine. I was going to forget about all this for a little while and pretend my life wasn't completely screwed up.

I raced down the wide, curving sidewalk of the complex until I got to Ozzi's building, climbed the three outdoor flights of stairs to his apartment, and raised my arm to knock. Before I did, though, his door flew open and he almost collided with me.

"I was just coming over."

"I couldn't wait that long." I threw my arms around his neck and kissed him hard. I pushed him backward into his apartment where he fumbled to close the door behind us.

Twelve minutes later, when we'd finished saying hello, he said, "I'm starving. Are you?"

Queasiness tiptoed around my edges and I knew I had to return to my screwed-up life whether I wanted to or not. "What did you have in mind?"

"Leftover meatloaf?" He pulled a clean t-shirt over his head. I loved the way the fabric stretched over his biceps.

"I'm in." I slipped on my clothes and followed him to the kitchen. "If you still have some of those heirloom tomatoes from the Farmers Market, I can't be responsible for my actions."

He held out a bowl full of tomatoes. "Go crazy."

Ozzi rummaged through the refrigerator until he found the meatloaf and one piece of leftover corn on the cob. "Arm wrestle you for it."

"If you loved me, you'd cut it in half."

"I love you so much, I'd let you have the whole thing."

"Sure. But only if I beat you arm wrestling."

"And they say chivalry is dead." He booped me on my nose with his nose, since his hands were both full.

I sliced tomatoes. He boiled water for the corn then placed slices of meatloaf to be heated in the microwave. When the water was roiling, he dropped in the two halves of corn. He zapped the meatloaf and dropped a mini-cob on each plate. I slathered butter over the corn, watching it drip seductively down the sides, eventually disappearing under the sliced meatloaf. Then I forked tomatoes next to them.

As we cooked and ate, I told Ozzi about my day, starting with the pregnancy suit and the Braid, and ending with Archie Cruz ambushing me and my social media blowing up this afternoon.

He had a forkful of meatloaf halfway to his mouth, but stopped it in mid-air. "Why didn't you tell me?"

"It just happened a couple hours ago. And I was trying to forget about it. Just wanted to have a nice, normal dinner with you."

Ozzi smiled, but said, "I think you won't see many days of nice and normal until you find Lapaglia."

"I suspect you're probably right." I stabbed my last bite of tomato a bit too aggressively. "I hate him."

"I do too." Ozzi made an elaborate show of stabbing his last bite of meatloaf over and over until it was a pile of crumbs on his plate.

I couldn't help but laugh. "But aren't you his Number One Fan and the keeper of his Wikipedia page?"

"Not after this." He used a finger to corral his meatloaf crumbs onto his fork. "I was, but no more."

I knew that to be the case after Saturday, but it was nice to hear him say it.

"He's dead to me."

"Don't say that."

"I didn't mean—"

"I know. But I've been thinking more and more that maybe he is ... hurt. I mean, nobody else seems to be worried about that, but what if he fell off the train, or was pushed off, or is shackled in some crazy girlfriend's basement? What if I'm the only one concerned about him and not just because he owes me money? His wife doesn't care. The train people don't care. The cops don't care. Maybe his girlfriends care, but I'm not seeing it." Being with Ozzi and eating a good dinner had me in a sturdier state of mind. I planted my palms solidly on the table. "How 'bout you use your vast Wikipedia knowledge for good and help me figure out where he might be?"

Ozzi stood and carried our dishes to the sink. "I've been thinking about that."

"And?"

"And I haven't really come up with anything."

I helped him load the dishwasher. "Maybe you're too close to all the facts you know about him. What if you just started telling me all the weird and arcane information you know, and we can try to sort it out together. See if it's useless trivia or not."

"Okay. Like what?"

"Like anything." I washed off the table while he cracked his knuckles like he was preparing to play Rachmaninov's Prelude in G Minor.

"He was born in Paramus, New Jersey."

"Automatically makes him highly suspect." We sat down next to each other on the couch. I tucked my legs up under me and leaned against him.

"His mom was Dona Donatelli." At my blank look he added, "A fairly influential watercolor artist. Left the family when Lapaglia was just a kid."

"Any siblings?"

"Nope, just him."

"What else?"

"Let's see." Ozzi stared into spaced, accessing his mental filing cabinet. "He writes his first drafts longhand with a blue Bic pen. After his assistant types it up, he destroys the handwritten version."

"Hm. That's interesting. So there's no actual proof he

writes his books." I told Ozzi about my conversation with Annamaria.

"So his wife could be the actual author? That's wild."

"Maybe. What else?"

"His friends from high school grew up to have interesting careers, too, like—"

"Butcher, baker, and candlestick maker?"

"Close. Olympic swimmer, FBI agent, and one of the shuttle astronauts."

"Wow. I have a friend from high school who almost got to sing the National Anthem at a Sky Sox game. And another who got caught shoplifting. By my dad, actually. That was some special kind of drama."

"I can imagine. We weren't friends or anything, but a guy I went to school with lost on Dancing With The Stars."

"Cool."

"Yes, but I don't think this is getting us anywhere." Ozzi stood to get his laptop. He sat back down and placed it on his right knee and my left. He pulled up the Wikipedia page, scrolling until he came to a list of live links to interviews Lapaglia had given over the years.

"Here. Read these while I go whip up some brownies. Maybe they'll tell you something." He slid the laptop completely on to my thighs then kissed me. "Nuts, right?"

I rolled my eyes at him. He knew very well my issue with nuts. It tickled him no end when I had to relinquish something delicious Barb had baked with nuts. A long time ago I'd told her I was allergic, but over the years she'd forgotten. In fact, she spun it all the way around and apologized to me when she baked something without nuts, thinking that I loved them. No way was I going to tell her, though. It wasn't her job to remember my allergies.

While Ozzi banged around his kitchen making nut-free brownies, I read online interviews with Rodolfo Lapaglia. They covered all the same basic information—age, education, titles and synopses of the many books he'd written—but some wanted to ask him more targeted questions. One wanted to focus on how he got his start in publishing. One wanted to focus on the niche he created for himself in writing thrillers about the mob. One was a round-up piece of famous people from Paramus, New Jersey. Who knew there'd be so many? One even wanted his favorite recipe, clearly using Lapaglia's celebrity to get more eyeballs on her cooking blog.

By the time Ozzi got the pan of brownies in the oven and plopped down next to me, my eyes were crossing.

"I'm not finding anything very useful."

Ozzi pulled the laptop toward him. "Want me to read to you?"

"Mm-hm." I pointed to the one I was going to read next. Then I closed my eyes and snuggled down so my head rested comfortably against the back of the couch.

He began reading the next interview.

I listened for a while, but the questions and answers sounded so similar to the other interviews I found it hard to pay attention. But something caught my attention. "Wait. Go back."

Ozzi read, "*What is the biggest problem with being such a famous author?* Lapaglia says, *I'm pigeonholed. I'm stuck writing the same types of books over and over—*"

I pulled the laptop over so we were sharing it again. I scrolled up to the previous article. "Look. He says a version of that same thing in every interview, even when he's not asked about it." I pointed to some text. "*I'd love to do something different, but I can't.*" I scrolled to the interview above that one. "*My fans and my publisher expect the same thing from me each time.*" I clicked on another interview. "And here. *I can't go anywhere, I can't do anything. I'm just a hamster on a wheel.*"

I closed the lid of the computer and thought for a minute.

"What?"

"I don't know. But I think that's important. He says it in

every interview. He's not happy. If I can believe his wife, they probably don't have a very happy life in Nebraska." I looked at Ozzi. "I think he disappeared himself."

Ozzi mulled over my words for a bit. "But why not just get a divorce and start a new life? Why all the drama?"

"This mob guy ... the Braid. It's probably no secret the mob is after him. I mean, his books are not at all complimentary to them and maybe he does know too much about them. That's what the Braid accused me of when we got into that hair-pulling contest."

"Hair-pulling contest! You make it sound like it was a girl fight at a slumber party." Ozzi pulled me close, subconsciously trying to protect me.

I shook him off, not wanting him to think I was worried about the Braid. "I told you. I gave as good as I got. I've got the height and weight advantage over that weasel. Don't worry about me."

"I do worry about you."

"I know. But don't."

"Just be careful."

"Ozzi, my love, I'm not going to go looking for trouble. I am trying my best to stay away from him. But I can't hide in my apartment and I've got to find Peter. I've learned that hiding doesn't actually help anything anyway. Not when most of my friends were murder suspects, not when my dad was killed"—the oven timer went off—"not when people put nuts in my brownies."

He knew that meant it was time to change the subject and check on the brownies.

I followed him into the kitchen, inhaling deeply the chocolate aroma floating from the oven, and watched while he poked the middle of the brownies with a toothpick to see if they were done. "I'm all over the place with theories. Lapaglia fell off the train, or Martina is holding him hostage, or the mob whacked him, or his wife did, or his wife's boyfriend did." I shook my head. "But the more I think about it, the more I think he disappeared himself, Oz. For some reason he didn't feel he could just get a divorce."

"Maybe he doesn't know his wife has a boyfriend. Maybe he thinks he and his wife are happy." He made quick cuts to create nine perfectly symmetrical brownies.

"I suppose that's possible. But when I talked to her it seemed very clear they were not."

"Well," Ozzi said, sliding a brownie on a small plate. "You know how stupid men can be." He handed me the plate.

"These smell fantastic." I kissed him. "Clearly, he hadn't made her enough brownies during their time together."

"That makes him stupid."

FOURTEEN

I spent the night at Ozzi's, only half aware that he'd received a call in the middle of the night and left, mumbling something about a glitch in his software. I assumed it had literal meaning.

He returned, coming up behind me just as I locking his front door.

"Ugh, I was hoping you'd still be here," he said.

"Technically I am."

He rubbed a hand over his bleary face. "What?"

"Never mind." I unlocked his door and ushered him into his apartment. "Straight to bed with you, mister. You've got about four hundred hours of sleep to catch up on. You've been working too many hours on this project." I pushed him down the hall toward the bedroom. "Are you hungry?"

"No. Ate all night."

"Anything healthy?"

"Nope." He kicked off his shoes, then dropped his pants. His phone bounced out of his pocket and I picked it up.

"Can I turn it off so you can sleep?" I closed the drapes. "Expecting any more emergencies?"

"Is that an oxymoron?"

"I'm turning off your phone."

"But—"

I moved to his nightstand. "I'm setting your alarm clock for eight hours. Then you can wake up and check your phone for any emergencies. I'll leave it on the coffee table."

"I'd argue with you, but I'm too tired."

I kissed him, tucked him in, and left the room, closing the door behind me. I turned the ringer off on his phone and set it on the table before making my way to critique group.

I hadn't planned on going today, since I didn't have any pages to submit. Plus, I felt scattered enough that I probably wouldn't give any constructive feedback to anyone who was diligent enough to submit pages today. But it occurred to me that my critique group could help me think through this real-life plot twist I found myself in. After all, I asked them for brainstorming help all the time. The only difference here was that it wasn't for one of my fictional mysteries.

As I drove to the exit of my apartment complex parking lot and waited for traffic to clear, I looked to my left and saw Nova sitting in front of Espresso Yourself like she was the doorman. Doorperson. Doordog. She was so cute I had to fight the urge to turn the steering wheel that direction in order to go visit her. However, I knew that Kell would have breakfast and delicious hot coffee waiting when I got to his house. Visiting Nova would be a balm to my soul, but would make me late.

I bumped into the driveway of Kell's McMansion a little bit early. I thought back to all the times I got here late for our meeting. For many years I detoured a few miles out of my way so I could drive past the parking lot where my dad had been gunned down when I was a teenager. I rarely stopped, just wanted that connection and maybe some answers. I got those answers recently so I'd been able to drive straight to Kell's without the detour. I also didn't have much of the tremor that had developed after Dad's murder. That meant I didn't have to change clothes after spilling something on myself, which so often had made me late.

A light tap on my window made me jump. Kell's twenty-something valet. Before I opened the car door, I flicked my dad's old locker key hanging from my rearview mirror. *Miss you, Dad.*

"Hello, Miss Russo. Looking lovely as always." He held his hand to help me out, which I took.

"Thank you, Tyler. How are you today?"

"Just fine, ma'am."

Ma'am. Ouch. He was probably only five years younger than me. "Stay in the air conditioning today. It's gonna be a hot one."

"Will do, ma'am." He slid into my seat and drove it off to Kell's garage, which I imagined to be as big as an auto showroom, and just as pristine. I never had to go looking for my car after our meeting because all our cars were lined up waiting for us, like we were VIPs in some obscure Literary Parade.

Everything at Kell Mooney's house was fancy. Except Kell. He opened the door wearing wrinkled khakis that were a size too big. The side of his round balding head still had traces of what appeared to be sheet marks. He was just finishing buttoning his shirt.

"You're here early!" Kell stepped aside to let me in.

"I know. It's like I'm a grown-up or something."

"How's that working out for you?"

I thought about all the turmoil in my life lately. "Not that great, actually. But at least I have that time management thing whipped."

He placed a comforting hand in the middle of my back and steered me toward the solarium, even though I could get there blindfolded, I'd been here so often.

The side table was groaning with food, as it always did for our meetings. Kell's staff had learned to put out everyone's favorite breakfast foods: yogurt and pastries for me; one soft-boiled egg and half a piece of whole wheat toast for Cordelia; AmyJo's cheesy bacon and eggs; doctor-recommended oatmeal with berries for Heinrich; Thaddeus "Einstein" Eichhorn's assortment of individual boxes of sugared cereal; Jenica's new-found obsession with chicken and waffles; and of course, Kell's cottage cheese.

I couldn't picture Kell ever eating anything other than bland cottage cheese. Not that his personality was bland, but his thrillers—all unpublished—certainly were. I thought of them as milders.

I've often wondered what would happen if I chose someone else's favorite food. I mean, it was all served buffet-style for anyone to take. Nothing was labeled with anyone's name, but would it create some scary Mad Max-type dystopian domino effect? Would we devolve into a demented Lord of the Flies alternate universe? It might be a fun social experiment, but I suspect Cordelia would be polite and simply say she'd already eaten. Jenica would roll her eyes then stare unblinking until whoever had her chicken and waffles relinquished them back to her. Nobody would choose Einstein's cereal or Kell's cottage cheese. AmyJo would surprise everyone by using her fork to stab anyone who came close to her bacon and eggs and Heinrich would revert to his native German, spewing a scary phlegm-laced diatribe. And then he'd scrape half his food onto the plate of the offender because maybe they really wanted it.

Yes, someday I must attempt this, but today is not that day.

I dropped my bag on the floor by the empty seat next to Cordelia and greeted her. She stopped delicately tapping the shell of her egg long enough to smile up at me. "Good morning, dear." When she went back to her task, her two-inch diamond studded cuff bracelet slid, allowing me a glimpse of the small but shocking red tattoo of the devil playing bass guitar on the inside of her wrist. She didn't try to hide it, but didn't flaunt it either and it always took me a bit by surprise. To see her walking into a high-end shop or spa, you'd never know she was a Led Zeppelin fan or wrote the filthiest erotica known to mankind.

I loved that about her and wished I had anything enigmatic about me.

As I carefully held a porcelain cup under the spigot of the coffee urn that probably cost as much as my car, Einstein and Heinrich walked in together.

Einstein made no eye contact, as was his custom, but Heinrich bellowed, "Good morning, *liebling*" at me.

Heinrich walked behind Cordelia, greeting her by pressing his palms against both of her upper arms then kissing the top of her head. She smiled up at him.

AmyJo arrived next, followed soon after by a dragging Jenica.

AmyJo stopped to hug everyone and dispense small but heartfelt compliments in her wake. When I first saw her do this, when we were both freshmen at Drake, I thought it was an affectation. But after living in Des Moines for a few weeks, where I met more and more Iowans, I realized AmyJo was simply a very nice person. Very midwestern. Very polite. And maybe the teensiest bit needy.

Jenica wasn't quite awake yet and we all typically gave her a wide berth until after breakfast. This morning, however, I couldn't help but notice the funny juxtaposition of her lacy anklets with tiny pink bows peeking over the tops of her Doc Martens. I mentioned them and was rewarded with her heavily kohl-rimmed eyes narrowing in my direction. I quirked my mouth in chagrined apology and studied my yogurt choices for today.

As usual, AmyJo, Kell, and Heinrich chattered while everyone else responded when necessary. Heinrich and AmyJo veered into dangerous territory when she said that she didn't particularly care for the movie he told her he watched last night. Heinrich let loose with a phlegm-soaked rebuke of her opinion, her ancestors, and her future children.

We were all used to his German-tinged outbursts, but I, for one, breathed a bit easier after he kissed AmyJo on the head when he went to refill his coffee.

I was grateful nobody had brought up my problems. It was pleasant to pretend none of my chaos had happened. But I knew it couldn't last much longer.

After AmyJo had caught up on everyone's doings over the past week, at least those who were awake and willing to share, she turned to me. "I'm surprised you came today. Do you have pages for us, after everything that's happened?"

I brought them up to speed on the fiasco that was my current life. I left out everything about the Braid and Peter O'Drool, though. "So, no, I don't have any pages ready, but maybe I could run something by you guys before we actually start the meeting?"

Everyone seemed agreeable.

"I'm mulling over a theory, trying to suss out this real-life story like I would a fictional one. What do you think it would be like to be really, really famous? How would you sketch out a character like that?"

"Like Lapaglia?" Heinrich pronounced it with a respectable amount of phlegm.

"Yes."

Cordelia said, "I'd want to hide. That's why I use a pseudonym for my books. I don't need or want fame."

"Remember Princess Diana? Chased by paparazzi everywhere she went. So dangerous. So sad." AmyJo bowed her head reverentially.

"Sucks," Einstein said.

"What ... Princess Diana?" AmyJo asked him.

"Everything. Sucks to be him," he answered.

"It probably doesn't *all* suck," AmyJo mused. "He's rich. I bet he never has to convince his agent or editor into publishing whatever he wants to write. I'm sure his publisher pays for his book tours—"

"And arranges them," I added, more than a little bit jealous.

"But he can't pick his nose or fart on a beach somewhere without social media going nuts. If he did, he'd create a cottage industry in meme creation," Jenica said.

"I wonder when was the last time he had a real vacation," Kell said. "I know I need at least two every year, one in Europe and one someplace tropical. Gotta recharge those batteries, eh?" He glanced around the table for agreement, forgetting that only Cordelia was mega-rich like he was.

Bless his heart, though. At least he had the decency to blush right to the top of his bald head. In his defense, he'd happily take any of us along with him if we'd ask.

"The vacation thing is real. Ozzi and I were reading some interviews where he said pretty much the same thing. More than once."

Heinrich nodded. "If I were this Lapaglia I vould vant *aus*. Gone. Vamoose."

He butchered Lapaglia's name so badly, if I didn't already know who we were talking about, I would have been confused. But he said exactly what I'd been thinking. "So, do any of you think he disappeared himself?" I asked.

I looked in turn at everyone as they nodded.

"Unless he offed himself," Jenica said.

"Or got offed," AmyJo added darkly, adding a slow slashing of her neck in case we didn't understand her meaning.

I sighed. "Oh, goody. I love when we have consensus. Lapaglia either skipped out, killed himself, or got murdered."

We got ready to move from the solarium to Kell's library. Immediately his household staff was there to clean up after us. They were spooky in their efficiency.

Jenica read her rhyming picture book text to us, which

was surprisingly good. The topic, though, I had problems with. It didn't seem to me that Burning Man would really speak to pre-schoolers.

Next, we tackled chapter fifty-seven—!!—of AmyJo's angsty young adult high fantasy romantic comedy coming-of-age. I still, even one-third of the way through, didn't find it particularly romantic or funny. And really? Star-crossed gryphons? I chose my words very carefully to say maybe she could consolidate the action from about chapter thirty or so to this one when the "meet cute" happened. "You know, tighten up the plot a bit. The backstory of her meeting Medusa isn't really germane to the story." Most everyone else said something similar.

Heinrich cleared his throat of some *excess* excess phlegm, which was a sign he was preparing to say too much. And probably too bluntly. I shot him a warning glance, and cut my eyes at AmyJo, who looked dazed, her rigid posture signaling she was on the verge of shellshock.

He took my hint, seeing she might not be sturdy enough to hear his opinion and nodded imperceptibly. He smiled and said, "I'm loving your use of past participles, *liebling*. Soon you'll be grammar Nazi around here!"

I still hadn't decided if a German "grammar Nazi" was funny or politically incorrect. Normally I feel like I'm fairly woke, politically, but these were strange times.

Last to present was Cordelia, so we all discussed her newest erotica short story as we always did, wearing crimson blushes. Except Heinrich. Nothing embarrassed him, as evidenced once again by his cringe-inducing questions.

I was glad when the meeting was over, because I had to concentrate extremely hard on everyone's work. The dull throb of a burgeoning headache began to take its toll. Giving constructive and kind critiques took all my focus on a good day, but was almost impossible when I had something like Peter O'Drool and Lapaglia weighing on my mind.

Driving home I smiled at the memory of Heinrich's mispronunciation of Lapaglia's name. It wasn't that difficult and I had said it several times. My smile tightened, though, when I thought back to my interactions with Lapaglia's girlfriends. When Lakshmi spoke of him I was almost positive she called him "Rodney" and Cecilia called him "Ron," even though his name was "Rodolfo." Maybe I just misheard.

I puzzled over it for a few miles. Was it possible they really didn't know his real name? Why would that be? Mistake or by design? And whose design? Lapaglia misleading them? Them misleading me?

I still believed it was quite plausible that Martina was hiding him, but maybe I was wrong. Maybe it's one of the other girlfriends. Or none of them.

When I got home I decided to try something. If it worked, great. But if it didn't, nothing bad would happen.

Theoretically.

FIFTEEN

When I turned my phone back on, I saw that texts and voice mails had started to come in about Peter O'Drool, crowding out the nasty trolling ones about my debut on Archie Cruz's news show. I was fairly certain none of them would pan out, since I didn't think any of them were from the Braid, but I'd tackle them just in case, after I set my plan in motion.

For once I didn't actually want to talk to Martina, so I texted her. *His train comes in at 3pm today.*

Then I texted Lakshmi to "pick up Rodney" and Cecilia to "pick up Ron" at 3pm.

Whoever doesn't come to pick him up is clearly the one hiding him. They might run, of course, but that was a chance I was willing to take.

Assuming they all saw the texts.

I had time before I needed to head down to Union Station to find an inconspicuous spot to spy on these women, so I began scrolling through the messages about Peter O'Drool.

I returned calls and texts telling me when and where they'd seen pugs. Most people came right out and asked the amount of the reward and I told them it would depend on how quickly they led me to Peter. None of the callers seemed legit, but I dutifully marked all the sightings on a map of the area I'd downloaded and printed out.

Map in hand, I trudged up the stairs, assuming that Don and Barb had been getting similar phone calls.

As I reached out to knock on their door, it opened and Barb almost ran into me.

"Oh, hello, dear," she said. "You're just in time, if you want to go with us."

"Where?"

"To meet a psychic at Espresso Yourself. She says she wants to help find Peter." Barb saw Don and I share a skeptical look. "Oh, stop that, you two. I know it's far-fetched, but we haven't had any luck with anything else. What have we got to lose?"

"Fifty bucks?" I suggested.

"Nope. She said no charge." She looked at me. "So are you coming?"

"I wouldn't miss it."

I shoved the map in the back pocket of my jean skirt and we walked over to the coffee shop. Don held the door and Barb stepped in first with me right behind her. I was highly skeptical of this outing and scanned the room. There weren't many people, so it didn't take long for me to spot a woman wearing enormous sunglasses and swaddled in a leopard print head scarf also wrapped around her neck. She was rummaging in her purse and hadn't seen us yet.

I yanked Don and Barb back out the door and marched them around the corner, away from the windows.

"Don, that lady was there when Peter got snatched. You said hello to her. She had on a different scarf." They both started around the corner but I held them back.

"She was there? Are you sure?" Barb asked, eyes darting.

"Almost positive. She looks just like Gloria Swanson in Sunset Boulevard."

"She does!"

"She must know something about Peter," Don said.

"What should we do?" Barb said. "I want to go punch her in the nose!"

"I have a better idea. But you'll have to wait here while I run back and get something."

"Hurry. We said we'd meet her five minutes ago."

"I don't think she's going anywhere. But if she comes out, walk up like you just got here and stall her until I get back. When you see me, Barb, meet me in the restroom."

"Ooh!" Barb bounced on her toes. "We're hatching a plan!"

I raced back to Ozzi's apartment and let myself in quietly so I wouldn't wake him up. I scribbled a note that said, *I have your phone over at Espressos. If you wake up before I get back, come over there*. Then I grabbed his phone and ran back to the coffee shop.

Barb and Don were still outside when I got there. I handed Barb Ozzi's phone. "Do you know how to text?"

"Don't be silly. Who would I text? Don when he's sitting right next to me on the couch?"

I thought about last night when I texted Ozzi while he was in the bathroom to ask if he wanted beer or wine with dinner. "You'd be surprised how often that happens."

"People," Barb said, shaking her head.

"I'm going to give you a quick lesson because she saw me with Peter."

"She saw me with Peter too. That's why she called," Don said.

"No, I think she has ulterior motives of some kind. But I'm going to sit at a different table where she can't see me, but hopefully I'll be able to hear your conversation. If I think of any questions I want you to ask, I'm going to type them on my phone and send them to Ozzi's phone. All you have to do is read them when they pop up on the screen. The ringer is already off, so you won't accidentally get any of his phone calls. Just leave the phone in your lap with the screen where you can glance down at it. You don't want her to see it, though. Just in case."

"You're very smart, dear." Barb patted my hand.

"Thank you, but so are you guys. I'm not expecting to have to weigh in with anything, but if she says something I want to explore further, I just want to be ready." I was hoping she could be tricked into giving specifics about the Braid, or Lapaglia, or anything that was going on.

"Okay? You guys ready?"

Barb got serious. "I hope she really is psychic or at least is here to tell us where Peter is."

Don nodded and put his arm around her while they entered Espresso Yourself. I waited a couple of beats then made my way behind the Gloria Swanson lookalike while Don and Barb walked up to her table.

"I'm Don and this is Barb. I'm sorry we're late."

"Not a problem at all," she said.

"And you are ...?"

"I am your psychic. Please, sit. Would you like coffee?"

If she were psychic wouldn't she already know that? I thought with irritation. *It's like she's not even trying.*

"That would be nice, thanks." Don pulled out the chair directly across from the psychic and Barb sat in it. Don sat between them. I scooted my chair over so I could see Barb better. I caught her eye and she nodded slightly. All systems go.

Lavar came over carrying mugs and a coffeepot. He saw me and started to say something, but I put my finger to my lips. He winked and ignored me, just like I wanted.

Nova did not, however. She came up next to me and sat. When I didn't respond quickly enough, she dropped her chin to my thigh. I rubbed her face then bent down and whispered in her velvety ear. "I'm working right now. Go keep an eye on this lady for me."

Nova padded over and sat just behind Barb's chair, facing the psychic. She stared unblinking until the woman said to Lavar, "I am uncomfortable with this ... creature here."

Lavar showed great restraint and simply finished pouring their coffee while saying, "Nova, sweets, go lay down." Nova stood and curled up on her rug in the corner, but kept her eye on the psychic.

After they were settled with their coffee, the psychic spoke. "You probably want to know why I called you."

"You must be psychic." Coming from anyone but Don that would sound sarcastic, but he said it with a twinkle in his eye and good humor in his voice. He was mounting a charm offensive.

"Ah, yes, well."

I couldn't see her face, but I bet she gave him one of those tight, condescending smiles devoid of all warmth.

She continued. "I wanted to meet with you today because I saw your Lost Dog posters"—she held one finger in the air and interrupted herself with an indelicate sneeze—"and wanted to offer my help. I've had ... great success in the past finding lost things and hope to do so again. So, let's begin, shall we?" Don and Barb both nodded. She stretched out her hands to them both. They grabbed hers and each other's. She tilted her head so far back I thought she'd be looking at me upside down.

Behind the counter I saw Lavar nudge Tuttle and tip his chin toward her. I shook my head and again, put my finger to my lips. They continued to stare, but tried to be inconspicuous.

Finally, the psychic brought her head down. I wondered if her eyes were open or closed, but who could tell with those sunglasses on.

"I see the letter L. Does that mean anything to you?"

"I like a nice limoncello now and again." Don said. "Oh, and we went to the Cheyenne Mountain Zoo and saw a lemur a few months ago."

"We had leftovers for dinner yesterday," Barb added.

I closed my lips against the smile that formed.

The psychic took a deep breath and looked heavenward again. "I'm getting a map ... it looks like ... West Virginia ... no, it's New Jersey. Definitely New Jersey."

"Peter is in New Jersey?" Barb leaned forward while one hand fluttered to her throat.

Don took back Barb's hand and squeezed it a bit.

"Do either of you have ties to New Jersey?"

"No," Don said flatly.

I texted Barb. *She's fake. She doesn't know where Peter is.* I saw her glance down at her lap. She looked straight at me, then frowned at the psychic.

The psychic again looked up and remained quiet for a few moments before lowering her head. "Books. I'm in a room surrounded by lots and lots of books...They look like thrillers, maybe suspense...Does that mean anything to you?"

Don pointedly looked to the bookstore side of Espresso Yourself and tilted his head at the psychic. She either didn't see or she ignored him.

It was clear to me she was pumping them for information about Lapaglia. But why? If she saw the Braid steal Peter O'Drool, why wasn't she interested in him right now? I hoped neither of them would take the bait.

I began a text to Barb, but before I got a few words in, Don said, "Books? Hm. We used to read quite a bit, the both of us, but you know how it is. The eyes go. We watch more movies than we read books, nowadays. Wait, are you seeing Peter surrounded by books? He never reads thrillers, though. He's more a non-fiction fan."

I clamped a hand over my mouth. To the psychic's credit, though, she remained nonplussed.

I thought of something and texted Barb. *Ask her if she sees a man with a silver braid. Tell her he came to you in a dream last night.*

Barb glanced down at her lap and frowned. She said, "Any opinion about the integration problems?"

I checked the message I sent.

Barb cleared her throat but didn't take her eyes off the phone in her lap. "Do you see a man with a silver braid? He came to me in a dream last night."

The psychic did not raise her head this time. "No, nothing like that."

I texted again, but Barb spoke before I pressed Send. "Are you joining us for load testing tonight?" Barb paused then added, "There was also a woman named Tiffany in my dream."

I leaned back and caught Don's eye to see if he knew what Barb was talking about. Integration? Load testing? I gasped and clamped a hand over my mouth, just as quickly removing it to text Barb. *You're getting Ozzi's texts from work too! There must be a problem at his office!*

Barb said, "You're getting .... Oh." She looked up and smiled brightly at the psychic. "Sorry. I'm having a senior moment. Will you excuse me a moment?" She let go of both the psychic's hand and Don's and headed toward the restroom. I followed her.

When we closed the door behind us she laughed. "Oh, good grief. That was ridiculous."

"You recovered nicely," I said. "So proud of my little nerd."

"I'm old, not stupid." She handed Ozzi's phone to me and I saw a dozen messages scrolling past. "So what do you think that was all about? It sounded like she was pumping us for information about that author."

"That's what I think too. But I'm not sure why." The messages kept scrolling. "I gotta get this phone back to Ozzi.

Looks like his project is blowing up." I held the door for her. "Unless you really have to ...?"

"No, just had to leave the table before I started laughing. Let's go."

I sent her off ahead of me so I could get a photo of the psychic. But when I turned the corner she was gone. Barb was standing by Don's side as he threw a few bills from his wallet on the table.

Lavar and Tuttle hurried over. "Landsakes, *who* was *that*?" Lavar asked.

"A psychic," Barb said.

"A psychic, my a...unt Sally!"

"Your Aunt Sally is a psychic?" Barb cocked her head at him and he blushed. I never actually knew black men could blush until I met Lavar.

"No ... I just ... I meant ..." Lavar looked at me for help.

"She's old, Lavar. Not stupid. She knew what you meant."

Barb laughed and placed her tiny hand on his bulging forearm. "Some people say cursing is the sign of a small vocabulary. But I think it's a sign of a creative thinker. You keep doing you."

"Be that as it may, what was all that?" Tuttle asked.

Don shrugged and looked at me. "As soon as we figure it out, we'll let you know."

I didn't want to drag Lavar and Tuttle into this, whatever this was. "Just somebody trying to scam a couple of worried pet owners."

"Pete not back yet?" Lavar's brow wrinkled and he drew Barb into a bear hug. I always worried he'd crush someone with his exuberant love.

"He'll be back," I said, more confident than I felt. "I've gotta get Ozzi's phone back to him. See you guys later."

I hurried back to Ozzi's apartment, debating with every step whether I should wake him up or not. By the time I got there, I decided it wasn't my call to make, no pun intended. I woke him, explained briefly what happened and brewed some coffee. Before I left I scrambled him some eggs and buttered two pieces of toast, making him promise to eat before he rushed to his office.

Back at my apartment I checked the clock. Still plenty of time to get to Union Station. I remembered the map of the city in my pocket and took it with me upstairs to Don and Barb's.

"I meant to show you this earlier." I unfolded the map on their dining table and smoothed it. "I've been getting some calls about Pete and have been marking them on here. I'm going to start checking them out."

"We've had some too." Don rewound then played back the ancient answering machine next to their landline. As we listened, if any locations were mentioned, I marked them on my map. I was disheartened to hear most of their callers wanted to know the amount of the reward too. I was also disheartened to hear how many calls they got asking them to buy pet insurance, contribute to mega-churches, and support the NRA.

When the messages were finished, Don handed me a piece of paper. "We quit answering the phone for fear we'd be on it when something important came in about Pete. But these are some of the things people told me."

I added those locations to my map and assured them I'd check them out. I could do many of them on my way to Union Station. Deep down, I knew Peter wouldn't be in any of them because I was convinced not one of these callers ever saw him—or any other dog, for that matter—before they called, asking about the reward. Maybe it was a mistake to have put that on the flyers. But maybe, just maybe, someone saw the Braid with him, or could give us the license plate of his matte black El Camino, or had actually scooped him up when the Braid wasn't looking, in some miraculous moment of psychic phenomenon.

Yeah, right. That could happen.

"If you talk to anyone who calls, be sure and ask if they saw a car. I want to know about any black El Caminos with matte finish. There can't be too many of them around. But don't describe the car to anyone. Make them describe it to you."

I planned my route between home and Union Station, noting with a scowl that nobody had given their actual home address in their messages. Just "at the corner of this and that" or "outside the gym on 5th."

Oh, Pete. Please be okay.

As I expected, none of the marks on my map showed me Pete or the El Camino. The few people I spoke with confirmed my suspicions, that none of the callers had any real connection to the locations they gave. I was more sure than ever the callers were opportunistic scammers.

Arriving at Union Station, I exchanged the map for my *I heart Denver* baseball cap and threaded my hair through the opening in the back.

I sat outside with one leg crossed on an out-of-the-way bench under the canopy and watched to see who, if anyone, would show up: Martina, Lakshmi, or Cecilia. I didn't even know if a train would be coming through. Would they look it up and see through my ruse? My foot bounced so much I had to place it flat on the ground so as not to knock me off the bench. It kept bouncing so I walked inside to the timetable on the wall and studied it to see if there was an estimated time for any arrival. It showed a passenger train coming from Memphis on its way to Seattle. I returned to my inconspicuous bench and tried to be equally inconspicuous as I scanned the crowd.

The train pulled in about ten minutes early and began disgorging passengers. The area became crowded with happy reunions and beleaguered tourists so I stood on the bench, balancing against a concrete pillar I could also peek around.

The third car of the train was directly in front of me, about twenty yards away. The station was behind me. The outdoor plaza was busy with more than just the train passengers, exactly like when Ozzi and I were here on Saturday. People walked through the plaza from all directions because Union Station was also the hub for the bus terminal and the light rail trains around Denver. Everyone was busy getting to or from some place. Except me. I stood hugging the concrete pillar, hoping to see whichever of Lapaglia's girlfriends were going to show up.

The arriving passengers were beginning to thin out and they let the departing passengers waiting in the snaking line begin to board.

I prepared myself for the eventuality that none of the girlfriends would show up when I heard voices I recognized behind me.

"I wonder why she wanted us down here," Cecilia said.

"You can't imagine the song and dance I had to do to get the afternoon off work," Lakshmi said in her pixie voice.

"I know. Me too. She better have a good reason for this stupid field trip."

I assumed they were talking about me. I kept my back to them and watched as they rounded the corner to my right, strolling toward the train. No sign of Lapaglia and it didn't sound like they expected him here. They sounded more curious as to why I texted them, which, admittedly, made more sense. I watched them as they stopped close to the train, scanning the area, probably searching for me rather than Lapaglia.

The departing passengers had mostly wound through the snaking queue and had climbed on to the train.

Still no Martina, though, which made me believe my theory about her hiding Lapaglia might be confirmed. I climbed down from the bench, brushing the concrete dust from my hands, and headed toward Lakshmi and Cecilia. Before I finished mentally composing my apology for getting them down here on a workday, I saw Martina stalk up to them, chest ricocheting between chin and belly. They spoke quietly, but by Martina's twisted face, I knew she was angry. I wanted to get closer to hear, but I also wanted to see how it would play out. I stepped behind a concrete pillar closer to them and peeked around it. Still couldn't hear. I searched the area but there was nowhere closer to them where I wouldn't be fully exposed. Maybe I could lean against those trash bins or bend down to tie my shoe over there—

The Braid was taking long strides in my direction, his eyes trained on me like lasers.

SIXTEEN

I didn't want to draw his attention to the three women I had tricked to get down here. He had been violent with me and maybe with all of them too. Perhaps he'd been stalking me this whole time and didn't even know they were here. I wanted to keep it that way.

I eased around my pillar, hidden from his view. I prayed he'd come around behind me. As soon as he moved in that direction, I took off at a sprint toward the train. I knew the sudden movement would draw his attention to me and away from the girlfriends. And maybe it would draw the girl-friend's attention, too, and they wouldn't be caught by surprise by the Braid if he decided to accost them.

I raced up the steps of the first train car, thankful it was unattended, expecting to travel back several cars and jump out again where I'd be less exposed. If I timed it right, I could disappear back into the station or veer toward the light rail trains or the underground bus terminal.

Fighting the crowded aisles from the first car to the second, I earned more than a few expletives along the way. "Sorry!" I said to all of them, but I knew they did not accept my apologies. Fighting to open the door between car two and car three, I was just about to put all my effort into it, when I saw the Braid fighting his way through the crowd in car three right toward me. He didn't even bother with apologies to the people I knew were cursing at him and his rudeness.

I turned around to make my way back through car two, which was even more crowded now. It seemed everyone who had been finding their seats earlier had now commenced opening all of their carry-on luggage to extricate everything they needed for the duration of their trip.

I glanced backward. The Braid was almost to the door between the cars. There was no way I was getting through that crowd in front of me. Just then a woman emerged from the restroom. She barely got out before I pushed past her and dove inside. "'Scuse me! Emergency!" She didn't need to know what kind of emergency it was. She could use her imagination, but it probably wouldn't include the Braid. I slammed the door and locked it behind me. I leaned on it to catch my breath.

I heard angry voices, recognizing the Jersey Shore accent of the Braid. I couldn't hear whom he was arguing with. It might have just been a cranky traveler, but I hoped it was a train employee who would throw him off.

Suddenly the train lurched, knocking me into the sink, almost literally. If there had been water in it, my butt would be soaked. I reached across the toilet and opened the tiny porthole window. The train was backing out of the station. The Rockies in the distance slowly inched by.

Seems I was headed for destinations west. How soon would they kick me off? Would they at least wait until the next station? What would happen when they discovered my credit card was maxed out and I couldn't buy a ticket even if I wanted?

The train was creeping along, but I didn't dare leave the safety of the restroom since I had no idea if the Braid was still on the train or not. If he was, I knew he'd be waiting right outside this door. Thinking he was leaning on the other side of it made me scramble closer to the window. The restroom was minuscule, but at least with the window open I was getting a hot breeze and a picturesque view. My personal observation car.

I wondered how long I could sequester myself in here before someone jimmied the door open. The rail yards were a part of Denver I never saw. As we picked up speed, I knew we had cleared the station and were officially on our way.

I kept my fingers crossed that the Braid had been thrown off before we left Union Station and that I could jump off at the next stop. I decided to make the best of my unfortunate situation and tried to get comfortable. With my feet on the closed toilet seat, I was able to perch on the edge of the insufficient counter running around the sink and gaze at the Colorado landscape pass by the window.

I called Ming to report another Braid sighting. The connection was bad and I felt I had to whisper, in case the Braid was listening at the door. Eventually, I got Ming to understand who I was and why I was calling. He told me he had no information for me.

"Would you tell me even if you did?"

He either pretended he didn't understand me, or he really didn't. Either way this conversation was over, but not before I heard the words "active imagination" through the static.

The handle on the door jiggled, immediately followed by loud open-palmed banging. My heart seized and I covered my head with my arms.

"I'm in here!" I yelled, embarrassed by my overreaction. "Might be awhile." I didn't know if they heard me, but the jiggling and banging stopped. I went back to gazing out the tiny window. The hot air felt good on my face, but wasn't refreshing. I wondered where exactly the next stop was and how I was going to explain to Ozzi I needed him to pick me up there.

I also wondered what it meant that all three girlfriends came to Union Station. Were none of them harboring Lapaglia? Or were they curious as to what I had planned? Planned, however, wasn't quite the right word. My plan, such as it was, didn't go much further than seeing who showed up, then confronting the girlfriend who hadn't showed up.

I stared out the window, a bit hypnotized by the rhythmic clattering of the wheels on the tracks. As the train slowed a bit around a curve, I saw a huge billboard for a resort. It had a drawing of a rustic-looking cabin and the tagline, *Lose Yourself in Lost Valley—escape for a day, a week, or a month.* It listed the amenities, which seemed quite appealing, especially the spa and daily happy hour. *I'd love to go there.*

With a jolt, I realized that every time Lapaglia took the train to and from Denver, which Annamaria said he did a lot, he saw this sign, maybe more than one, if train billboards were the same as highway billboards.

Did Lapaglia finally take the sign's advice?

SEVENTEEN

After lots more rhythmic clattering, some more banging on the restroom door, and perhaps a bit of nodding off on my part, I felt the train rumble and screech to a stop. I couldn't see the name of the station due to some ancient cottonwoods drooping leafy branches over the sign. I knew I had to get off the train here, though.

Unsure if the Braid was on the train with me or not, I opened the door a crack and peeked out. A swarm of people wearing matching blue baseball caps with "Anderson Family Reunion" stitched across them crowded the aisle, clearly gathering their belongings to disembark here. I tugged my blue *I Heart Denver* cap down as low as I could and hurried to join them. I insinuated myself between two pre-teen girls and an older woman, perhaps their grandmother. The two pre-teens held hands and were fidgety with excitement. I suspected they were cousins who didn't get to see each other very often, because why would you be that excited with your sister?

The older woman struggled with a suitcase. She said, "Brianna, would you help me get this down?"

"Let me get that for you." I sprang to her side, lifting

down the bag and using it to shield my face from the Braid, should he be nearby.

"Why, thank you so much!" she said. I ushered the two girls in front of me and she followed behind. I hurried off the train behind the two girls who took off after some other members of their group already waiting in a knot by the door into the station.

I dropped the suitcase next to them and yanked open the door. The older woman called, "Thanks again!" and waved at me when I turned my head. I waved back then ducked inside the station. The ladies' room was just inside and I zipped into it, locking myself in the stall nearest the door. Lots of women came in and out. The other two toilets flushed, sinks ran, hand dryers whirred.

But soon it was silent and I knew I was alone. I realized I had better avail myself of the facilities just in case. How inconveniently stupid to have been locked in two separate restrooms for hours and not take the opportunity to do some availing.

I crept out of the stall, washed my hands and face, and then inched open the restroom door, peering out with one eye. Nobody. I stepped around a dry erase sandwich board sign handwritten with arrival and departure times next to a huge faux ficus tree. I checked the clock on the wall. The train had continued on its journey ten minutes ago.

I didn't hear any voices but wasn't convinced the Braid wasn't skulking around here somewhere just like I was. I squinted through the plastic leaves of the ficus but didn't see anyone. Wary, I noted all the exits.

I took one cautious step and then another. Still nobody. No voices. In front of me stretched two rows of rustic wooden benches, ornate arms bisecting them at regular intervals. Antique-looking light fixtures hung from the ceiling, fan blades rotating lazily. An empty fireplace broke up the wall to my right, ash and soot stains crawling on the brickwork in all directions. Beyond the benches was a curved archway with dark wood trim around it.

The whole room harkened back to the Old West. I took a few more tentative steps, fully expecting the Braid to jump out at me. But he didn't. Either he got off the train before it left Denver, or he didn't see me get off here and was on his way west to Seattle. I was glad I had thought to close the door of the restroom when I hustled off the train. Maybe he thought I was still there.

Feeling more confident, but still a tad jumpy, I made my way through the archway toward the ticket office. Hanging above the window was a carved wooden sign that read "Lost Valley Station."

My heart clutched a bit. If this was Lost Valley, maybe I could check out the resort and see if Lapaglia did wind up there. It was a long shot, but it made a certain kind of sense. As much sense as anything did these days.

On the other side of the ticket window, a man rested his legs on a desk, blue jeans and cowboy boots crossed comfortably. He leaned back in his chair, fingers interlaced behind his head. I softly cleared my throat but he didn't move. I tapped my fingernail on the counter. Unsure, I struck the silver bell.

The poor man jumped and almost fell from his chair. "Dang! Where'd you come from?"

"I'm sorry. I was on the train that just came in."

He stood, brushed off his embarrassment, and straightened his chair before coming to the window.

"Can I get a cab out to the resort?"

"Why don't you just take their shuttle?" He pointed out the sign. "It's the only thing out here." He narrowed his eyes at me. "Why didn't you get on the shuttle with that nice family going out there?"

"It was full."

"No, it wasn't."

I blushed at my stupid lie when I already had a stupid truth at the ready. "It left when I was in the restroom."

Now it was his turn to blush. He reached for the phone and mumbled, "I'll call out there and tell him he's got another passenger. Shouldn't be too long."

I thanked him and walked to the front of the station to wait, but was driven inside after about five minutes by extreme heat and aggressive flies. Flies with no understanding or concern for my personal space. Autonomous gangsters bent on the total destruction of my unflappable serenity. Flies so committed to my discomfort they had surely raised their tiny fists and swore an oath.

After many minutes of contemplating the probable futility of investigating the Lost Valley Resort, and a near-decision to simply take the next train back to Denver, the door to the station whooshed open. A pale, well-groomed man who looked like he just stepped out of the pages of Newly-Transplanted Cowboy Monthly called out a greeting to the train agent, then walked toward me with his hand outstretched. In his other hand he carried a small paper bag with the Lost Valley Resort logo printed on it.

"Alan Fraser, owner of Lost Valley Resort. Hear you need a ride."

"I'm Charlee Russo and I do. I'm sorry to drag you all the way back here."

He handed me the bag. "I'm sorry to hear about your troubles."

Confused, I opened the bag. Inside was an assortment of over-the-counter remedies, Pepto-Bismol, Imodium, Midol, ibuprofin. Heat crept up my neck and settled in my face. The train agent must have told him I was in the restroom for an inordinately long time. I couldn't very well explain I was hiding, so I swallowed my humiliation and simply said, "Thanks."

He followed me toward the exit but said, "Let me just

grab your luggage."

"I don't have any." Seeing the bewilderment on his face I added, "I like to travel light."

"We have a gift shop at the resort, in case you find you traveled a bit too light." A smile played on his lips, almost hidden by his reddish goatee and mustache. "Shall we?" He swept an arm toward the door.

"Can I ask you something first?" I said, digging in my bag. I pulled out the picture of Lapaglia. "Do you know this man? Would he happen to be staying at your resort?"

He didn't even look at the photo. "I can't divulge my guest list. We have a very strict privacy policy. I'm sure you understand."

"Sure. I get it." *Don't like it, but I get it.*

He walked a step-and-a-half ahead of me so I was able to study him without being rudely obvious. The population of the world would be completely self-conscious if they knew how many writers studied them for traits for our character files.

Alan Fraser was not what I expected in an owner of a rustic western resort. Red thinning hair, first of all. I couldn't name one ginger cowboy. No cowboy hat. Jeans with a razor-sharp crease right down the center of each leg. How do you even do that? Ornate western-style shirt with too many sequins, probably mail-order from someplace in Thailand instead of the iconic Rockmount Ranch Wear store in Larimer Square in Denver. And worse yet, two-toned wingtips instead of boots.

As if he could read my mind, at the van he motioned me up the stairs and said, "I'm from Manhattan."

Not sure what the correct response was, I decided no response was probably best. Anything I said would come out judgmental, perhaps even rude, even though that wouldn't be my intent. If he were a character in a book, I'd appreciate the juxtaposition and wonder if the author was planting some sort of foreshadowing image in my head, or drawing subtle attention to something dubious about him, or maybe just messing with me. Good thing he wasn't a character in a book, I guess.

I stepped into the van and took a seat in the second row.

Alan Fraser had the radio turned low to a twangy country station. The way he hummed along and quietly sang incorrect words out of sync perfectly illustrated his Manhattan-ness. He seemed to be trying on this cowboy persona and it didn't fit very well. It reminded me of when I used to stagger and scuff around in my mom's high heels as a child.

He turned from a paved road to a rutted dirt road. We bumped along and I watched the silvery-green rabbitbrush, the low-slung sumac with their orange-red berries, and the occasional purple flowering sage pass by. He shifted gears and the van struggled as the terrain rose in elevation. Before long, we rounded a bend and the semi-arid landscape morphed into something more befitting the Colorado mountains. Stands of pine trees and aspen stretched in a patchwork panorama before us.

As we traveled, we chatted politely. He told me about falling in love with Colorado and trying his hand at innkeeping. I told him I wrote mysteries. I hoped he would slip up and say, "What a small world! I have Rodolfo Lapaglia staying here, too," but no such luck. All he said was, "I enjoy a good mystery" without mentioning any of mine.

He slowed the van as we came upon a driveway to the left. He turned and we passed under a huge ranch sign spanning the entrance. A massive log was anchored across the top of two equally massive logs set deep into the ground on either side. The words "Lost Valley Ranch" cut from shiny black metal dangled from chains.

It looked decidedly more western and rustic than Alan Fraser ever could. We drove another half-mile or so and he pointed out the horseshoe pits to the right and beyond that, a chuckwagon heading across the prairie. It was the most bucolic thing I'd seen since we left the Lost Valley station twenty minutes or so earlier.

"Chuckwagon supper tonight. Barbecue, beans, cornbread, a nice pinot noir, the works. Sign up and they'll find you a nice horse to ride out there." He turned to look at me. "You ride?"

I hadn't been on a horse since I plodded around in a circle on the back of a sad swayback at the Renaissance Festival. Her ennui had seeped upward through the saddle and settled in my eight-year-old bones. By the time we'd made the requisite six laps, I had nodded off twice. "Not really."

"We also have a hayride that goes out there."

That sounded worse. I never understood the allure of a hayride. Hay is uncomfortable, pokey and itchy, full of dust and pollen and possibly hantavirus. Its only purpose around humans was to make them sneeze. But I didn't want to hurt his feelings. He was only trying to be helpful to his guest. "Maybe. I just sign up?"

"Yes'm. At the front desk."

That *yes'm* sounded like something he'd been practicing.

He parked the shuttle van under the portico in front of the resort which, up close, looked much more stylish than rustic. We remained outside, walking to the end of the main building, and he pointed in the direction of the cabins while he listed the amenities—all electric, wifi-enabled, air conditioning, room service—the patio area with outdoor kitchen and propane grills if I wanted to cook any of the fish I caught, and the huge, very inviting kidney-shaped pool with hot tub.

When he finished, he escorted me to the front desk, introduced me to Maggie, the clerk, then clicked his wingtips together, doffing the nonexistent hat on his head. "I'll leave you to it, then. Enjoy your stay."

I watched him go with a bemused smile then turned to Maggie. "Wingtips?"

EIGHTEEN

She laughed. "Yep, wingtips every day. Says boots hurt his feet. But he's the nicest guy I've ever worked for."

"Probably because his feet don't hurt."

"Ha! Probably." She brightened up her efficient hospitality face and started clicking her computer keyboard. "So ... checking in?"

"Um ... not really. I don't have a reserva—"

"Oh, please don't worry about that. It's the middle of the week. We have cabins available."

"No, I mean, I'm not expecting to stay." I placed my bag of pharmaceuticals on the counter.

"Then ... why are you ... here?"

"It's kind of a long story."

She nodded, knowingly, but she couldn't possibly know.

I didn't want to tell her I was looking for Lapaglia, because if he was here, I'd want to catch him by surprise. "I actually just kinda got stuck on the train and ended up at the Lost Valley station. I didn't know where else to go, so I was maybe going to hang out here and wait for my boyfriend to come pick me up? But he won't even be off work for hours, and then to drive up here might take ....?"

"From Denver? Couple hours. More with traffic."

I sighed. I wasn't even sure Ozzi could get away, what with his integration problems and load testing. Either way, he wasn't going to be happy with me, especially if I tried to confront Lapaglia on my own.

"Well, if you decide later you want a cabin, you just let me know and I'll set you up right nice."

"Would it be possible to get a sandwich or something out by the pool? It looks gorgeous out there." I was hungry, but I also had a half-baked scheme maybe I could order food with Lapaglia's name and they'd confirm he was here someplace. Or not. Regardless, I was still going to order something. I was starving. And if Lapaglia was here, he could sure as heck pay for my meal. He owed me that, at the very least.

"Absolutely." She reached under the counter and handed me a menu. "Just take this out there and call whenever you're ready. The number's on the back."

I traipsed down a long hallway, past the restaurant, past the bar, past the coffee kiosk, past the gift shop, head on a swivel watching for Lapaglia the entire time, but there was nobody around. Maggie was right. It was dead here.

When I exited at the far end of the building, I found myself on a wide concrete sidewalk that meandered through the trees, huge hundred-year-old pines, stately blue spruce, and stands of tall, skinny aspen with their peeling white bark and leaves shimmering and quaking despite very little breeze. The shady sidewalk led toward the cabins.

Wherever the sidewalk forked, there were wooden signs with the cabin names chiseled into them and an arrow directing guests the right way along a dirt path. The first cabin was just off the sidewalk, but the other three were hidden among the trees.

The first sign I came to listed *Lodgepole, Spruce, Bristlecone,* and *Ponderosa*. The sign reading *Lodgepole* was nailed over the door of the cabin closest to me. It was closed up tight and nobody was around. I followed the arrow down the dirt path toward *Spruce.* If I didn't know three more cabins were back here I would never have guessed it.

The Lost Valley Resort was beginning to grow on me. This would be a great place for a writer's retreat.

I found myself treading lightly, almost tiptoeing along the path. It was so tranquil out here. Suddenly, *Spruce* cabin loomed in front of me and I heard a woman gasp. I gasped in response.

"Oh my, you scared me!" A middle-aged woman sat on the porch clutching a paperback to her chest.

"I'm sorry!"

At the same time we both said, "It's so quiet here!" then laughed.

I continued on toward *Bristlecone* and *Ponderosa.*

"Step on a twig next time," she called after me.

"Will do!"

Both cabins seemed empty, so I took the path behind. I was glad I wouldn't have to pass by *Spruce* again and disturb that poor woman trying to read. I picked up a twig and carried it, thinking if I needed to, I could warn someone of my presence by snapping it with my hands. I wasn't sure that would be any less startling, though. Might even be more alarming. I tossed it aside and decided instead to simply swing my bag and the laminated menu in a slightly exaggerated manner. The slap and crinkle of the paper might do the trick. I didn't want to be responsible for giving anyone a heart attack.

The next fork I came to pointed toward cabins named *Penstemon, Lupine, Larkspur,* and *Columbine.* This time, since I was behind the cabin area, *Columbine* was the most out-of-the-way of this pod. I heard kids playing. As I approached, five kids ranging in age from toddler to pre-teen, all completely covered in joyful vacation dirt, ran right up to me.

"Wanna buy a mud pie?" a boy around six asked.

"Or a moothie?" the toddler asked.

"Ssssmoothie," a pre-teen girl corrected, elongating the missing sound.

"A mud pie and a smoothie," I said. "Sounds delicious, but I don't think so." I patted my belly like I was Santa.

"Why not?" A little girl with half a front tooth sprouting put her hands on her hips and stared at me.

I knew her type. Bossy. Demanding. Awkward. She reminded me of me.

"Because I have work to do."

"What work?" she asked.

I couldn't very well tell her I was stalking someone so I said, "I'm a writer."

"For books?"

"Yes, for books."

"I like books. But only books with pictures. Do you draw pictures in your books?"

"Only when I was bored in Poly Sci."

"What?"

"Nothing. No, I don't draw pictures in my books."

"Why not? Lots of people make pictures in their books. Like Mr. Ronny."

"I don't know Mr. Ronny."

"Why not?" She stamped her bossy little foot.

The pre-teen rescued me from the interrogation. "He's in that cabin over there." She waved vaguely. "He's an"—she struggled to come up with the word—"illustrator. That's what he said it's called when you draw pictures for kid books. He wanted our opinion on them the other day. Mom let us go."

"He was a good draw-er," the toddler said.

"Nuh uh. He was a poopy draw-er," the bossy snaggle-toothed girl said.

A shy boy stepped around the pre-teen and pulled his

finger from his mouth long enough to say, "He brung us ice cream."

"Oh boy. I bet that was fun," I said.

"We're going on another hike today. I'm going to be Line Leader," Little Miss Bossy said.

"That sounds like fun too."

They all nodded and we stared at each other for a while, having run out of discussion topics. "Okay, I guess I better let you get back to your pie and smoothie making now."

They ran back to the mud puddle they'd made and the older girl goosed it with a bit more water from a bucket.

I followed the path from the kids at *Columbine* to *Larkspur*, then *Lupine*, but they both seemed empty. When I got to *Penstemon*, I greeted a young couple watching me from their porch. A bottle of wine sat on the table between them. They both had their feet on the railing, she was barefoot with a bright red pedicure, he wore flip flops.

"Nice out here, eh?" I said.

"Sure is," she said.

"We're on our honeymoon," he said, puffing out his chest a bit.

"Congratulations." I continued on my way.

When I'd passed them I heard the girl say, "Geez, you don't have to tell *everyone*. And would it kill you to wear a shirt sometimes?"

Yeah, that marriage was made in heaven.

Back on the concrete sidewalk, I had a choice to make. I could continue walking around all the cabins in a far-fetched attempt to see if Lapaglia was here, or I could head back toward the pool area and a sandwich. I decided on the sandwich since I didn't know how many more cabins there were. I might need sustenance. Besides, the notion that Lapaglia decided to vacation here seemed more than a little ridiculous now that I was here. Just my imagination working overtime, and maybe a little wishful thinking.

I followed the sidewalk back toward the main building, where I'd seen some bistro tables earlier. I settled into one and opened my menu, deciding on the cheapest thing on the menu, an $18 Reuben sandwich. I called the number on the back of the menu and they told me it would be about fifteen minutes. I settled in and tried to figure out what I'd say to Ozzi when I called him. I couldn't put it off much longer. I thought about calling AmyJo instead, even though I was fairly certain she worked tonight. Would she want to drive all the way out here after work? I snorted. Regardless of what she wanted, I knew if I asked, she'd be here. That's the kind of friend she was. Calling my brother was out of the question, though. Lance would interrogate me and wring every secret from my cold, dead body.

The reunion family from the train came and rearranged several tables and chairs, noisily scraping them on the concrete to form a massive compound worthy of Kennebunkport. The kids all wore swimsuits. The adults had a loud gossipy conversation about family members who hadn't joined them for this reunion. The kids ran around giggling and bopping each other with pool noodles.

I picked up my things, trying to be inconspicuous and not rude, and moved to the opposite side of the huge patio area. I passed through the section with the three covered gas grills where Alan Fraser told me I could fry up any fish I caught. All the patio enclaves—the bistro tables, the pool, the grills with nearby picnic tables—were strategically designed so no matter where you were on the patio, each outdoor party still had privacy from other guests. It was truly a delightful and majestic space. I was headed for the umbrella-covered tables behind the huge outdoor kitchen, complete with two built-in smokers, a couple of stovetops, and an impressive pizza oven, outfitted for any guests who enjoyed cooking while on vacation. It was a gorgeous amenity, with its intricate brickwork running almost the length of the outdoor area, but I couldn't imagine any scenario where I would be so inclined to utilize it. I barely cooked at home. And wasn't the point of a vacation to go someplace where people did things for you?

As I arranged myself, I saw the happy noisy family walking toward the pool followed by a cadre of waiters from the restaurant carrying many silver trays of food. I couldn't hear them at all anymore.

About a dozen tables away, I saw a man with his back to me, painting at an easel. He must be the illustrator the children had told me about.

I decided to introduce myself while I waited for my lunch and decide for myself whether he was a good or poopy drawer. I scuffed my sneakers on the concrete to make a bit of noise so I wouldn't startle him. I knew when I got in my 'writing zone' I fell into a kind of tunnel vision trance. More than once, someone had accidentally spoken too loudly, causing me to jump and shriek, scaring the bejeebers out of everyone in the vicinity.

I didn't need to freak out some poor guy on vacation.

Scuff, scuff, scuff.

The man looked up at me.

I looked down at him. He wore a bolo tie with a silver clasp in the same design as Martina's logo and Tiffany Isaac's necklace in the photo Detective Ming showed us.

I felt my mouth turn into a cartoon O.

NINETEEN

"Lapaglia?" I reached out for him, just to see if he was real. He flinched and drew back. "What are you—why are you—" I couldn't settle on a single question until my gaze landed again on the bolo tie he was wearing. The silver slide was definitely the same curlicue design as Martina's logo and Tiffany Isaac's necklace. "Where did you get that tie?"

He hadn't taken his eyes off me, but continued to shrink back. His hand fluttered to his tie. "It was a gift. It's not for sale. Who are you?"

He didn't even recognize me? "I'm Charlee Russo."

He relaxed and broke eye contact, picking up his paintbrush. "Ah, Miss Russo. Enjoying the resort? I must say I quite—"

"What are you doing here? Why didn't you show up at our event? You left me holding the bag for all those costs! I'm up to my eyeballs in debt now! Everyone hates me! I was on the news!" That last word came out more as a wail than a word. I didn't mention Peter O'Drool being dognapped because I didn't want to tip my hand that I was going to deliver Lapaglia directly into the Braid's hands at the first opportunity. But it suddenly occurred to me I had no idea how to contact the Braid. A bridge to be crossed.

Regardless, I expected Lapaglia to be remorseful, concerned with the financial travails he caused, maybe not even understanding what had happened, jumping up to fix everything. But he was nonplussed. In fact, what's less than nonplussed? Was that even possible? Because that's what he was.

Staring at him brush vibrantly colored paint over his canvas, I could feel my rage beginning to grow. It began in my sweaty feet, tingling my toes, knocking my knees, clenching my butt, pounding my heart. My forearms pulsed with each squeeze of my fists.

I had to sit down. And far enough away that I wouldn't inadvertently punch him in the throat. He continued to make nonplussed streaks of color while I pulled out a chair across from him.

Trying to keep my voice low and even I said, "How could you just ditch out on our event and leave me holding the bag? I don't deserve that. And using all those women ... Lakshmi, Martina, Cecelia? They don't deserve that either. And your wife? Neither does she."

"Yes, Annamaria is a saint."

I wondered if she knew about his girlfriends. I thought about my conversation with her and how she used the term *rendezvous* and didn't seem to care that he'd gone missing. "You need to come back to Denver with me. Today. Now. And make everything right."

He tilted his head and assessed his work, teddy bears at a picnic. "Nah. I'm digging it here. Don't want to go back. I wished for a different life and I got it."

"A different life? Why? What's wrong with your old life?"

"I'm tired of writing mob stories. But when I told my publisher, they said they didn't care what I wanted. So I blogged to my fans, expecting them to rally to my defense so I could prove to Penn & Powell that they'd follow me. But those ingrates." He held his brush in midair and looked over at me. "After all I did for them. All those books I wrote simply to entertain them. What did it get me?"

"A huge income? Fame? Accolades? World renown?"

Lapaglia stuck his tongue out and blew a raspberry. "Not everything it's cracked up to be."

"Some of us would like to see what fame and money is cracked up to be. But thanks to you, I probably never will."

"Count yourself lucky, then."

"I DON'T count myself LUCKY—" I felt my rage start tingling my toes and clenching my butt again so I took a deep breath. "What exactly is it you want?"

A ridiculous grin spread over his face. "I want to write and illustrate children's picture books. Independently."

A million thoughts jitterbugged in my brain. None of this made sense.

"What are you talking about? You did all this to me so you could—" I made a conscious effort to refrain from making fists. "You just want to write in a different genre?"

He nodded and went back to his painting, ridiculous grin still on his face.

"Lots of authors write in different genres." I felt like I was explaining the alphabet to a coffee cup. "You just need a pseudonym for one of them. And authors publish books traditionally, like with Penn & Powell, but they also publish independently. They're called 'hybrid authors.' You don't need to go underground to do this. People do it every day."

Lapaglia was so taken aback by this revelation he dropped the paintbrush in his lap but made no move to retrieve it. "What? People do this? Why didn't anyone tell me?"

"Perhaps because you're a huge recluse who goes out of his way not to meet anyone or involve yourself in the community of writers?" I concentrated on drawing slow, steady breaths in an effort to avoid an assault charge. Instead of punching him in the throat, I opened and closed my fists repeatedly.

He regarded me like a scientist might study microbes. After a few moments, he shrugged and picked up his paintbrush. "You don't realize how hard it is for me—"

"I read your interviews where you moan about not being able to go out in public. What about traveling to Denver constantly? What about being here? What about your girlfriends?"

He looked away, maybe with a flicker of regret or remorse on his face. "I'll go back eventually. I need them."

I let out a noise, part ill-humored laugh, part indignation. "Don't get your hopes up. They all know each other now. Your jig, as they say, is up." I waited for his denial or bluster or whatever philandering jerks do when they're caught, but he didn't react. Finally I said, "Why are you here? Why Lost Valley Resort if you need your girlfriends so much?" I stretched out *need* and *girlfriends* so sarcastically I felt like I was fourteen again. I wouldn't be surprised if a full bloom of acne had erupted all over my face.

Lapaglia sighed and wiped his hands on a rag. "I knew my jig"—he paused and rolled his eyes—"was up when I saw you and Martina talking on Saturday when the train came in."

So he *was* pretending not to recognize me. The weasel.

"Every time I come to Denver I see signs for this place so I got back on the train and hid in the restroom."

One hundred percent of the participants in this conversation had hidden in the train restroom between Denver and the Lost Valley Resort. It made me wonder how many other people had done the same thing over the years.

A waiter carrying my food stopped near the table where I'd left my purse, the menu, and my pharmaceuticals. I called to him, "Yes, that's me. Just leave it there." He nodded and I saw him slip the bill underneath the tray.

"Martina thinks I'm your secret girlfriend and she wants to kill me."

He waved my worry away. "A simple case of mistaken identity."

"Easy for you to say. She looks mean."

"Marty is a peach. A pussycat. A marshmallow."

I let that roll around in my brain a bit. *Marty* does sound softer and nicer than *Martina*. I wonder what she calls him. Wait. I groaned, remembering how they all used different names to refer to him. "You gave all those women a different name for yourself. You're just using them to help with this new picture book career of yours!" My hand fluttered to my throat as I put it all together. "Lakshmi is a children's librarian, Cecilia is a graphic designer, Martina is a marketing expert. You ARE a jerk!" I stood up so fast I knocked my chair over. "You're not interested in these women. You're just picking their brains and using their skills to help you produce and sell your picture books!"

He ignored my outburst and went back to painting, swizzling his brush in a dab of paint the color of blood. "Says you."

I had to move away from him because a thick rage was bubbling up and I didn't think I could control it right now. Before I went back to my table, I leaned in close to Lapaglia's ear. "I will get the money you owe me"—I silently added *and I will get Peter*—"today."

He never turned around, just continued painting. Either he had no intention of reimbursing me or he was just waiting for me to tell him how much. Or maybe I had terrified him. I doubted it, but it gave me a little puff of satisfaction.

I bit into my Reuben while I calculated what he owed me, both compensatory damages as well as punitive. He owed me, dammit.

At one point I thought he was getting up to come over and beg my forgiveness, throwing himself on my righteous mercy, but he only angled his chair to get out of the sun. He didn't even seem concerned that I might broadcast his location to the world. He *should* care about that, if he'd been the one to come face-to-face with all those furious workshop participants.

I was too livid to call Ozzi or anyone else to come get me, or Penn & Powell to tell them I found their Golden Boy Jerk. I needed to wait until I could modulate my tone and my words, and probably not in public, just in case I misjudged. I ate half my sandwich, but didn't taste any of it, while I stared daggers into Lapaglia's back.

The family reunion family made a noisy departure as they hurried to get to their trail ride on time. Watching them with their easy camaraderie and playfulness as they chased each other out of the area calmed me down the teensiest bit. Not everyone was horrible. Just Lapaglia.

As I picked up the other half of my $18 Reuben, dangling a single strand of sauerkraut, I saw a flick of silver way up near the front of the outdoor kitchen. Something about it told me it wasn't a bird. It seemed familiar somehow. I stared, straining to identify whatever it was.

No. It couldn't be.

The Braid was sneaking up on Lapaglia from around the front of the outdoor kitchen. He hugged the brick. Lapaglia painted, oblivious to his presence. I reached up slowly and tilted the umbrella over my table so it blocked me completely. Then I slid out from behind it and moved quickly, with my head down, to the opposite side of the outdoor kitchen. I tiptoed the entire length of it hoping the Braid wouldn't double back and run into me.

I reached the short end of the brick structure. Unless he'd moved, which I didn't suspect since I hadn't heard any voices or scuffling, the Braid was still peering around the corner to the left, while I was on the right. Only about eight feet of brick wall separated us.

I pressed my back against the bricks and squinched my eyes. There was no one in the long patio area or beyond it outside the main building. I knew if I screamed or caused a ruckus, both men would disappear. But if I could deliver Lapaglia to the Braid, he'd give me back Peter O'Drool. He promised. That was the deal.

Slowly, like a well-trained ninja, I inched forward.

TWENTY

I realized I didn't want to hide from the Braid. I wanted to sneak up behind that jerk Lapaglia and deliver him into the Braid's grateful hands. I reversed direction and snuck back the way I'd come. I crossed the patio toward the table where my lunch sat but I didn't stop. Instead I continued on to where Lapaglia sat, preoccupied with painting his teddy bears.

By the time I reached Lapaglia from behind, the Braid had sprinted up to him from the side. We each clamped a hand on his shoulders at the same time.

"Here he is!" I raised my free hand, offering the Braid a high five.

Lapaglia tried to stand but we both pushed him back into his seat.

"What are you doing here?" The Braid scorched me with his eyes.

"I found him for you."

"You did not do jack. I found him myself." The Braid pushed me away and I fell to the concrete.

This was the last straw on my last nerve. I was done being pushed around by old men, literally and figuratively. I scrambled to my feet, looking, I'm certain, like a honey badger with nothing left to lose. The full fury of my frustration and rage shot through me, bestowing Wonder Woman strength which I used to leap onto the Braid's back and ride him like a rodeo bull, one arm around his throat, the other wrapped around his hair like reins.

The faces of all those judgmental cops at my Dad's funeral all those years ago flashed across my memory. Detectives Ming-Like-The-Vase and Campbell-Like-The-Soup, smug and condescending, questioning me about the murder of my agent. Those patronizing cops in Portland assuming I was a nut-job who watched too many movies. Lapaglia, entitled and arrogant, ruining my career, my credit, and maybe my entire life with his selfishness. And now the Braid, dognapping, backstabbing, double-crossing mobster, clearly with no intention of keeping his promise to me.

I held tight to that ponytail, surprised that my fury hadn't ripped it from his head completely. I never asked for any of this and I was sick of being dropped into circumstances out of my wheelhouse. How dare these men shake my comfort zone to the core!

We galloped all over that patio with him trying to buck me off. I was a bitch on wheels with a full tank of gas. Lapaglia simply stared, mouth wide open.

The Braid lost his balance when I hooked my foot around the leg of one of the propane grills and knocked his legs out from under him. I collapsed on top of him. His face smushed into the hot concrete. I straddled his back, my knees pinning his arms. I attempted to loosen the bungee cord holding the cover on the grill but couldn't quite reach. I didn't dare lift a knee off the thrashing mobster beneath me.

I yelled to Lapaglia to grab the cord. He did so without a word, still gaping at the scene before him. I tied the Braid's hands behind him. With my newfound superhuman strength, I yanked him to his feet by the back of his collar and dropped him into a chair. I splayed one palm on the Braid's chest, commanding Lapaglia to grab another bungee. I used it to lash the Braid to the chair, winding it tight around his chest. Breathing hard, I got the third bungee and fastened his ankles to the legs of the chair.

Leaving him in the sun, I stepped into the shade of an umbrella, Lapaglia at my side.

I brought the thunder, I thought, chest heaving, quoting AmyJo's favorite song. She'd be proud. I began to collect myself, willing my breathing to slow.

The complacency had finally disappeared from Lapaglia's face. It thrilled me to see he was now a cross between terror and shame, and what I hoped was culpability. All of this was his fault and the sooner he recognized that, the better off we'd both be.

The Braid, however, had pasted a sneer on his face. I needed him to understand the depth of my emotion at this moment. But how? Then I spied a pair of gardening shears propped in one of the many alcoves of the brick kitchen structure. I walked casually to it, praying my hands wouldn't shake as I picked it up, and that my voice would work when I figured out what to say.

As I ambled toward the Braid, opening and closing the shears with my hand, testing them out, Lapaglia's eyes widened. When I stopped next to the Braid, my knee almost touching his, I thought I saw a flicker of concern pass over his face. *At least he's paying attention.*

I bent down, my mouth next to his ear. "Where's Peter O'Drool?" I spoke in my normal voice, swollen with pride I hadn't squeaked.

The Braid turned his face toward mine. I saw no worry or concern anywhere on it. He stared in an alpha dog manner, but I held his gaze, no worry or concern on my face either. I hoped. Then he made a dismissive *pfft* sound and turned his attention to Lapaglia.

"Rodolfo." The Braid stretched out the second syllable. "It is time to confess."

I couldn't believe the Braid was trussed up like a Christmas goose and still thought he was in charge. Curious about the confession, however, I kept my mouth shut. But I did snap the shears a couple of times to remind them both that technically, I still had the upper hand.

"Confess what?" Lapaglia's face had returned to his previous nonchalance.

"Confess that you murdered my cousin."

"What?" Lapaglia blanched.

"He murdered who?" I asked, stunned.

"My cousin, Tiffany." The Braid kept his eyes on Lapaglia but spoke to me. "She called me, but I couldn't talk and let it go to voicemail. When I listened to it, she mentioned Lapaglia's name. The next day I learned she had been found murdered in Denver."

I looked from the Braid to Lapaglia who hadn't moved a muscle. I realized he might try to bolt at any moment. I stepped toward him, waving the pruning shears. "Get me those other bungee cords."

Lapaglia never looked at me, just moved mechanically toward the other grill and removed the cords securing the cover. He handed them to me, still without meeting my eyes.

I dragged a nearby chair, placing it four feet away from the Braid's. Pointing with the shears I commanded, "Sit down."

Lapaglia sat.

I began to get scared. This was too easy. As quickly as I could, I tied Lapaglia to the chair the same way I'd tied the Braid. Lapaglia still hadn't looked at me, simply stared at the concrete.

"Now talk." I gestured at Lapaglia's chest with the shears.

He didn't move.

The Braid started to speak but I pointed the shears at him and he shut up.

"Lapaglia." He still didn't respond so I gently poked him in the chest with the tip of the shears. He looked up at me. "This man just accused you of murdering Tiffany Isaac, who he says is his cousin. Don't you have anything to say to that?"

"I didn't do it." He looked at the Braid with disbelief. "Tiff's dead?"

The Braid glared at him.

"You have three seconds to tell me what's going on. And then I'm calling the cops," I said.

"I don't know. I just talked to her the other day."

"What did you talk about?" I asked.

"Nothing. She told me she'd seen the photos online from the Dark Dagger Awards."

The same ones I'd seen. "What about them?"

He looked me directly in the eyes. "I'm not sure. She wasn't making a lot of sense, talking fast and disjointed. Told me a story about sitting in a sushi bar with a friend years ago, when they were in college. They were procrastinating homework or something and talking about how nice it would be to trade places with two women sitting near them."

The Braid made a noise in his throat. "She told me the same story," he said, looking up at me. "She also told me that my name has been linked with Lapaglia's, that I am the one accused of feeding him inside information about the family."

"Whose family?" I asked.

"*The* family. The Zaminskys," the Braid said.

"Who are they?"

Lapaglia answered. "A crime family. He works for them."

"And you know this because ....?"

"Everyone knows this," Lapaglia said.

I didn't know it, but I kept that to myself. I asked the Braid, "Is this true?"

"Yes."

"Are you feeding Lapaglia inside information?"

The Braid didn't answer but shot me an angry look.

I looked from one to the other, becoming more and more exasperated with them. I wanted to call the police, but I wanted to know what was going on just the teensiest bit more. Besides, they were trussed up tight. I had plenty of time. I pointed my shears at one and then the other. "Remember when I went all spider monkey a little bit ago? Fair warning, I'm fixin' to do it again if you don't tell me what's going on." I opened and closed the shears. "In great detail."

The Braid and Lapaglia glanced at each other, neither wanting to explain. Finally, the Braid spoke.

"Someone is setting me up to make it look like I am feeding stories to this hack so he can write his books." He jerked his head at Lapaglia, who quickly glanced away. "The information is sensitive and not many people would know it. Unfortunately, I am one of them. Lapaglia will be accompanying me back to Jersey to tell them who has been spoon-feeding these stories to him to prove I was not involved. If he does not come with me, I will be forced to kill him to show he is nothing to me."

I thought about this for a moment. "So, either way you're in deep doo-doo. If your family thinks you're the snitch, you're a goner. If Lapaglia turns up dead, the Feds will think you did it and you're a goner." I mulled this over. "What's your real name anyway?"

"Cesare Silvio."

Lapaglia gasped. "Every email I got was signed *The Silver Fox.*"

I snapped my head toward the Braid. "You said you weren't the one feeding him information."

"I am not. Someone is setting me up."

I thought about what Don and Ozzi had told me about the character "Taffeta" in Lapaglia's books. "Was it Tiffany? Was she setting you up? She's your cousin, part of your crime family too."

"You do not know what you are talking about."

"Educate me."

"She is my cousin, yes, but we are not part of the Zaminsky family. I only work for them. Just because someone works for Walmart does not mean they are related to Sam Walton."

"Then what did Tiffany have to do with any of this?" I asked him.

"Yeah … what?" Lapaglia asked. "She's not really dead, is she?" His voice had a sad, resigned timbre to it.

The Braid scowled at him but answered me. "In her message she told me she was worried I was being set up for something and she did not want to see me get whacked."

I had no reason to believe him. In Lapaglia's book, Taffeta/Tiffany was a double-crosser. But if the Braid was telling the truth that she wasn't in the mob, then maybe "Taffeta" was someone else.

I turned to Lapaglia. "Who was Taffeta in your books?"

"Taffeta."

"Yes, Taffeta," I said impatiently.

Lapaglia frowned at me. "Taffeta … in my books … is … Taffeta." He spoke to me like I didn't understand English.

"Who was she based on?"

"Nobody. She's fictional."

"Don't play dumb, mister. You and I both know that fictional characters are often based on real people. Especially when they're handed to you fully-formed on a silver platter."

"Silver. You said it yourself. Ask the Silver Fox over there."

I turned to the Braid. "So how would Tiffany know anything about the mob if she wasn't in the mob?"

"I do not know."

"Does she have friends in the Zaminsky mob?"

"I do not know, but I hope she does not. They are ruthless."

"Unlike you, who spends his time feeding the hungry and building hospitals for the poor."

"You do not have to be sarcastic."

These men and this conversation were getting me all riled up again, and I still didn't understand any of it. If Lapaglia wrote those books based on stories he was given, someone had a *reason* for wanting him to write those books and include those stories. If "Mohawk" from the books is the Braid, and the story line was that he had to make things right with the mob, and here is the Braid wanting Lapaglia to go back to New Jersey to makes things right with the mob, then who was "Taffeta"?

If Taffeta was Tiffany, then maybe the Braid simply wasn't aware his cousin worked for the mob too. I'd seen enough gangster movies to know there were always plenty of secrets to go around.

But if it wasn't Tiffany, then it had to be someone else in the Zaminsky crime family.

I turned to Lapaglia. "Tell me again where you got the inside dirt on those mob stories."

"Emails signed *The Silver Fox*, like I said." He jerked his head toward the Braid.

"See? It is faulty information like this that will get me whacked. I never sent you any emails," the Braid said.

Lapaglia motioned to me to come closer to him. I squatted next to him, but warily, and only after making sure he was still tied tight. I also made sure he noticed I still held the garden shears.

"This is fishy," he whispered. "He killed Tiff."

"He says you killed her," I whispered back.

"I loved her. Why would I kill her?" The silver clasp of his bolo tie caught the sun every time he moved.

"Stranger things have happened."

"She never mentioned she had a cousin in the mob."

"Why would she?"

"You've gotta believe me. I didn't hurt Tiff." His eyes filled as he stared at me. "Which scenario makes more sense ... that a middle-aged author murdered someone in cold blood, or that a guy in the mob did? And notice how he never uses contractions when he speaks, like some Damon Runyon character?"

"I was thinking more like Kim Darby in *True Grit*, but so what?" I whispered, trying to keep one eye on him and one on the Braid.

"None of the emails sounded like that." He cut his eyes at the Braid.

"But would they? Do you talk exactly how you write in emails?" I mulled this over for a moment then nodded. *Yes, people generally sounded like their emails. Unless they were trying to disguise it.* "How long have you been getting mob stories from this Silver Fox?"

"Years," he whispered. "At least ten."

To me, that ruse didn't seem sustainable over so long. Months, maybe, but ten years?

As if giving voice to my thoughts, Lapaglia mimicked the Braid. "I do not think that a mook such as this could have been behind such a plot."

I shook out my legs and turned back to the Braid, speaking in my normal voice. "Let's talk about Tiffany some more. Why would she have been murdered?"

He looked as sad as Lapaglia had. For a minute I felt sorry for him. Then I remembered Peter's kidnapping, the hair-pulling, and the potential whacking.

"I do not know. She was a good person. She drove for the senior center. She volunteered at the food bank. She recorded books for the blind. She had a podcast!" he wailed.

I recalled Detective Ming telling me and Ozzi that Tiffany had been seen around Union Station before she'd been found dead. I turned toward Lapaglia. "Perhaps she was waiting for someone to get off the train."

"Now you wait one second. You don't think I—"

"Was she another of your girlfriends? Did you kill her because she double-crossed you somehow?"

"Double-crossed me how?"

I thought for a minute. "Well, I don't know. Maybe *she* knew *you* were double-crossing the Braid here."

"Again, how exactly would that work? Somebody was feeding me information about the Zaminsky family, so logically the info had to come from there."

I was getting confused. "Maybe if Tiffany knew who was feeding you the info, and she confronted them, maybe they killed her?"

Lapaglia made a frustrated chuffing noise, but the Braid had a realization.

"If Tiffany found out that the information leaked to Lapaglia was being blamed on me, and if she knew who really leaked it, she would try to make it right. She would confront them." He looked stricken. "It is my fault she is dead. She was trying to protect me. She knew who was behind those 'Silver Fox' emails to Lapaglia."

"And it got her killed," I added.

The Braid began fighting against his restraints as he shouted at Lapaglia. "If you had a better imagination and came up with stories of your own, none of this would have happened!" He tried *bump-bump-bumping* his chair closer to Lapaglia.

I moved toward him, waving the shears to remind him I still had them.

He took a deep breath and stopped moving around. "Again, Lapaglia. I ask you to confess. Do not make me break your kneecaps," the Braid snarled.

"It doesn't look like you're in any position to break

anybody's anything." I waved my hand at all the bungee cord.

The Braid and Lapaglia bantered back and forth about people I didn't know and things I didn't understand about the mob. While they accused, threatened, and cajoled, I kept an eye on them, but stepped away, set the shears on a table, and pulled out my phone. I very calmly explained to the 911 dispatcher that two men at the Lost Valley Resort might have information about a murder that occurred in Denver and they should send someone out right away. I added that one of them was also a dognapper.

The dispatcher seemed completely unfazed by our conversation—but that was her job. She said she'd send someone right out.

I was happy to wait for officers to take these two off my hands. Let them sort it all out.

But I still needed to know where the Braid stashed Peter. I interrupted their bickering. "Where are you hiding Peter?"

"Who's Peter?" Lapaglia asked.

"The dog he kidnapped to force me to find you." I glared at the Braid and he glared back. "Which I did, by the way."

"He stole your dog?" He glared at the Braid too. "That's low man, even for a mobster."

"Pete's not my dog." I jabbed a finger in the Braid's direction. "He stole a precious pet from an elderly couple. Peter is their only joy."

"They will get over it." The Braid broke eye contact and looked at his feet.

"Low, man." Lapaglia slowly shook his head. "Low indeed."

"Almost as low as you leaving me holding the debt and the PR mess from the event you ditched," I snapped.

"Actually, I think stealing a dog is much, much lower." Lapaglia turned to the Braid. "You should give that dog back."

"You should give her money back."

I scooped up the shears from where I'd left them on the table, then opened and closed them. The raspy, grating sound caused the Braid to flinch.

I could use his fear to get answers about Peter O'Drool.

TWENTY-ONE

I raised the clippers, pretending to inspect them. "Sharp," I said. I lovingly turned them over and over, purposely keeping them very near his face. I had absolutely no intention of using them. What was I gonna do, lop off his fingers? Impale him? The idea was laughable, but I didn't want either of these two men to know that.

I also didn't want either of them to see my hands begin to shake so I sidled around behind the Braid. He twisted his head to keep me in view, but he couldn't. He snapped his head the other direction and his long silver braid hit my arm. I grabbed it near the base of his scalp. With my other hand I made the *snip-snip* of the shears near his ear, where he was sure to hear it.

"Do not even think about doing that," he said.

"Tell me where Peter is." I pulled his hair tighter and rested it inside the shears.

"Nev—"

"What's going on here?" Alan Fraser, the owner of the resort came around the side of the outdoor kitchen and bellowed.

Startled, I snipped off the Braid's braid.

I stared at it in my hand. It was like holding half a rat. I thought about my hair looped through the opening in the back of my baseball cap. The urge to touch my own ponytail was overwhelming, but my hands were full of shears and half a rat so I had to settle for shaking my head and feeling the comfort of my hair tickle my shoulders and back.

Archie Cruz, that smarmy news guy, pushed his way around Alan Fraser. I saw the 35mm camera around his neck and quickly hid the shank of hair behind my back.

Alan Fraser reached for Archie Cruz' arm. He hissed, "You were supposed to stay out of sight!" But Archie Cruz kept coming.

Alan Fraser gaped at us, his face blotchy with anger. "I *said,* what's going *on* here? I got a report of some kind of ruckus."

Gone was the mild-mannered guy who brought me from the station earlier. He noticed the gardening shears in my hand. I could tell he wasn't sure of what I'd done—or was about to do—but he knew he didn't want whatever it was to happen.

"Hey," Archie Cruz said, peering closer at the Braid tied up in the chair. "You're that mob guy from the wanted posters. Cesare Silvio, right?" He moved closer and grasped what he could of the Braid's hand pinned behind him. "Thrilled to meet you, sir."

"Likewise." The Braid gave a diminutive wiggle of his fingers.

"Thought your hair was longer." He studied the Braid's head, whose hair now fell in an uneven pageboy around his face.

Alan Fraser held out his hand for the shears and I placed them in his hand. "This is the last time I'm going to ask. What ... is going ... on?"

I stepped away from the Braid, hiding the braid behind me. "This man has attacked me on more than one occasion."

"This woman has attacked *me* on more than one occasion. And she assaulted my hair!"

"It was an accident, but I'm not sorry. This man stole a dog from an elderly couple."

"I never!"

"You did, you liar. And this man—" I gestured at Lapaglia — "might have murdered a woman in Denver."

"I did no such thing. And I demand you untie me."

"Wait for the police," I told Alan Fraser. "I already called them."

"You did what?" Alan Fraser already had his phone out. He dialed, then after a moment spoke into it. "Hey, Michaelson. Did you just get a call from up here?" He listened for a bit, then said, "Tell them to turn around. It was just a misunderstanding. Everything here is fine."

"No, it's not!" I yelled toward the phone, but he'd already disconnected.

Alan Fraser knelt to untie the Braid's feet. "This will not do," he said to me. "I cannot have you tying up people on the patio of the Lost Valley Resort. That would be very bad for business."

"Where would you like me to tie them up, then? These are bad guys!"

"I can't have this kind of publicity." Alan Fraser kicked the first loose bungee away from the Braid's chair and worked on the bungee wrapped around his torso.

"I thought that's why you called me, to get publicity," Archie Cruz said.

Alan Fraser pulled the second bungee off and kicked it aside. "Yes, to show that the reclusive Rodolfo Lapaglia chooses Lost Valley Resort to write his books." He shot Lapaglia a dirty look then tapped the Braid on the shoulder to indicate he should lean forward. "NOT to rendezvous with low-level mobsters." He finished untying the Braid's hands and rested a hand on his shoulder. "No offense ... Mr. Silvio, was it?"

"None taken." The Braid rubbed his wrists as he stood.

"What about your very strict privacy policy?" I asked sarcastically.

I received no answer from Alan Fraser, just a silent blush running up the back of his neck.

"You can't have it both ways," I said. "You can't claim to give your guests privacy, and then call the media up here to report on it."

"And you can't tie up my guests right on my patio!" Alan Fraser's face was like an overripe tomato as he untied Lapaglia. It clashed with his hair.

Lapaglia and the Braid kept a wary distance from each other.

I wasn't sure what Alan Fraser was thinking. He called Archie Cruz to take paparazzi photos of Lapaglia ... were they both going to make money off them somehow? And even when he found out the Braid was in the mob and Lapaglia might be a murderer, he still untied them and told the police to stand down? Was he a bad businessman or a bad person? Or both?

Despite his phone call, I still expected the police to show up any minute. Would they really turn around and not investigate a call like mine?

Before I even saw him move, the Braid was in front of me.

I gasped.

He held out his hand.

I didn't move.

He flicked his fingers toward my hands behind my back. I placed the braid in his hand. He removed the elastic and handed me back the shank of hair, which I immediately dropped on the patio, strands swirling and fluttering to the concrete. The undefined fluttering edges made it look like a discarded snakeskin. He studied it sadly, then walked away, using the elastic to make a puny ponytail of his hair. When he finished, he shook his head. Half the hair escaped from the elastic.

"Oh, that's gold!" Archie Cruz exclaimed, hurrying after the Braid with his camera to his face.

The Braid grabbed Archie Cruz' camera lens and shoved him, hard. Cruz slammed into the concrete.

The Braid pivoted toward Lapaglia, grabbed him by his tricep, and began marching him across the patio. "You are coming back to New Jersey with me and telling them everything."

Lapaglia struggled to get away but the Braid held him tight.

"Okay, everyone stop right where they are. This has gone far enough!" Alan Fraser spoke loudly and with authority, but nobody stopped. He raised his voice. "I'm calling the cops!" He pulled out his phone, punched at it, then spoke into it. "I changed my mind. Get up here NOW!"

Lapaglia broke free from the Braid's grip and ran, disappearing into the trees.

The Braid tried to go after him, but Archie Cruz got back in his face with the camera and began clicking. Alan Fraser race-walked toward the building, still talking into his phone.

The Braid got a wild look in his eye, finally accepting he wasn't in charge of the situation. He began sprinting down the patio.

I chased after him. "Wait, wait! You have to tell me where Peter is! I got you to Lapaglia before the cops did."

The Braid kept running. "I did not get the information I needed!"

"That's not my fault!"

The Braid never broke stride and was almost to the corner of the building.

"Just tell me where Peter is and I'll go get him. Please?" I yelled, running faster. I came around the corner and saw the

Braid climbing into the driver's seat of the shuttle van. "Is Peter at least safe?" I called to him.

"Of course he is. I am not a monster." He started up the engine, floored it, and fishtailed away from the resort.

Alan Fraser burst out of the building and skidded to a stop. "Where are you?" he screamed into the phone. I wanted to point out they'd have been here by now if he hadn't called them off earlier. He stalked back into the building.

I stood, sweating in the summer heat, trying to make sense of everything that just happened.

I worried about Peter O'Drool. Would the Braid return him, now that he'd found Lapaglia? I know he didn't get the information he wanted, or Lapaglia, but that wasn't Peter's fault. Surely he wouldn't hold all this against a fat little pug. Surely not. But might he be vindictive enough to hold everything against the woman who cut off his hair, even though she totally didn't mean to? I groaned. Why did I have to threaten him with those shears? Why did that idiot Alan Fraser have to come around the corner right then? And why wouldn't the Braid just tell me where Peter was? He was using him for leverage against me to find Lapaglia and I found him. Isn't there some kind of gentlemen's code? Honor among thieves and all that?

An odd sound captured my attention and I turned to see Lapaglia galloping through the scrub on a big brown horse. He held the reins in one hand and with the other hugged a suitcase precariously balanced across the saddle horn and his lap.

I screamed after him, "You are the worst thing to happen to the world since Twitter!"

~

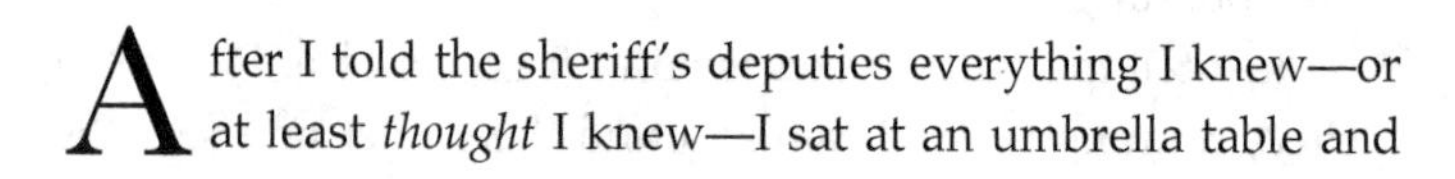

After I told the sheriff's deputies everything I knew—or at least *thought* I knew—I sat at an umbrella table and tried to work up the courage to call Ozzi and see if he'd come pick me up. He would, of course, no question, but he was upset with me. I knew this because he'd told me as much in the three increasingly frantic voicemails he'd left me. I had already texted him a quick, "I'm fine," but still. He'd used words like *reckless*, *stupid*, and *impulsive*. More than once.

And he wasn't wrong.

But I was so tired, and I knew I couldn't make him understand why I'd even gone to Union Station today, much less explain how everything went sideways.

During the long drive back to Denver, I didn't want to have to defend the indefensible, even though it had made so much sense at the time.

Instead I'd called AmyJo. I explained where I was, giving her the least amount of information I could get away with and still get a ride home. She said she'd be there as soon as she could.

I settled into a shady chaise lounge and called Ozzi. "Can you talk?"

"Where are you?"

"Still at the resort."

"Do you want me to—"

"AmyJo's on her way, but I'll probably be home pretty late."

"You know I'd come get you."

"I know. But you're so busy and …"

"And you don't want me yelling at you."

"Even if I deserve it."

"You don't deserve it. I was just worried about you. I'm not angry. So tell me everything."

After I filled him in and he promised to be waiting at my apartment when I got home, I hung up, closed my eyes, and waited for AmyJo. The resort was so quiet and peaceful. I was the only one by the pool, or anywhere, for that matter. Those kids must have gone on their hike, otherwise I couldn't imagine why they wouldn't be splashing in this glorious pool. The family reunion family must still be on their trail ride or maybe at the chuckwagon dinner. I began to suspect this resort was much larger than I realized, with many more activities.

I listened to the sweet song of the meadowlarks, the chittering of the squirrels, and the gentle quaking of the aspen leaves in the breeze. But nothing drowned out the refrain *I had them right here* that kept whistling through my brain.

Reckless, stupid, and impulsive or not, I was so close to delivering Lapaglia to the Braid, allowing me to ransom Peter. Small consolation to think I might have helped the police solve a murder instead.

I heard footsteps pounding across the concrete. I opened one eye, knowing it wasn't AmyJo, but hoping it was.

Geez. Archie Cruz. Why doesn't he crawl back under his ambush-news rock and leave me alone?

I turned away from him and willed myself to be invisible. Didn't work.

"Where is he? Lapaglia." He was breathless.

"Gone. For good, I hope. Why?"

"His wife was murdered."

TWENTY-TWO

"What?" An icy wave crashed over me. I just talked to her the other day. "Where? When?"

"At their house in Nebraska. Sometime Monday or Tuesday. Package bomb. Where is he?"

My mind skittered. Monday and Tuesday was when Lapaglia was unaccounted for. Unless he really had been at the Lost Valley Resort since Saturday. I jumped up and dashed to the ladies room for privacy from Archie Cruz's stare. I called the number in my history that I used to order my sandwich and asked to speak to Alan Fraser.

I got transferred to the front desk.

"I'm sorry. He's gone for the day," Maggie said. "Might I be of assistance?"

It was probably better that way, what with Alan Fraser's privacy policy. "Can you tell me when Rodolfo Lapaglia checked in?"

"Um ... I'm not really supposed to—"

"He's not a guest any longer. He's checked out already."

"Still ..."

"Listen, I understand there are privacy concerns and I appreciate you abiding by them, but this is serious. It's a matter of life and death." I hoped she heard the urgency in my voice and didn't think too hard about how life and death would apply to someone's check-in date. Especially if he'd already checked out. By now, surely she knew about the goings-on here today.

There was a long pause and I held my breath.

She spoke quietly, almost a whisper. "What was his name again?"

I whispered back, "Rodolfo Lapaglia."

"Pardon me? I can't hear you."

I repeated it louder, which seemed wrong, since she was whispering.

Her keyboard clattered. "Nobody checked in with that name in the last month."

I replied in a whisper. "He used a fake name."

"What? A word game?"

She had misunderstood me, but yes, he was definitely playing games, and I had no idea what name he might have checked in under, so I said, "The guy who stole the horse. When did he check in? What name did he use?"

Maggie was quiet for a long time. I assumed she was looking up the information. Instead she whispered, "I'm sorry I couldn't be of more help," then returned to her perky customer service voice. "Thank you for calling the Lost Valley Resort!"

I hung up and slumped against the wall. The Blow-O-Matic 3000 hand dryer roared to life. I jumped away from it and banged into a stall door, which slammed backward and then forward again, ricocheting into my face. I put my hand out to stop the door, then sat down on the closed toilet seat and readjusted my baseball cap.

I'd bet all the money Lapaglia owed me that he hadn't been at the Lost Valley Resort since Saturday. Was Alan Fraser covering for him? Why? Did Lapaglia zip back to Nebraska to kill Annamaria? Did he actually mail a package bomb to his wife? Archie Cruz must have made that up. Nobody gets killed by a package bomb, especially in Nebraska.

Lapaglia's voice prickled my memory. *"Yeah, Annamaria is a saint."* His statement sounded much more sinister now. Did my imagination add a sneer to his voice?

Were his girlfriends involved in his wife's murder? Did he convince one of them to go to Nebraska? Someone could drive to his house and be back in Denver the same day. But I couldn't picture mousy doormat Lakshmi killing anyone. And Cecilia would have to explain to her controlling husband where she was going and where she'd been, unless she called in sick or something and did it during working hours.

And Martina? Who knows? Of the three girlfriends, my money was on her. I slid her business card from the small outside pocket of my purse and stared at it, waiting for it to offer up some answers. I stared at it so long that my vision swirled and my mind wandered, but suddenly everything snapped back into focus.

I knew what I had to do, even without complete information. I reached forward and locked the restroom stall door. I contemplated calling Detective Ming, but instead looked up the number for the Denver Police Department's anonymous tip line.

"Are you investigating the Tiffany Isaac death as a murder or an accident?"

"Why do you need to know?"

"I might have information."

"And your name is?"

"Isn't this the *anonymous* tip line?" I took a deep breath, unsure if I was doing the right thing or not. "I heard that Annamaria Lapaglia was found dead in Nebraska and I just saw Rodolfo Lapaglia at the Lost Valley Resort outside Denver. I think maybe the two murders are connected."

"How would he kill someone in Nebraska all the way from Denver?"

"That's your job to figure out, isn't it? I'm just giving you some information to investigate. Lapaglia might be on the train. Talk to Alan Fraser at the resort and the sheriffs up here. He stole a horse, but maybe just rode it to the station."

"Who stole a horse?"

"Rodolfo Lapaglia!"

"Ma'am, I would really appreciate knowing your name."

"I can't ... not just yet." I disconnected. Staying anonymous for now was the right thing to do, I was sure. I needed to talk to Lapaglia's girlfriends before dragging them into something so potentially public. Maybe even dangerous.

I opened the restroom door and jumped when Archie Cruz loomed in front of me.

"Geez, you took long enough. You okay? Bad news gives me the runs, too."

Ugh. I'd forgotten all about him. "That's not what I was—never mind. Why are you still here?"

"Where should I be?"

"I don't know." I pushed past him. "Maybe finding some other poor slob to ambush?"

"Yeah, sorry about that. But you gotta admit, that was some good optics for the four o'clock news."

I would admit nothing of the sort. "It was mean and unnecessary. I didn't steal anyone's money. It was all Lapaglia's fault."

"And now he's disappeared and his wife is dead." He stared intensely at me for an uncomfortably long time.

"You think I—"

"Nah, I'm just kidding." He shrugged. "Hey, I was just doing my job. Got a tip from a viewer and then you show up nine months preggo *and* with beer, well, there's not a producer on earth who wouldn't run that. We couldn't have staged it better if we tried."

"Mean. And. Unnecessary."

"Yeah, I owe you one."

TWENTY-THREE

Even though I got home really late and Ozzi was sound asleep in my bed, I was up early the next day.

Driving home from the resort, AmyJo and I had talked through everything, trying to figure out what I should do next. We both agreed that locating Peter O'Drool was contingent on figuring out how all these puzzle pieces fit together. We just couldn't figure out how. Or if we had all the puzzle pieces. Or what the final picture might look like.

This morning, I'd been guzzling coffee and using the full force of my research skills to find some link between Tiffany and any of the characters in my little drama.

Knowing that Tiffany Isaac was definitely involved, I began by searching for information about her. The recent articles about her murder popped up, but they had nothing I could use. But I also found a twelve-year-old society column article from a newspaper with the title *Wedding of the Decade*. It wasn't Tiffany's wedding, but she was one of the bridesmaids. There was a small photo online, showing eight bridesmaids paired up with eight groomsmen. The caption didn't include everyone's full name, just their first initial and last name. I found *T Isaac,* standing next to *V Zaminsky*. So she did know someone in the mob family.

I played a little mental Scattergories. Girl's names that start with V—go. Vivian. Victoria. Valerie. Vanessa. Vera. Virginia.

As I sipped my coffee, I realized I had the full force of the internet at my fingers. I typed *V Zaminsky* in the search bar.

Several articles about Velvet Zaminsky filled the screen.

I thought about Cecilia's pejorative *velvet mafia* comment. At the time I had assumed that's what she'd meant, but she hadn't actually said that. She'd actually said "Velvet's mafia."

Velvet Zaminsky. Definitely part of the crime family the Braid had mentioned.

I went back to the Wedding of the Decade photo. I tried to enlarge it but it only got fuzzy.

One thing that wasn't fuzzy, though, was that Tiffany and Velvet knew each other.

I went back to the articles about Velvet Zaminsky. The first one that came up was about a mob trial in New Jersey where she had to testify. The trial was all about tax evasion, but as I scrolled, a large image filled the screen, making me gasp.

I opened a new tab and brought up the photo of Rodolfo and Annamaria Lapaglia at the Dark Dagger Awards. I put the photos side by side and studied them.

The resemblance between Annamaria Lapaglia and Velvet Zaminsky was remarkable.

I dug up more images of Velvet. Because she was from a prominent family, there were many photos of her through the years. I stacked them in age order on my computer desktop and clicked through them, like flipping pages of a photo album. The changes in her features over the years were subtle —thinning of the nose, cheek implants perhaps, hair color— but set out side-by-side like this they were obvious.

"First Tiffany and now Annamaria. This can't be coincidence."

I needed to set up a meeting with the girlfriends to tell them about Annamaria's murder, Lapaglia's disappearance, and Velvet's potential involvement. They might be in danger. Unless they were involved. Either way, I had to know. If I did it in person, I could see their reactions. One of these women might be the key to finding Peter O'Drool.

I began with Lakshmi. I explained my plan and added, "And I need you to call Martina. Make sure she has my number and tell her it's imperative she meet with us. At the very least, she *must* call me." I had to find out the connection between her logo, Lapaglia's bolo tie, and Tiffany's necklace.

Since both Lakshmi and Cecilia were working today, we agreed to meet at noon at a restaurant near both of them.

I got a terse text from Martina. "You're buying."

"Absolutely," I responded, even though I didn't quite know how I'd swing that.

Ozzi padded into the kitchen wearing boxers and a stretched out t-shirt, rubbing his face. He looked surprised to see me. "I didn't hear you come in last night." He kissed me on the head. "Didn't think you'd be up so early this morning."

"I have stuff to do. I didn't want to wake you up. I'm meeting Lapaglia's girlfriends for lunch at El Señor's." Reassuring him it wasn't reckless, stupid, or impulsive, I explained my plan while pouring him a cup of coffee and loading a plate with two slices of Barb's zucchini bread. I added another slice. "Hey, handsome ..." I placed his breakfast on the table then rubbed my hands on his chest. "Do you have any money I can borrow?" I nibbled his ear.

"Oh, I see how it is. You just love me for my wallet." He sat at the kitchen table.

"Not true." I cupped his pecs. "These are nice too." I straddled him on his lap. "So ... do you?"

"Mmm?" His eyes had rolled back in his head a little.

"Have any money I can borrow?"

He opened one eye and grinned. "I don't charge interest in the usual manner."

"That's a chance I'm willing to take."

~

At 11:55 I pulled open the door to the El Señor Mexican restaurant and saw Lakshmi, Cecilia, and Martina waiting for me. They'd already eaten three-quarters of a basket of chips and salsa.

"Didn't we say noon?" I asked.

"We needed a pre-meeting," Martina said. "Not sure we know what's going on. I never even knew about this one until yesterday." She jerked her head toward Cecilia. "So talk," she said to me. I felt resentment radiating off her.

Okay, so this is how it's going to be. I pulled out the fourth chair and hooked my bag over the back. I scooped a chip through chunky salsa and chewed, gathering my thoughts. "I told you earlier that Annamaria Lapaglia has been murdered—"

"I don't know who that is," Cecilia interrupted.

"She's the wife of the man you've all been having an affair with. You just know him by different names." I rooted around my bag for the photo I tore from his book jacket and passed it around. Lakshmi and Cecilia had seen it before and knew who I meant. Martina looked at the photo, then back at me.

"Tell me something I don't know." Her eyes narrowed and I suddenly worried for Lapaglia if she ever got her hands on him again.

Before she could interrupt I said, "He's an author of thrillers about the mob. I was supposed to do a writer's event with him on Saturday but he never showed up." I looked at Martina. "That's why I was at Union Station. Why were you there?"

Martina's gaze pierced right through me. I suddenly

wished that she'd continued avoiding me and hadn't showed up today. I nervously shoved chips and salsa into my mouth.

Finally Martina spoke. "I was there on Saturday to catch him in a lie. A few weeks ago he told me he was coming to Denver that day, but then hemmed and hawed and said he misspoke, that it was actually a month from Saturday, like he got the date wrong. Something about his voice on the phone made me suspicious so I did some digging. He told me his name was Ronald Donatelli. I didn't find him but I found a woman named Dona Donatelli—"

I remembered what Ozzi had told me. "His mother."

"—whose artistic style was very similar to his. And then I found out she had a son named Rodolfo Lapaglia, who, among other things"—Martina leveled her gaze and dropped an octave—"was coming to Denver to meet you."

"Okay, one last time, he wasn't coming to meet me. He was coming to do a writing workshop with me." I thought back to waiting with Ozzi for the train. "Wait! You were eavesdropping on us!" Then I remembered Martina's assault on me in the restroom. "I told you then that Ozzi was my boyfriend. Why didn't you believe me?"

"He wasn't acting like your boyfriend."

"What was he supposed to do? Jump me right there in Union Station? Who did you think he was?"

"Your brother."

"What? Why?" I was instantly skeeved out that Lance and I might ever act like we were—ugh—sweethearts.

"I Googled you too, when I saw about the workshop, and saw all that stuff about your family, you killing your literary agent—"

I looked at Lakshmi and Cecilia. "I did NOT kill my agent." I spread my gaze around the table, to include them all. "Let's get back to the matter at hand. By not showing up for that workshop on Saturday, Lapaglia made a ton of problems for me, so I've been looking for him. I found him yesterday but then he disappeared again. Afterward, I learned his wife had been murdered. I'm worried the three of you might be implicated and perhaps in danger yourselves." I let that sink in for a minute, studying their faces while I scooped another chip. Before I finished, the server came to take our order. I hadn't looked at the menu yet, but I didn't want to take the time. I ordered a chicken chimichanga. I'd eaten here before, but even if they'd changed their menu since then, no self-respecting Mexican restaurant would remove that. Deep-fried burrito with guacamole and sour cream on top? Yes, please.

After the server left, I told them the story about going to Lost Valley and finding Lapaglia and the Braid there.

Lakshmi remembered seeing me get on the train and wondered why. "You said he was coming into town. That's why I went down there. Why were you there?"

"I was trying to see which of you would come down. I thought one of you might be hiding him."

Martina snorted. "Nancy Drew much?"

"I'm just trying to get my money back. And a dog." Peter still hadn't been returned like I'd hoped. I told them about the Braid dognapping him to coerce me to find Lapaglia before the cops did.

"Why would the cops be after him?" Cecilia asked.

"Honestly, I don't even know anymore. It might have been a bluff. But when someone's holding you by your drag wig upside down on a chain link fence, nothing much makes sense."

They nodded knowingly as if they'd all been in a similar situation at some point in their pasts.

The server brought our food and we ate in silence for a bit.

"I said earlier that I'm worried you guys would be implicated in this. I know enough about murder investigations to know that the police will find you, so it's better to get in front of this earlier rather than later. And I want you to do it yourselves. I don't want to have to drag you into it."

Lakshmi and Cecilia looked worried, but Martina said, "I got nothing to worry about."

I wiped my mouth and fingers on a napkin then reached into my purse. I pulled out her business card. "I think you do. Maybe more than anyone. Your business logo is very similar to a bolo tie I saw Lapaglia wearing yesterday—"

"So?"

"And on a necklace worn by Tiffany Isaac, who, I think you all know, was also murdered recently." I finished the last couple bites of my lunch, wondering if I should have mentioned Tiffany. My hands shook a bit as I dragged a fork full of fallen lettuce and tomatoes through a smear of guacamole and into my mouth. I didn't really think one of these women was a murderer, but I've been monumentally wrong about people in the past.

Cecilia checked her watch. "I've got to get back." She and Lakshmi began gathering their belongings.

I held up my hand. "Just one more thing. The reason I wanted you all here was to ask you to go to the police with me."

"No way in hell," Martina said.

"I can't do that." Cecilia noticeably paled.

Lakshmi just shook her head.

"No cops are going to be knocking on our doors about this," Martina said. "We didn't even know this Lapaglia's real name until you told us. We're invisible." The server brought the bill and Martina handed it to me.

I put the leather check presenter on the table without looking at it. "Regardless, we all need to go to the police to tell them what we know." Then all this would be someone else's problem and I could look for Peter full-time.

"Nope." Martina pushed her chair back, grabbed her

wallet and phone and stood. She got right in my face. "And don't even think about giving my name to the cops." She left.

"You guys will, though, right?" I asked the others.

"I told you, I can't," Cecilia said.

Lakshmi just shook her head and hurried after Cecilia.

I stared after them, hoping maybe at least one of them would change her mind and come back. No such luck. I sighed and looked at the bill for lunch. A big smiley face covered it with a note that said *Paid*. I flagged down our server and asked about it.

"That couple over there paid it for you. Included the tip and everything." She pointed to a corner table where two people sat with their menus concealing their faces.

I collected my purse and walked over to thank them and ask why. As soon as I got there, they lowered their menus. AmyJo yelled, "Surprise!" then clamped a hand over her mouth. "That was loud," she whispered, blushing. Ozzi just grinned.

I pulled out a chair and sat. "What are you guys doing here?"

"I was worried when you told me what you were doing this morning so I invited AmyJo to lunch so we could spy on you. Figured you wouldn't be mad at me in front of her," Ozzi said.

"I'm not mad. And thank you." I sighed. "None of that went like I expected."

"What did you want to happen?" AmyJo asked.

"I wanted to scare them enough about Lapaglia, his wife getting murdered, the Braid, and Tiffany Isaac that they'd go to the police. But they won't. And that big gal threatened me again."

Ozzi rubbed brusquely at his stubble. "What did she say?"

I waved away his concern. "If they would talk to the cops, then I wouldn't have to. I mean, two women have been murdered. I can't just walk away from that."

"Then go to the police. Tell them what you know," Ozzi said.

I threw my hands into the air and accidentally banged my elbow on the table. "I've *been* talking to Ming and look where that's gotten me." I rubbed my elbow. "Besides, I'm not entirely sure what I do know. I told those deputies at Lost Valley everything I could about Lapaglia and the Braid, but what if I drag these women into this mess and get them targeted by someone? I couldn't live with myself."

"Who would target them?" AmyJo asked.

"I don't know. Somebody. Maybe the Braid? Lapaglia? Somebody I don't even know about?"

"Maybe you'd solve the crimes, though," Ozzi said quietly, covering my hand with his. "Maybe one of those women killed Lapaglia's wife. Or that Tiffany. Or both."

"I considered that but discounted it before, but now, maybe you're right. Maybe they did, with or without Lapaglia's help."

AmyJo pushed her plate aside and flopped a notebook on the tabletop. "Who's your best candidate?" Her pen was poised over the page.

"I don't know. Martina is crazy-jealous of everyone. The first time she saw me she told me to stay away from her boyfriend."

AmyJo scribbled notes then looked up. "Who else?"

"Lakshmi—that little one with the cute glasses?—she is pushed around by everyone. A real doormat. Maybe she had enough and snapped. And Cecilia, the other one, is petrified her husband will find out about her affair with Lapaglia. She said he's violent."

"Lapaglia?"

"No, her husband."

While AmyJo scribbled, I stared at the oversized sombreros stapled to the wall for ambiance. "Lapaglia is über-suspicious, running away and being so vocal about wanting to live a different life. I did call the tip line yesterday to tell Denver PD that I saw him at Lost Valley. Maybe they'll grab him up, he'll confess, and this will be all done."

"You wouldn't get your money back that way," Ozzi said.

"No, I sure wouldn't."

"I can see Lapaglia killing his wife." AmyJo tapped her pen on her bottom lip. "He's a jerk."

"He is indeed." I nodded. "But maybe it was the Braid. When I talked to Annamaria the other day she hinted that she did all the work on Lapaglia's books. The Braid kept wanting to know how Lapaglia knew so much about the mob—the family, he called it. What if the Braid found out Annamaria wrote the books? He'd go after her instead of Lapaglia."

"But how would that involve Tiffany Isaac?" Ozzi asked. "Or whoever might be setting up the guy you scalped?"

I let out a whoosh of air. "I don't know. It probably wouldn't. I need a nap."

"I need to get back to work," Ozzi said, pushing his chair back.

"Me, too." AmyJo stood. "This was fun, though. Thanks for lunch, Oz."

"Fun?" I stood, too.

"It's always fun to go out to lunch," AmyJo said. "Regardless of the reason. Plus, we didn't have to swoop in and rescue you."

"I dunno. That sounds kinda fun to me." Ozzi slipped his arm around my waist.

"I'm sure you'll have plenty of opportunities in the future. If history is any indication." I kissed him lightly on the lips.

Driving home, I debated whether to call Lance. I changed my mind fourteen times, but by the time I plopped down on my couch, it was a firm negative. I'd have to tell him more than might be prudent about my activities, plus it wasn't even a Colorado crime. Annamaria's murder was for the great state of Nebraska to solve.

Nebraska's murder to solve. Hmm. Maybe I could talk to Annamaria's boyfriend, Thomas Percy, and see if he knew anything I could use. Maybe he and Annamaria knew about Lapaglia's girlfriends. Maybe he killed Annamaria. Maybe Peter O'Drool magically found his way there and he was just waiting for me to call to collect him. I had nothing to lose.

Before I did, I called Barb and Don to see if Peter was back yet. Don answered.

"Not yet," he said.

"Find out anything more from Lapaglia's books?"

"Working on it."

I asked Don if, in the books, there was anything about Taffeta, who might be our Tiffany, being set up by anyone in the crime family.

"Charlee, these books are full of betrayals, double-crossings, set-ups, and all manner of skullduggery."

"That's what I was afraid of. Why couldn't Lapaglia write cozy mysteries so the characters are quirky and fun?"

"Mysteries have fun murderers?"

I sighed. "No, I guess not. Well, let me know if something jumps out at you."

"Just a matter of time."

I wished I had his confidence. "Fingers crossed."

I poured myself a glass of iced tea then found the number my editor gave me for Lapaglia's house in Nebraska. Maybe I'd get lucky and whoever answered would know how I could find this Thomas Percy.

I dialed. While I waited for it to be picked up, I decided if anyone answered I'd ask for Lapaglia. If he was actually there, that might mean he didn't kill her.

"Thomas Percy speaking."

Annamaria's boyfriend? "Um ... hi, Thomas. I was looking for Rodolfo Lapaglia."

"Not here."

"Not at the house or not in Nebraska?"

"Who wants to know?" I could hear the venom in his voice.

"My name is Charlee. I spoke to Annamaria a few days ago. I asked her if she knew where Rodolfo was, but I got the impression there was no love lost between them."

I heard him make a noise. Was he crying?

"You know she's ... dead," he said.

"Yes, I do. I'm so sorry."

"Did you know she was murdered?"

"Yes."

"Killed exactly like in one of his books."

My stomach lurched. That hit too close to home. The memory of being told my agent had been killed exactly as I had written in a manuscript washed over me. I shook off the past and fought to return to the present.

If Annamaria was responsible for Lapaglia's books, as she'd said, was this some kind of evil retribution? Coincidence? Was it even true?

The present swam back into clear focus. Thomas had apparently been speaking this whole time.

"I'm sorry to go on like this, but I don't really have anyone to talk to here. It's nice to talk to one of her friends."

A flush of guilt buzzed through me, but I didn't correct him.

"Annamaria and I were serious, but for obvious reasons, weren't really public about it." He paused. "I wish I had come right home that day."

"Where'd you go?"

"There was a glitch in the schedule—I work for the railroad—and I got back in town a day early. I went out with the guys for a beer. Since she wasn't expecting me, I didn't think a couple of hours would matter. How wrong I was."

It didn't seem that coming home any earlier would have stopped her from opening a package bomb. If anything, it might have killed him, too. But he didn't need to hear that from me.

"When was this, exactly?"

"Tuesday around four." He paused and I jotted a note to myself. "Thing is," he paused again. "I saw her in town and waved at her but she didn't seem to notice me. Later they told me that was impossible because it was an hour after she died." Long pause. "I think it was her ghost looking for me to say goodbye. If I hadn'ta gone to the Brickyard this never would have happened." His sobs broke my heart.

I tried to console him through the phone but we both knew it was ineffective. Before he hung up he said, voice shaking, "If you see that son of a—if you see Lapaglia, you tell him I will hunt him down if it's the last thing I do."

I sat, phone still in my hand for a long time. If Thomas actually killed Annamaria, he was one excellent actor. I wish I could have seen his face while he told me all that. Then I realized I could check his alibi pretty easily. An internet search quickly brought up the Brickyard and I called them.

I asked the man who answered, "Hey, were you working Tuesday afternoon?"

"I work every afternoon. I own the place."

"Do you remember Thomas Percy in there that day?"

"I already told some other cop yes, he was sitting here from at least two o'clock when I put in his order for a bacon cheeseburger and fries until he left around five. Thomas didn't kill Annamaria. Now leave me alone and get busy finding out who did."

Again, a flush of guilt shot through me. I couldn't help it if people made assumptions about me. I didn't tell Thomas I was a friend of Annamaria's and I didn't tell this guy I was with the police. But still.

I considered Thomas Percy's alibi. Eating a burger and nursing a beer all afternoon didn't preclude him from sending a package bomb to be delivered while he was conveniently out of the way. But his voice on the phone. His demeanor. His sobs. Nobody is that good an actor. I just couldn't believe he killed Annamaria.

It had to be Lapaglia.

I called our editor at Penn & Powell. "Steph, have you heard from Lapaglia in the last day or so?"

"No. Why?"

"He disappeared again. And did you hear that his wife was murdered?"

Steph screeched into the phone. "Are you freakin' kidding me? Charlee, I've got to go. Thanks for telling me."

The police hadn't called Penn & Powell yet. What did that mean? Have they already caught him? Did they get my anonymous tip? Are they chasing him?

I couldn't fathom the answer but there was nothing I could do about that. I could, however, check the alibis of his girlfriends, now that I knew Annamaria's time of death. With all the extra layers of scrutiny at the post office in recent years, I couldn't see how a package bomb could go through the mail. It had to be delivered in person.

I started with Lakshmi. "Where were you on Tuesday afternoon?"

"At work until six. Why?"

"Annamaria was killed at 4:00."

"And you think I did it?"

Actually, the vision of mousey Lakshmi killing anyone was so far-fetched it was laughable. "Not really. But now will you go to the police with me? I really think it was Lapaglia. You might have information for them, or worse, be in danger."

"I'm not involved in this. And if you give them my name I'll deny it."

For someone who most often resembled a doormat, she sounded quite adamant. Nothing I said could convince her and I think she actually hung up on me.

Next, I called Cecilia.

"I took the day off for my husband's birthday. We went to Elitch's. The water park and the rides. Sunburned my feet something awful. Why?"

When I told her what I'd told Lakshmi, her voice pitched upward and her words came fast, tumbling over themselves. "I can't get my name in the paper. My husband will kill me."

That didn't seem like hyperbole. "Keep your park passes and we'll take them to the police. There's probably security cameras all over Elitch's. Your alibi will be solid."

She calmed enough to put spaces between her words. "Charlee, there's no way I'm going to the police. I'd be in more danger from my husband than I would Lapaglia or some random murderer. No way."

No amount of begging, lecturing, or cajoling could change her mind.

I took a few deep breaths to prepare myself before I called Martina. I reminded myself I was doing all this to find Peter. And maybe to stop another murder.

"What do you want?"

"Where were you Tuesday afternoon?"

"None of your damn business."

"Martina, look, I know you don't like me, but two women have been murdered, possibly by the man you're having an affair with. I'm worried you might be next." I sounded more melodramatic than I wanted.

Apparently she thought so too because she snorted. "I can take care of myself."

"I don't doubt that for a minute. But I think you might have information the cops can use to snag him. And if you're not careful, they might sweep you up, too. You know, the girlfriend is always the prime suspect in the wife's death."

"What's *your* alibi?" She dragged the word out. "Aren't you furious with Lapaglia for cheating you out of a ton of money?"

A taste of bile crawled into my mouth. "That would make me kill him, not his wife."

"Says you. You better think long and hard about your intentions, missy."

Suddenly I didn't care if she was swept up in this fiasco. "Fine. I'll butt out." I wanted to slam the phone down, but settled for the *plink* of disconnecting my iPhone.

A rock formed in the pit of my stomach. *Could* a bomb get through the mail? It had happened before. And if it did, alibis didn't matter.

Not mine. Not anyone's.

TWENTY-FOUR

I washed my hands of Lapaglia and his girlfriends, leaving it up to the cops to follow up on my anonymous tip. I'd done everything I could.

It was time to concentrate solely on finding Peter O'Drool.

Even though he gave me the creeps, I emailed Archie Cruz through the *Your Advocate* tab on the Channel 29 website and asked if he had any information about where the Braid lived or visited when he was in Denver. If he'd been snooping around looking for a story, maybe he'd share. After all, he did say he owed me.

While I waited for him to respond, I started calling local animal shelters. Halfway through the second one, my phone pinged with a new message.

Archie Cruz responded. *Mob connections everywhere. Like chain stores.* Then he typed an address on east Colfax. I copied it into a search engine and up popped a map in a sketchy, mostly residential part of Denver. I raced over there.

I double-checked the address then stepped into a scraggly yard. A rusty chain link gate hung by one hinge. I froze, hoping Peter would race out to greet me when he heard the metal-on-metal screech, and not a Rottweiler or Siberian tiger or something.

Nothing raced out to greet me. I wasn't sure whether to be relieved or not.

I picked my way up the cracked and weedy sidewalk. Pushed the doorbell and it fell off the wall. I knocked on the door, not entirely sure I wanted anyone to answer.

Nobody did.

Putting my ear to the door, I listened for any dog-like sounds, but heard nothing. I stepped to the picture window, covered on the inside with a droopy sheet. There was a gap in the corner where I thought maybe I could see inside. I cupped my hands and pressed close against the glass.

"What are you doing?" A stern man's voice behind me made me jump and bang my face on the window where I left a greasy nose print.

I hurried away from the window, back toward the side-walk. I was relieved it was just a man pushing a stroller. "I was looking for my dog."

"A pug?"

"Yes! Do you know where he is?"

"I saw it with the lady who lives here. Don't know her name. Redhead. She works at the liquor store on the corner." He continued down the sidewalk.

I wanted to hug him. Instead, I hollered after him, "Thank you!" and rushed off in the direction he'd indicated.

I yanked open the door of the liquor store and was assaulted by the icy blast of a gung-ho air conditioner, but no Peter.

"Help you?" A redhead stood behind the counter chewing something.

"Yes. I'm looking for a cute little pug. I was told you might have seen him?" I was more than curious about any relation-ship she might have with the Braid. Was she part of the mob "chain stores" Archie Cruz alluded to? But I kept the focus on

Peter. Besides, I was done—finis, kaput, pfft—with agonizing over some lowlife mobster. And what if she clammed up if I mentioned him? Who knows what he might have told her about me.

She reached into a tin in front of her and plucked out a small pretzel. "Yeah, I seen him." She popped it into her mouth. "Lived with him for a bit but he was too demanding. Always wanted to go out but my gate is busted so I had to go out too, to keep him from running off after a rabbit. He also kept begging for these." She shook the tin. "And they're expensive! From the health food store." She held the tin out. "Want one?"

When I shook my head and started to ask about Peter, she said, "Go ahead. Treat yo self." She shook the tin at me again and I felt it was in Peter's best interest—and perhaps mine—to go ahead and take one.

"Mmm," I said. "Good pretzel." It was a perfectly ordinary pretzel but I didn't want to offend someone who had info about Pete. I looked around. "So is Peter, the dog ... is he here?"

"Nah. Gave him to my mom. She hates pretzels and has a fenced yard."

"Can I have her address?"

She shook her very red head. "Don't know it."

My heart sunk.

"But it's two blocks thataway, then one thataway," she said, pointing. "Has a swing set in the yard. Can't miss it."

I again resisted the almost overwhelming urge to hug my thanks. Instead, I jogged two thataways, keeping my eyes peeled for a swing set. Three blocks later I stood in front of a nicely maintained house and yard with what could only be described as a child's utopia. A two-story wooden play structure complete with widow's walk and pirate's mast filled most of the yard. The swings, slide, and monkey bars were empty, the yard quiet.

I rang the doorbell and heard the hopeful *ding-dong* inside. After a few moments, an elderly woman opened the door.

"Where's the kids?" She peered behind me.

I peered behind me as well. "The kids?"

"My nephew's kids. You're not delivering them today?"

"No, sorry. I think you have me confused with someone else. I'm here because your daughter told me she gave you a dog ... a pug?"

"She did do."

I grinned. "Is he here? Can I see him?"

"Nope. Gave him to my nephew's kids." She wrinkled her nose then pushed her glasses back upward. "That dog was a snore factory. And gassy to boot."

That definitely sounded like Peter.

"Can you tell me where I might find your nephew?"

She pointed to the sidewalk. "Coming along now."

I followed the direction she pointed and saw a young man with three school-aged girls in tow. As soon as they got to the gate, they burst through it and ran for the play structure yelling and putting dibs on their favorite activities.

"Where's that dog? Why ain't you walking him?" she asked her nephew.

"Ran away. Seems he don't like playing dress up."

I groaned. Back to square one.

"This lady lookin' for him."

He winced. "Sorry. He just bolted before I could get a leash on him. Cute little bugger too. Hope he's alright."

"Me, too. Was it around here somewhere?" I hoped Peter hadn't run out onto busy Colfax Avenue.

He pointed. "I live over that way. On Walnut. Ain't seen him since yesterday." He saw my face and again said, "Sorry."

"Thanks anyway." I gave them both my number in case Peter came back to either of them.

I almost asked what, if any, connection they had to the

Braid, but reminded myself I didn't care and it might change their behavior toward me. But it sure didn't seem like the Braid mentioned me to them. He either didn't care if I found Peter on my own, or didn't think it would be possible.

I turned and left them, moving the direction the nephew had pointed. I didn't hurry, though, worried what I might find. I decided it wouldn't hurt to ask people I passed if they'd seen him. Five people in a row said they hadn't, three ignored me completely, and one homeless guy called me "Mom" and tried to kiss me.

But the next lady told me she had, in fact, seen a dog in a Bronco cheerleading outfit running down the street yesterday. She didn't notice the breed, but confirmed it was pretty small. I followed the route she figured he took, after thanking her profusely.

"Hope you find it," she called after me. "But next time, afford that dog some dignity."

I didn't give up despite the fact that Peter probably wouldn't still be out here today if he'd been running around yesterday. I slowed my pace, trying to think like a pug. A flash of color in the gutter caught my eye. Wishing I had a stick, I cautiously poked it with my foot, knocking off a smashed Starbucks cup.

My heart sunk. A tiny orange and blue cheerleader's outfit. I toed it one more time, as if by doing so I could magically conjure Peter wearing it, standing in front of me.

I heard the squeal of brakes and an angry horn. I saw a brown blur race through the busy Colfax traffic and down an alley.

"Pete! Peter O'Drool!" I couldn't cross the heavy traffic in the middle of the street here, so I ran to the nearest intersection and jabbed the crosswalk signal until the light changed. I ran across, following the blur that could only have been Peter. I kept calling his name, but he didn't come back to me. I wasn't sure where he went, but I kept searching.

I turned a corner and there he sat on the sidewalk, eating half a bagel.

Relief flooded my body and tears flowed. "Peter! I'm so glad to see you!" He ignored me, intent on his street food. I knelt next to him and tried to pick him up, but he grabbed his bagel and danced out of reach.

I took a couple of steps toward him, coming up behind him. I scooped him up with one arm and held the bagel in his mouth with the other. "I'm not going to take it away. Eat the whole thing if you want. I just want you." I rubbed my cheek on his head.

"Oh, my gosh! Rambo!" A twenty-something girl with a neck tattoo ran toward me, holding out her arms. "Thank you for catching my dog!" She tried to take Pete from my arms but I held tight.

"This isn't your dog." We played tug-of-war with him.

"Yes, it is."

"No, it's not."

"Yes. It IS!"

"No. It's NOT!"

We had a standoff, four hands on Peter, four eyes boring into each other. Pete continued to snarfle on his bagel, oblivious to the confrontation.

"Prove he's yours," I said.

The girl let go. "Okay. C'mon." She jerked her head at me.

I followed her, matching her pace, but then I slowed. Why did she agree so quickly? Was she leading me into a trap? Was she a cohort of the Braid? With every step I got more paranoid. I hugged Pete tighter, feeling watched. Head on a swivel, I scanned as we walked, seeing danger everywhere, jumping at shadows.

I considered pivoting and taking off the opposite direction, but with an armful of Peter, I wouldn't beat this girl in a foot race. I saw how fast she ran up to us. And if she, alone or with the Braid, was using Peter to lure me, then he was still in danger. No way would I let go of him.

Maybe I could prove he was Peter, rather than having her prove he was Rambo.

I stopped in the middle of the sidewalk. "Wait. I don't know where we're going, but how 'bout I prove this is Peter O'Drool right here." I tapped my foot on the cement.

"We're just going there." She pointed at a run-down apartment building.

"Regardless." I bobbled Peter while digging out my phone. She held out her arms to hold him, but I clutched him tighter. I scrolled through a series of photos of Peter I'd marked as favorites over the years, including the one I used for his Missing Dog poster.

She shielded the phone from the glare of the setting sun and swiped through them. "Cute," she finally said. "But not Rambo."

Peter looked up, finished with his bagel. The girl traced the perfect inverted Vs formed by the wrinkles over his eyes and the single ridge above them. Using two fingers, she enlarged one of my photos of Peter and traced the two upside-down Ys on Peter's forehead.

My eyes darted between the dog in my arms and the dog on my phone. She was right. This was not Peter. Plus, his face and fur were darker than Peter's. The world began to get filmy. I used my shoulder to angrily brush away the tears that had sprung to my eyes.

I handed Rambo back to his owner.

She laid a hand gently on my forearm. "I'm sorry."

My mouth felt mushy. "Have you seen another pug around here?"

She shook her head, nuzzling Rambo. She must have seen my face redden and lip start quivering because she stopped loving on her dog. "Check the park." She gestured with Rambo. "You find stray dogs there all the time. Lots of good trash, isn't there, big boy?" She spoke in baby talk to Rambo, who responded by belching in her face.

I didn't think I could reassemble my heart there on the sidewalk and began to walk in the direction of the park. I had to double back to find it, but soon enough I was trudging through the grass. I picked up the stick I'd wished for earlier and used it to rustle bushes. All that accomplished was scaring up some quaking rabbits who froze before darting past me.

I plopped onto a bench and called Peter's name a few times, but I doubted he was here. I pictured him shimmying out of the cheerleading uniform and being so thrilled to be rid of it, he ran right into traffic. I closed my eyes against the dreadful image.

What are the other possibilities? Maybe animal control picked him up? Some kind person collected him up off the street, took him to a vet to see if he'd been micro-chipped, and they were in the process of contacting Don and Barb at this very moment?

I held tight to that image as I made my way back to my car.

My stomach churned. I trudged along the sidewalk taking deep breaths until I got to my car, bumping into people I never even saw. I probably looked like a street junkie. Downcast eyes. Dejected. World-weary.

If I'd only said no to that stupid event with Lapaglia none of this would have happened. Peter would still be safe with Barb and Don, Lapaglia wouldn't have come to Denver, the Braid wouldn't have used Peter as leverage over me. Maybe Annamaria would still be alive.

I couldn't stop thinking about Peter all the way home. Where *was* he? I couldn't bear to look up toward Barb and Don's apartment when I got there. They would have called me if he'd been found. I kicked off my shoes and fell into bed, exhausted.

Ozzi texted but I responded with a terse, "*In bed*" before shutting off my ringer.

I slept like I had dengue fever. Tossing and turning, kicking the covers to the floor, punching my pillow. I dreamed of Peter, his stubby legs trotting through our neighborhood, around the Lost Valley Resort, in front of the Brickhouse Tavern in Nebraska. When his face morphed into the ghost face of Annamaria, I woke with a jolt, my chest heaving.

It was the middle of the night, but I took a cool shower anyway.

Afterward I sat at my kitchen table bundled up in my chenille robe, hands wrapped around the warmth of a cup of herbal tea. I couldn't get the morphed image of Peter and Annamaria out of my mind. The tea wasn't helping. I left it on the table and shuffled to my office in the spare bedroom of my apartment.

Sitting at my desk in the dark, I opened my laptop. Something nagged at the periphery of me, some residue from my dreams. I wanted to see that photo of Annamaria at the Dark Dagger Awards with Lapaglia again. I couldn't bear the thought of scrolling through photos of Peter, but maybe a photo of her would get the disturbing morphed image out of my mind. I scrolled through the website until I came to the photos from the banquet. I saw a couple of different pictures of her. In one, she and Lapaglia were holding hands and looking straight at the camera. In another, she was alone, looking away from the camera, seemingly unaware she was in the shot. She stood in the background, not the focus of the picture, up against a dark curtain.

Something was different, though. I flipped back several pages to the first photo. In that one she's wearing a black boat neck dress. I could barely tell where her dress stopped and Lapaglia's black tuxedo began. But in the other picture, she's wearing a burgundy dress with a plunging neckline.

I went back and forth, squinting at them. There must have been a pre-banquet cocktail party with the nominees and then she had changed her clothes for the ceremony. Or perhaps they were held on different evenings. I searched the pages for captions but there were none. I dragged both photos to my desktop to make it easier to study them side by side.

The burgundy color could be mistaken for black, under certain lighting conditions, but there was no way those necklines were interchangeable. One high, one low. Definitely different dresses.

I zoomed in on the black dress photo, scrutinizing Annamaria. Enlarging the photo pixilated it and turned her a bit fuzzy, but I could see her dark hair done up in a classic chignon.

Next I zoomed in on the photo of her wearing the burgundy dress. Silver earrings hung from her lobes and a matching necklace dropped into her cleavage. Her hair was down in this one, a little longer than shoulder-length, held back on either side by two ornate silver combs. I squinted at the image, enlarging it a bit more, but it was immediately too much. The details became impossible to discern. I stepped it back a notch. Those combs. Something about them. I tried making the image a bit darker and then enlarging it again.

I leaned closer to the screen. I couldn't be completely sure, but the design on the combs seemed to match the design on Lapaglia's bolo tie, Martina's logo, and Tiffany's necklace.

Was it my imagination? The fuzzy enlargement? The late hour and bad dreams?

I wrestled with it until exhaustion took hold of me and I stumbled back to bed. I did sleep, but it remained fitful and I was glad to wake up.

The first thing I did was study those photos again.

I knew it was early but called Thomas Percy anyway, hoping he wasn't at work on a train someplace.

He answered on the first ring, trepidation in his voice. "Hello?"

"Thomas? Are you okay? It's Charlee Russo."

"Oh. Hi. Sorry. I haven't been sleeping well. I keep having dreams about Annamaria. And again yesterday I thought I saw her at the market."

"I'm sorry I woke you."

"Frankly, I'd rather be awake."

"This might sound random, but did Annamaria ever wear combs in her hair? You know, the decorative kind?"

He sucked in his breath. "Annamaria never wore jewelry of any kind. Adornments, she called them. She always said baubles detracted from a woman's inner beauty."

"Not even when she dressed up?"

"What do you know about that comb? Why are you asking?" He lowered his voice. "They found one at the crime scene."

It was my turn to suck in my breath. "Can you describe what they found?"

"No. The police have it. What's this all about?" He spoke louder and quicker.

"I don't know yet, but I'll tell you when I can."

Would Thomas know how Annamaria looked when she dressed up for a fancy awards dinner?

The design on that comb was taking on a life of its own in my mind. Why would it have the same design as Lapaglia's bolo tie, Martina's business cards, and Tiffany's necklace?

It wasn't random. And Lapaglia was the link.

I called my brother. "Lance, I can't tell you why right this minute, but can you get me a photo of the silver hair comb the Nebraska cops found at the scene of Annamaria Lapaglia's murder?"

He made a non-committal noise.

"Can you get it?"

"It would make me a happy camper to know why." He didn't sound anywhere near happy camper status.

"You send me that photo and if it shows what I think it's going to show, then I'll tell you. Otherwise, it's just me having a bad night's sleep."

He made that non-committal noise again. "Where do you think I work? Do you think there's this one big happy police department nirvana where cops from all fifty states sit around eating donuts and waiting for calls to come in so we can solve crimes like on Scooby Doo?"

"No, but I—"

"I work for the Denver PD, Space Case. I'm not a detective. I'm a patrol cop. In Dennnnverrrr."

"I don't need a lecture. You could have just said no, you know." I paused. "Can you at least tell me if you guys picked up Lapaglia?"

"No." He disconnected.

He sounded awfully grumpy. I probably woke him up, too. Wait. Did he mean they didn't find Lapaglia or that he couldn't tell me?

I texted him. *Is Lapaglia in custody or not?*

Not.

I made coffee and watched it drip into the pot. With each drip I became more and more convinced that the only plausible answer for all this matching jewelry was Rodolfo Lapaglia. He had to be involved in both murders. He was the common thread. And he's still out there, at least according to my brother, the patrol cop. In Dennnnverrrr.

It was wishful thinking on my part to hope that Lance had some sort of contact with any Nebraska cops. Would have been great, though.

I watched the rest of the coffee finish dripping into the pot. As I filled a cup, a text pinged. I glanced at my phone and sloshed coffee on the floor.

A photo of a silver comb filled the screen. The curlicue design matched. The photo faded.

I lunged for my phone, jabbing at the message icon. I stared again at the comb. No message from Lance, just the photo.

How did you get this? I texted.

An animated gif of the Scooby Doo gang appeared and began dancing.

TWENTY-FIVE

I hated waking up Ozzi, but called him anyway. Maybe he was already awake.

He wasn't.

"I'm so sorry to wake you up, but I need your help with something. Can I come over?"

When I got there he was looking blurry. I should have brought the coffee. I pushed him gently on to the couch and sat next to him with his laptop open on my lap. "Can we test out your new facial recognition technology?"

Ozzi immediately perked up. He pulled the computer to his lap and opened up a program. He started to explain how it all worked, but I interrupted him. "Go to the Dark Dagger website and pull up the most recent awards dinner." He opened a new tab. When the page loaded, I pointed to the two photos of Annamaria, the one with Lapaglia and the one with her in the background. "Download those." He did. "I want to see if these are the same woman."

He studied the downloads on his desktop. "Of course they are. I can tell just by looking. You don't need—"

"Humor me."

He clicked and clacked across the keyboard, running the

photos through the magic software. He tried to explain what was happening, but realized he was speaking a language I didn't understand and stopped. When the program showed the results—*100% Match*—I felt like I got punched in the belly. I made him test it again, then a third time, asking him to explain each step.

Still, the photos matched. The software he and his team had been working on for so long believed unequivocally that the two women in the photos were the same person.

But I did not.

"Your software is wrong. I know for a fact they are two different women."

"For a fact?"

"Maybe not a *fact* fact. But they are."

"Charlee, I don't know what to tell you, but—"

"Didn't you just the other day have some horrible glitch? Maybe it's still not working."

He stared off into space. I knew that look. He was working out a problem in his mind. Everything had dropped away, and he was seeing computer code, line by line. Suddenly, he raced for the door. "I've got to check something!"

"Oz! You need pants!"

While he got dressed, I got more and more excited that he'd find his software glitch and my theory would be vindicated. I packed up his computer case and handed it to him Dagwood and Blondie-style as he ran out of his apartment.

I ate a piece of toast with butter and jelly while I thought about Lapaglia and his girlfriends. By the time the last bite was gone and I'd licked the sticky from my fingers, I had a plan.

TWENTY-SIX

First, I called the anonymous tip line again and explained all about the bolo tie, the necklace, and the combs. I omitted details about Martina's business card for now. Then I left a voice mail for Detective Ming with the same information. I made sure to include and enunciate clearly the phrases, "I know you think I'm crazy, but I'm not," and "I'm trying my best to be a good citizen."

Next, I sent a group text to Lakshmi, Cecilia, and Martina, giving them one last opportunity to do the right thing. I typed:

You can't deny that the man you now know as Rodolfo Lapaglia is a creep. He cheated me out of a big chunk of money, he cheated his fans who came to hear him teach a workshop, he cheated on his wife and each of you, he lied to you about his identity, and I'm pretty sure he's a murderer, maybe twice over. I think we can prove this, and if my plan works, you can be long gone before the cops get there. If you don't step forward, some other poor woman may die ... maybe even one of you. Do you want that on your conscience? And even if he's not involved in murder, should he get away with making you all look like fools and using you the way he did??

I held my breath and hit send. I didn't care if the cops

nabbed Lapaglia or if we did, but it was clear someone had to and it didn't seem like the cops were on it.

The first response came from Cecilia, a selfie with her eye blackened and the message, *Bad guys deserve bad things. I'm in.*

Ten minutes later Martina texted. *Fine.*

After I'd showered, Lakshmi's response awaited. *Okay, if you all think that's best.*

Tepid, but I'd take it.

The first step was for someone to contact him. Cecilia volunteered and told him his page proofs were ready and they needed to meet. He replied to her message so quickly that it was clear to me he'd circled back to Denver after he escaped the Lost Valley Resort. I wondered where he parked the horse.

The trap was set to lure Lapaglia to the Aurora Motor Coachettes, a vintage motel I drove by all the time. It wasn't seedy enough to be worrisome, hadn't turned into weekly housing for the almost-homeless, nor had it been gentrified by hipsters. Best of all, it had a secluded barbecue area behind the corner room, which I booked for Friday night. The owner had seemed especially grateful when I offered an extra twenty to keep the rooms on either side empty as well.

When I got there, I could have saved my twenty bucks. Saved Ozzi's twenty bucks, that is. The only people on the premises were a retired couple who had parked their RV at the far end of the property.

I circled the motel by foot, making sure my plan would work exactly as I'd imagined. Sturdy chairs around the fire pit. Easy access from the motel room. Quiet.

I passed through a breezeway to the front of the motel and wiggled the key in the room door. I glanced at my car parked several spaces away, not that Lapaglia knew what kind of car I drove, but I didn't want to spook him with too much activity.

The room was tidy, but smelled musty. All the furnishings

were out of date, spanning many decades and design trends. I had no doubt that sleeping in that bed would send me straight to a chiropractor. Luckily, I'd be doing no sleeping here.

I closed the door and kept the curtains drawn. The room was gloomy so I turned on both the heavy baroque-style lamp on the nightstand, and the macramé swag lamp hanging over the small table in the corner.

Hands on hips, I walked through my plan to make sure it would work, now that I'd seen this long, narrow room. Bathroom and closet in the rear on either side, and the sliding patio door almost directly opposite the front door.

It was perfect.

Cecilia would greet him at the front door, but Martina, Lakshmi and I would be waiting out back.

We planned to tie Lapaglia up out there to force him to watch his three girlfriends symbolically and literally destroy his picture book—at least in print shop proof form—in the fire pit as punishment for lying and using the three of them. After that, I was going to send the women on their way, then call the cops to come get him. I flipped open the lock on the patio door. We'd want to head out back as soon as we heard Lapaglia show up.

The other women arrived well ahead of time, making sure to park at the far end of the motel like I'd asked. Martina brought pizza and beer while we waited for him. Cecilia and I sat at the wobbly mismatched chairs on either side of a scratched table. Lakshmi sat cross-legged at the foot of the bed, and Martina leaned against the headboard.

We went over the plan one last time. I was in the middle of explaining how the zip ties worked to lash him to a chair when Cecilia expressed doubts.

"Do you really think he killed somebody?" She stretched the *really* from here to Kansas.

"Yes, absolutely," I said. "There's that bolo tie he was

wearing that matched the design on Tiffany's necklace, those silver combs, and—" I turned to Martina. "And the logo on your business cards. Why do they all match? What's the significance?"

Martina stiffened. "What are you implying?"

"Nothing. I'm just asking a question."

"Not that it's any of your business, but he was wearing that tie when I met him. I liked the design, so I copied it for my logo."

I studied her face. Was she lying? "I thought Lapaglia started his relationship with you because you had a marketing business?"

Martina reddened. "He did."

"Then why didn't you already have a logo?" Cecilia asked suspiciously.

We all stared at Martina until she knew she had to answer. "Okay, fine. I wasn't a marketing professional"—she used air quotes—"at all until someone introduced me to him that way. I worked at a big marketing firm, but in the payroll department." She shrugged. "I'd been toying with the idea so I thought this would be as good a time as any to start my own business."

"So you plopped a logo on a business card and rented a post office box at Pandora's." I bit the point off a slice of pizza and tried to hide my envy at her audacity.

Martina shrugged again.

"Ballsy," Cecilia said.

Quiet until now, Lakshmi said, "How else do people start businesses?"

She got me there, but that wasn't the point. "Regardless of how Martina started her marketing business, there's still the question of the bolo tie, the combs, and that necklace. There's a link there and the only possible explanation is Lapaglia."

"I still can't see him killing anyone, much less two people," Cecilia said.

"Me neither," Lakshmi added quietly.

"Gotta agree," Martina said, mouth full of pizza. "I've been thinking about it since you called, and it just doesn't make sense to me. Yes, he's a piece of .... philanderer and user of our good natures for which I'm willing to punish him, but I don't think we should get the cops involved."

"Me neither," Lakshmi said again, a little bit louder. She wiped her mouth on a paper napkin and began clearing the trash.

"That's what I've been thinking, too," Cecilia said. "I don't mind if you guys want to punish him by destroying his manuscript and illustrations, but I think we should leave it at that. Not go to the police." She paused. "He was actually really nice to me, even with all the using and lying. Way nicer than my husband." Her fingers brushed her black eye. "And I seriously doubt that our names will come up at any point." She handed Lakshmi her plate and crumpled napkin. Lakshmi nodded and smiled.

I felt my fists clench. "I don't think Tiffany or Annamaria would say he was actually really nice to them while he was killing them."

"Show us your proof," Martina said, holding out her hand. When I didn't place anything in it she said, "Exactly. You have nothing. You're playing a dangerous game of chicken, and I'm the head hen."

Whatever that means. "You guys are missing the point. We're not going to execute the guy. All we're going to do is get the three of you some well-deserved revenge, and then I'm calling the cops to come and pick him up. They'll investigate and gather the rest of the evidence."

"And we'd be part of the evidence," Cecilia said softly.

"He can't be a murderer," Lakshmi said. "He just can't."

"Why not?" I asked.

"Because ... because ..." She swept her arm to include

everyone. "Because we *know* him! We can't possibly know a murderer!"

Cecilia and Martina murmured and nodded their agreement.

I stared at them, stunned. How could they not see what I see? And how could I possibly make them understand that everyone had secrets, even people close to you.

I took a swig from my beer bottle and told them the story about the murder of my agent. Satisfied that would illustrate my point, I let them chew on that while I stood up and added my trash to the pile Lakshmi collected. When I turned back, Martina had slipped into the chair I'd been sitting in.

"Sorry," she said. "My back's killing me. That bed sucks." She picked up my phone lying on the table and squinted at it. *"You were right,"* she read. *"Different women."* She set it back down. "What kind of name is Ozzi?"

He fixed the software glitch! I was right. Velvet was at the Dark Dagger Awards that night too. I had no time to celebrate or figure out what to do with that information because in the next breath Martina said, "Let's take a vote. All in favor of not calling the cops tonight raise your hand."

Three hands shot up in the air.

"We have to!" I said.

"No," Martina said. "We don't."

I paced the length of the small room, twice, stopping in front of Lakshmi. "You can't go along with them," I said.

"I don't want to be involved with the police," she said.

I turned toward Cecilia who looked away and said, "If my husband finds out about any of this ...."

I knew it was futile, but I stepped toward Martina and held out my hands, palms up. "I'm begging you."

She stared at me long enough that I thought she might change her mind. But then she rolled her eyes and said, "You're such a drama queen. Besides, if the cops take him, you'll never see a dime of any reimbursement from him."

Crossing my arms, I felt my fingernails dig into my palms. Of course she was probably right about never seeing that money, but this has gone beyond that now. What about the greater good of humanity? My money problem wasn't as important as putting a murderer behind bars. Why couldn't they see that?

I needed to get out of there, get some air, clear my head. I stuffed the plates and napkins into the empty pizza box. I removed the two remaining beers from the cardboard carrier and filled the spaces with empties. I reached for Martina's but she grabbed it first.

"I'm not done!"

I snatched up the trash and slammed the motel door behind me, knowing that I didn't have much time to convince them. I just had to figure out a more compelling argument. I stomped down the sidewalk toward the dumpster. The clanging of the dumpster lid when I deposited our trash caught the attention of the retired couple sitting under an awning in canvas camp chairs in the weeds. I returned their wave but veered away, taking the well-trod dirt path leading behind the motel.

I was still furious and hadn't formulated a more compelling argument, so I kicked and chased a rusted can the length of the motel, not stopping until I reached the fire pit behind the room where the backstabbing, scaredy-cat women waited.

I dragged off the plywood square used to keep unobservant people from falling in the open pit, which I presumed was not building code compliant. I stared into the abyss of the brick-lined pit dug into the ground. Layers of black soot lined the inside. How many fires had been laid in here? How many ritual manuscript cremations?

How was I going to convince them to let me call the cops? Could I do this without them? Would the cops even believe me? What if we tied him up, burned his manuscript, and then we all left? Then I could still call the cops and the women would be none the wiser.

That might work. No, it wouldn't. He'd be screaming all our names at the top of his lungs. I shook my head. Lapaglia was going to be here soon. I had to get everyone back on track with some kind of plan. The fire was the key. I needed to remind them what he did, how he abused their trust. Once we started with the ritual burning of his manuscript, they'd remember what a deplorable human he really was.

I searched the area looking for the woodpile the motel owner had alluded to when I told her we'd want a fire tonight. I felt in my pocket for the matchbook with the motel's name on it that she'd tossed to me earlier. I carried four skinny logs and an old newspaper to the fire pit. I criss-crossed the logs like I remember my dad doing when we went camping. I wadded sheets of yellowed newsprint, brittle with age, poking them strategically under the logs.

I briefly admired my handiwork, wondering if my dad would have been proud, then struck a match, lighting each wad of paper in turn. It was time to convince them our scheme was solid and get Martina and Lakshmi out of the room before Lapaglia got here. They'll see this bonfire blazing and remember why they wanted to do this in the first place.

Tires crunched over the asphalt of the parking lot. I hurried to the corner of the breezeway and peeked out. I saw Lapaglia get out of the driver's seat of an El Camino with a black matte paint job. The Braid's car? A woman slid across the front seat and followed him out the driver's side.

When I saw her face, I clamped a hand over my mouth.

TWENTY-SEVEN

Annamaria? Velvet? The woman turned sharply toward the breezeway, as if she'd heard me. I ducked further back, keeping my hand over my mouth.

She was pressed up tight next to Lapaglia and speaking to him in a quiet voice. I strained to hear. It was all mumbling until I heard him say, "Velvet, please don't do this."

I peeked around the corner again and saw her hold out her hand. Lapaglia dropped the keys in her palm. She pocketed them then slipped her arm through his, leading him to the door of the motel room.

Suddenly Thomas Percy's words made perfect sense. He hadn't been seeing Annamaria's ghost, he was seeing Velvet. Velvet was pretending to be Annamaria and they were falling for it. She fed the mob stories to Lapaglia. She set up the Braid. But why? Why was she here? Why were they in the Braid's car? Because they killed him too?

Lapaglia and this Velvet were clearly in cahoots.

Now the two of them show up here, together. Why? To murder Cecilia? She was the only one Lapaglia expected to be here tonight. I offered a silent prayer of thanks that Lakshmi and Martina were both still in there with her. I hoped they were anyway. I hurried back to the greenbelt and peeked in the sliding door at the back of the room. They were all there.

I studied the scene, trying to imprint everything on my memory so I could give the police a perfect description when I called them. Lapaglia wore a gray golf shirt and black trousers. Velvet wore a pale pink stylish capri-style pantsuit, with a dark pink shell, and matching slingbacks.

I'd left my phone inside, but I knew there had to be a phone nearby, in the office, or maybe with the RV couple. I knew I had to call immediately, since Cecilia—perhaps all the women—were in danger.

I peered more intently through the sliding glass door. Something didn't seem right. Cecilia didn't look like she was in danger, in fact, nobody did. Lapaglia and Velvet stood so close they looked like conjoined twins. Glacially slow and church mouse silent, I slid open the patio door so I could hear what they were saying.

"Does it look like I'm dead?" Velvet laughed. "Don't be silly. Just a huge misunderstanding. My boyfriend was just being dramatic because I got back together with my husband, Rodolfo, and went on a romantic getaway. Thomas freaked out. That's why Rod and I vowed no more affairs. Only the straight and narrow for us now. Right, dear?"

Lapaglia mumbled something but he did not look like he was back in some happy marital bliss. In fact, he looked a little like he might throw up.

"And when Rod told me he was meeting you here, Cecilia, I had to tag along and explain that your affair must come to an end, now that we're working on our marriage. How lucky I am that you're all here at once!"

Martina explained to her how they had all been duped by Lapaglia and hadn't even learned his real name until recently. She started explaining the bonfire plan.

Suddenly Velvet raised her index finger to interrupt. Then

she sneezed. Sneezes were like fingerprints. No two were alike and I'd heard that sneeze before ... at Espresso Yourself!

Velvet was the psychic who met with Don and Barb that day. She had been trying to track Lapaglia. And now she had, along with all of his girlfriends.

My pulse quickened. For whatever reason, Velvet killed Annamaria and was pretending to be her. And now she was going to kill Lapaglia and his girlfriends!

I needed to get the cops here right now. I pushed back from the sliding door but must have given it a little shove. It squeaked. Everyone turned toward the sound.

I didn't have time to get away. I zipped toward the fire and grabbed a smoldering twig, using it as a poker by the time Velvet came out the sliding door.

"Oh, hi!" I gushed, overly friendly. My only hope was to pretend I'd been out here the whole time and that I was oblivious.

She stood a few steps away, hands in her pockets, watching me stoke the fire. Showers of sparks danced on an arc into the air. I kept tight hold of the smoldering stick.

I poked at the fire a few more times. When I looked up, I saw the necklace around her throat. It was exactly like Tiffany's in the photo. I willed myself to remain perky and calm. "Ooh! Love your necklace! Where'd you get it?"

"I made it. It's my own design. I make jewelry." She glanced back through the sliding door and gave a slight wave.

They must have been watching us. I hoped one of them would call the cops, but the women thought she was Annamaria. But surely Lapaglia would tell them she wasn't. Would they believe him?

"You're a jewelry designer?"

"Just a side business." She glanced again at the patio door.

"Do you have this design on ... other pieces? I don't really, um, wear necklaces." Lame. She was going to get suspicious.

"Yes. I can stamp it on any of my silver pieces, earrings, bracelet cuffs, hair accessories."

I needed to make sure. "My friend Tiffany has a necklace just like this one." Present tense.

"Yes, that poor girl loved my designs."

Past tense. Aha! Trapped her with my cunning rhetoric. But wait. Tiffany's murder was on the news. I poked the fire again while I thought of my next move.

Time ran out, though, because at that moment Velvet pulled a gun from her pocket and waved it at me.

Without thinking I said, "You're going to kill me like you did Tiffany?"

"She was annoyingly nosy, too." Velvet aimed right at me. "Too smart for her own good. She figured it out."

"Figured what out?" If there was one thing I'd learned recently, it was that criminals liked to brag about, or at least explain, their crimes. They all seemed to think somehow they were the victims.

"She figured out I wanted to escape my life and start over."

I remembered at Lost Valley how Lapaglia told me and the Braid about his last conversation with Tiffany. "You've wanted someone else's life since that day in the sushi restaurant in college. You're playing the long game."

She laughed. "You might be too smart for your own good too. Did you figure out I even got a nose job?" She caressed the side of her nose.

"But why? Why not just move to Wisconsin or Berlin or wherever? Open your jewelry store and live your life."

Velvet grimaced. "If only I could. The Family wouldn't allow it. I know too much about too many things. If they thought I was dissatisfied or worse, disgruntled, they'd kill me to keep me quiet."

"So you had to make it look like the Braid, er, Cesare Silvio was feeding information to Lapaglia."

She pointed the gun at me. "I recognize you now. You were at that coffee shop with the old couple."

I pointed my stick at her. "Yes. And you were trying to find Lapaglia. So now that you have, why don't you take him and get out of here?" The smoldering stick trembled in my hand. "And could you quit pointing that at me?" I gestured at the gun.

She looked at the gun in her hand, shrugged, and lowered it. Now she aimed it at my foot. "My work here isn't quite finished."

"What work is that?" I shuffled a bit to the side so the gun aimed at the ground next to me.

"Well, for starters, I'd like to kill Lapaglia and pin it on his harem. Just like I'm pinning Tiffany's murder on him."

"Why?"

"You don't need the details, but let's just say I was a bad girl and he's the only one who might tell my family."

"Yeah, families can be ... unforgiving."

"Ha! You don't know the half of it." Her brittle laugh hung in the air.

"But at least they let you borrow the family car." I thought about the Braid accusing me of knowing so much about the mob. "Did you kill Annamaria because she actually wrote the books?"

Anger flashed on Velvet's face. "*I* was the one who wrote those books. I planned out every line, delivered every story to him." She waved her gun toward Lapaglia unseen in the motel room behind us. "*I* should have won that Dark Dagger award."

"Then why kill Annamaria?"

"That was actually a mistake. Why would someone open a package bomb addressed *Personal and Confidential* to someone else?"

"Because they didn't know it was a bomb?"

"I suppose. It was unfortunate, though. I regret that. I

don't often make such mistakes. Gruesome business, murder."

"Why'd you go to Nebraska if you sent a package bomb?"

"Oh, honey, don't mess with the U. S. Postal Service. They will catch you every time. The only way to deliver a package bomb is in person." She smiled indulgently like she was explaining the ABCs to a toddler.

My skin turned to gooseflesh. This lady was a cold-blooded killer. And I was having a conversation with her. Maybe that meant she liked me and wasn't planning on killing me. After all, I wasn't part of Lapaglia's harem.

"But like I said, Tiffany was annoyingly nosy, too." She raised the gun again and pointed it at my face.

I lunged to the side and snatched up a folding aluminum lawn chair, holding it in front of me like a shield. Like that would protect me. I held it rigidly between us, wildly hoping she was bluffing. At the exact moment I saw Velvet's finger twitch, I dove out of the way, chucking the lawn chair sideways at her.

She was knocked off balance and stumbled right into the fire pit. She shrieked. I heard a *whoosh* and saw flames licking at her pantsuit.

I screamed and dragged her out by her arms, rolling her in the grass, batting out the flames. I sprawled on top of her, pinned her tight, now that her capris weren't burning.

Popcorn noises and the acrid smell of hot metal assailed my senses. The gun was in the fire.

"How many bullets?" I screamed in her ear. I flattened myself on top of her, not really caring what the number was at this point, not really. I restrained her in my terrified superhuman pancake embrace until the popcorn noises dissipated and I was sure all the bullets had discharged.

Martina sidled out the sliding door holding Lapaglia as her shield. Lakshmi and Cecilia inched forward behind them.

Lakshmi and Cecilia spoke simultaneously.

"Are you okay?"

"What happened?"

Martina peered around Lapaglia into the flames. "Thank God for deep fire pits."

"Get off me!" Velvet struggled under my weight.

"No. Not until I know what's going on. And I'm sure no more ammo will go off." I twisted my head to look at Lapaglia, still being held hostage in front of Martina. "You start."

"I don't know what's—" he started.

Martina shook him. "Don't you dare lie to us."

Lapaglia looked at me sitting on Velvet. "Fine. It was Velvet feeding me all that information about the mob so I could write my books. But somebody found out so she double-crossed Silvio—the Braid—and pinned it on him. He wanted me to go back to Jersey and confess to clear his name. But I'm pretty sure even if I did, he would have whacked me."

"Did you know she wants to whack you, too?" I asked him.

"The gun in my ribs gave me a clue," he said.

I remembered seeing them get out of the car and how they stood so close together in the motel room. She was holding that gun on him the whole time. What a cool customer she was.

"Why does she want to kill him?" Martina asked.

"If I had to guess, it's because he's the only one who can blab that she was doing the informing on the mob. She's ruined the Braid's credibility, maybe even killed him too," I said, thinking about her driving up in his car.

Velvet bucked hard under me, trying to throw me off. When she couldn't, she wrenched her head sideways.

I bent toward her face. "Unless Lapaglia was wearing your fancy hair comb, I bet most of the evidence points to you being at the crime scene in Nebraska. And I bet package bombs throw off a lot of other evidence. Plus, you have all of us as witnesses to your confession." I pressed her more firmly into the weedy grass. She snuffled and sneezed as the individual blades poked into her nose.

Velvet struggled to get away but I held her tight. She seemed to relax a bit, probably coming to grips with the fact she was trapped.

"You really killed Annamaria and Tiffany?" Lapaglia asked her. "I thought you were different. What kind of monster *are* you?" Lapaglia's question came out like a whine.

"Different than other mob killers?" I looked at him, incredulous. "And while we're asking questions, how did you not notice the resemblance between Velvet and your wife?"

"I never saw her until today when she accosted me on the way here."

I must have loosened my grip on Velvet at this surprising statement because the next thing I knew I was seeing stars, just like in a cartoon. The back of her head came up again, this time catching my nose instead of my forehead. Nausea gripped me as my vision narrowed to a pinprick. I'd never felt so much pain before. My muscles turned to pudding and I rolled off her. She scrambled away before Lakshmi or Cecilia even knew what had happened and could react.

She sneered at me. "Big mistake. Watch your back." Velvet disappeared around the corner of the breezeway.

Nobody spoke for several moments. Martina kept a tight hold of Lapaglia's upper arms.

When my pinpoint of vision widened a bit, Lakshmi and Cecilia helped me struggle to my feet. I probed my nose to see if it was broken. It didn't seem to be bleeding, but I couldn't believe that was possible, based on the pain factor.

The fire crackled, sending me back to the grass, belly first, hands over my head. When I realized it was just a knot in one of the logs, I slowly pushed myself up to a sitting position. The bright white from the shower of sparks disappeared and it seemed darker than ever, even though the sun hadn't set yet. Maybe I was blacking out. I rolled onto my back and closed my eyes.

"Hands in the air!"

Two police officers rounded the corner from the breezeway with guns drawn. A third escorted a handcuffed Velvet.

We immediately complied, me from my position flat on my back.

The one holding Velvet said, "We have a report of shots fired."

With my hands straight up in the air, I used one finger to point into the fire pit. "The gun's in there." I rotated my finger and pointed at Velvet. "It was her."

Two more cops, one female, came around the corner, guns drawn. They patted us all down for weapons, then holstered their guns. One heaved me to my feet.

The first officer holstered his gun too. "What's going on here?" he asked, staring straight at me. I didn't know why I looked like the ringleader here.

"I think you'll find that lady"—I pointed at Velvet—"has murdered Annamaria Lapaglia and probably has her passport, IDs, and credit cards in her possession somewhere. She also killed Tiffany Isaac."

The officer pulled out a notepad.

Lapaglia looked as if he was going to throw up. "I've caused a lot of trouble, haven't I?" he whispered.

"Ya think?"

Two of the officers carted Velvet away.

The female officer leaned close to Cecilia. "Where'd you get that shiner?"

Cecilia took a deep breath. "Husband."

The officer glanced at Lapaglia. "Him?"

Cecelia shook her head and stared at the ground. Suddenly she looked up and said, "I want to press charges. I want him to pay. Just like him." She jabbed a finger in Lapaglia's direction.

The officer patted Cecelia's shoulder then took some quick photos of her eye with a cell phone. "After we finish up here, we'll take care of you."

After making sure I didn't need medical attention, they sat us down in lawn chairs while they processed the scene and asked us questions. I drew the short straw and ended up next to Lapaglia.

He leaned toward me. "As soon as they give me my phone back, I'm going to get those funds—and then some—transferred to you as thanks for saving my life."

"But not because you owe me? Dillhole."

Martina, Cecilia, and Lakshmi all chimed in, rallying to my defense, nonstop expletives rained down in a steady stream until the female cop raised a hand to quiet us.

"Why's he a dillhole ... and all those other things?" she asked.

Martina told her the whole story of how he used each of them and lied to them, how he'd screwed me over with the workshop event, and ended with, "Can we burn his manuscript?"

The police officer looked each one of us in the eye and finally said, "I'll help."

She and Cecilia went inside to collect the pages.

I turned to Lapaglia. "If you never saw Velvet until today, how'd you get the bolo tie from her?"

"I didn't get it from her. It was a gift from Tiffany. She said she asked a friend to make it. If only—"

"Yeah, yeah, yeah, if wishes were horses. Do you have any way to contact Cesare Silvio? Do you think he'd give back Peter even after I tied him up and accidentally cut off his braid?"

One of the cops, who I thought was engrossed in writing his report said, "You did what now?"

I sighed and told him the story of how the Braid was after Lapaglia and kidnapped Peter O'Drool to make me help locate him. "But even though I did, he disappeared instead of returning Peter to me."

"No honor among thieves anymore." The cop pursed his lips.

"That's what I said!"

One of the other cops added, "Is he that mob guy? Didn't we get a call about him?"

The female cop came out with Cecilia who carried the manuscript pages.

"Hey, Delgado." He addressed the female cop. "What was that mob guy's name the FBI called about?"

"Cesare Silvio," she said.

"Where is he?" I shouted. "I need him to tell me where Peter is, the dog he kidnapped."

"Long gone." She helped herself to some pages from the stack of papers Cecilia held. Lakshmi and Martina did the same. "By the time the sheriff's department near the resort called the task force, he'd already hopped a plane."

"Back to Jersey?" Lapaglia asked.

"Nope. Direct from Denver to Frankfurt. Disappeared into eastern Europe by now, I bet." She fed pages into the fire with the others. "He'll turn up eventually."

"Not soon enough for Peter, though." I slumped in my seat.

After a few minutes of staring into the fire, I turned toward Lapaglia who flinched each time a page of his manuscript caught fire.

"Why did Alan Fraser at Lost Valley tell the cops not to come when he found out I'd called 911?"

Lapaglia didn't take his eyes off the fire. "Didn't want bad publicity, probably. Or maybe he has a healthy fear of the mob. Who knows."

Who knows indeed.

"Why weren't you a registered guest there?"

"Alan Fraser was using me, so I used him too. Told him I didn't want anyone tracking me there."

"That makes no sense. He wanted the publicity of having you there, but he wanted to keep it a secret?"

"He called Archie Cruz. He wanted to control the publicity."

I shook my head, watching as the women burned Lapaglia's manuscript and illustrations. Lakshmi, Cecilia, and Martina began dancing around the fire pit like the witches from Macbeth. They were truly enjoying themselves; this was a very cathartic experience for them.

The police officer tossed her remaining pages in the fire and grinned as they fluttered down and blazed. Then she turned away from the fire and leveled her index finger at Lapaglia. He had a resigned look on his face and I hoped he learned his lesson.

I was glad the murders were solved, the Braid was out of the country, and that everyone—me included—would get their money back from the cancelled workshop. Hopefully Lapaglia would honor his word to add a bit more so I could pay Ozzi back and cover all the overdraft fees sure to trickle in on my account.

But I'd give every dime back and live in abject poverty forever if only I could locate Peter. How could I go home and face Don and Barb? A tear slipped out of the corner of my eye and slid down my face before I could swipe it away.

The female cop noticed because she said, "Hey, Schwartzman, can these ladies be excused?"

"You got all their info?"

"Yes, sir."

"Then cut 'em loose."

~

I couldn't bear going home so I steered my car toward the park where I'd unsuccessfully looked for Peter before. It was the only place I could think of to go. I parked on the street and walked the last couple of blocks. I passed a health food store and did a double-take when I saw a display of those tins of fancy pretzels that lady said Peter kept begging for. On a whim, I veered inside and with the last of the cash Ozzi had loaned me, bought one as a tribute to poor Peter.

The world had slowed and everything seemed cold, despite the summer weather.

The cashier chattered as she took Ozzi's money from me but I didn't hear a word she said. I was filled to the brim with melancholy and guilt that I didn't know what to do with.

At the park I sat on a bench and watched ducks swim in the pond across the way. Beyond that was a pick-up game of basketball.

Watching the sunset normally made me feel so serene, but tonight it smothered me with gloom. I took the cellophane wrapper off the tin of pretzels. I popped open the lid and ate one. Maybe my blood sugar was too low.

On a whim, I shook the tin and called Peter's name. If this was a movie, he'd come charging out of the lengthening shadows, backlit and beautiful, and make a slow-motion leap into my arms like he'd just been waiting for me to come and get him. I shook it again. Called him.

Nothing.

This was not a movie.

I ate a few more pretzels without tasting them, staring at the basketball game until the players left the court. Despondent or not, I couldn't delay the inevitable any longer. As nice as Barb and Don were, I'd have to move from the apartment complex. Every time we'd see one another, all those dreadful emotions would come roaring back. The stress of losing Peter would kill us all.

I stood from the bench and brushed salt and pretzel

crumbs from my lap. The park was poorly lit and now with the sun mostly down, I had to walk carefully over the uneven grass.

A rabbit rocketed out from under a nearby bush and scared the bejeebers out of me. I twisted my ankle and bobbled the tin as I fell to my knees. The lid flew off. Pretzels rained down like a summer hailstorm.

A blur streaked by. Still on my hands and knees, I let loose a streak of inventive curses directed at those frolicking rabbits, but maybe bottled up and aimed at Lapaglia, the Braid, and Velvet, too. I collected my wits for a moment, then rolled to my butt so I could brush the dirt from my knees and check for bleeding. I pulled out my phone and shined the flashlight on my knees.

I heard snuffling behind me. Rabbit? Skunk? Raccoon? Slowly rotating the light toward the sound, I quickly ran through a mental checklist of weapons I could use to fight off whatever it was. Maybe my keys, but I'd have to dig them out. The quickest, handiest, and probably most ineffective was the pretzel tin. I transferred it to my right hand and raised it above my head.

When I'd fully rotated, I came face to face with Peter O'Drool, snarfing up pretzels from the grass.

"Peter!" I yelled.

He didn't quit chewing but did a sort of wiggle-walk in my direction. I scooped him up and kissed him over and over on his wrinkled little snout. He licked my cheek then wiggled to get down, back to his treasure trove of treats. But before he did, he bounded under a bush and dragged his filthy rainbow-colored flamingo out, dropping it at my feet.

I sat next to him, hand on his collar, and called Barb and Don.

ACKNOWLEDGMENTS

I'm very grateful I have talented and generous friends who agree to read drafts of my books and offer constructive—and oh-so kind—feedback to me. You'd be reading a very different book if not for MB Partlow, Jessie Cornwell, Karen Whalen, Trina Burgermeister, Ann Perramond, Amy Drayer, and my agent Jill Marsal. Any mistakes you find are obviously theirs and theirs alone ….

Subscribe to Becky Clark's *So Seldom It's Shameful News* for contests, giveaways, sales, sneak peeks, and other behind-the-scenes shenanigans at BeckyClarkBooks.com.

ALSO BY BECKY CLARK

— Dunne Diehl Novels (with Ted Hardwick) —

Banana Bamboozle (#1)

Marshmallow Mayhem (#2)

— Mystery Writer's Mysteries —

Fiction Can Be Murder (#1)

Foul Play on Words (#2)

Metaphor for Murder (#3)

— Crossword Puzzle Mysteries —

Puzzling Ink (#1)

Punning With Scissors (#2 May 2021)

Fatal Solutions (#3 Nov 2021)

— Nonfiction —

Eight Weeks to a Complete Novel—Write Better, Write Faster, Be More Organized

Lazy Low Cal Lifestyle Complete Cookbook

Reading Maniac—Fun Ways to Encourage Reading Success

ABOUT THE AUTHOR

Becky Clark is the seventh of eight kids which explains both her insatiable need for attention and her atrocious table manners. She likes to read funny books so it felt natural to write them, too. She's a native of Colorado, which is where she lives with her indulgent husband and quirky dog, who looks and acts remarkably like Nova in this book.

Becky loves to present workshops to writing groups and is a founding member of the Colorado Chapter of Sisters in Crime. Visit her on Facebook and at BeckyClarkBooks.com for all sorts of shenanigans.

PRAISE FOR MYSTERY WRITER'S MYSTERIES

Foul Play on Words (#2)

"So good I wanted to read it twice! It has everything I love in a funny mystery: characters I care about, a plot that grabs me from page one, voice, and laughs galore. Clear your day, because this laugh-out-loud comic caper mystery is a one-sitting read!" —*Jess Lourey, Anthony, Agatha, and Lefty Award–nominated author of the Mira James Mysteries*

"Clark is the queen of the subtle misdirect and the casually dropped clue. I gave myself a resounding 'I could have had a V-8' head slap when I reached the end and realized she'd given me everything I needed to solve the mystery without me ever knowing it!"—*Kristi Abbott, author of the Popcorn Shop Mysteries*

"The backdrop for Clark's witty, engaging mystery is a writers' conference where everything that can go wrong does so, in a hilarious way. You'll both sympathize and laugh along with heroine Charlemagne 'Charlee' Russo as she balances saving the conference from total disaster with the dangerous task of rescuing the kidnapped daughter of a close friend." —*Ellen Byron, award-winning author of the Cajun Country Mysteries*

"Another winning entry in this wonderful series, *Foul Play on Words* is a clever, compelling mystery. The intriguing plot will pull you in immediately, and the engaging sleuth with quips at the ready will keep you laughing all the way through. A must-read for fans of humorous cozies!"

—*Cynthia Kuhn, award-winning author of the Lila Maclean Academic Mysteries*

"*Foul Play on Words* is irresistible. A perfect combination of comedy and suspense. Mystery writer Charlee Russo narrows down a long list of oddball suspects at the wildest writers' conference of all time. Every word is funnier than the word before. A must-read." —*Gretchen Archer, bestselling author of the Davis Way Crime Capers*

"*Foul Play on Words* is hilariously quirky with a side of neurosis. The misadventures of being a mystery writer were never so much fun." —*Libby Klein, author of the Poppy McAllister Mystery Series*

Fiction Can Be Murder (#1)

"A promising series debut." —*Booklist*

"The charming heroine and the supporting cast shine in Clark's fun and funny solo mystery debut...which doesn't take anyone too seriously in the best way possible." —*Kirkus Reviews*

"Cozy fans should enjoy this funny and affecting view into a mystery writer's life." —*Publishers Weekly*

Charlee Russo is my new favorite amateur sleuth! Wickedly witty author Charlee takes us along on her wild ride to prove her innocence in the murder of her literary agent, a murder based on the plot of one of her own books! Giving readers an inside look at the writer's life, Becky Clark pens a funny, clever page-turner of a mystery and I can't wait for the next one in this terrific new series!" —*Jenn McKinlay, bestselling author of the Library Lover's Mysteries*

"Becky Clark wields a witty pen, writing about an author who is plunged into her own mystery." —*Marty Wingate, author of the Potting Shed mysteries*

"Becky Clark is a hilarious new talent in mystery fiction. With a mixture of humor and plot, *Fiction Can Be Murder* pulls back the curtain on the creative writing process and exposes the homicidal thoughts that take place while writing a book." —*Diane Vallere, bestselling author of the Costume Shop mysteries*

CPSIA information can be obtained
at www.ICGtesting.com
Printed in the USA
LVHW081350310721
694224LV00029B/890